A Pacifica Resort Novel

Love *and* Reservations

DEE ROLLINGS

Love and Reservations: A Pacifica Resort Novel (Book 2)

First paperback edition May 2024

979-8-9861581-4-3 (Ebook)

979-8-9861581-5-0 (Paperback)

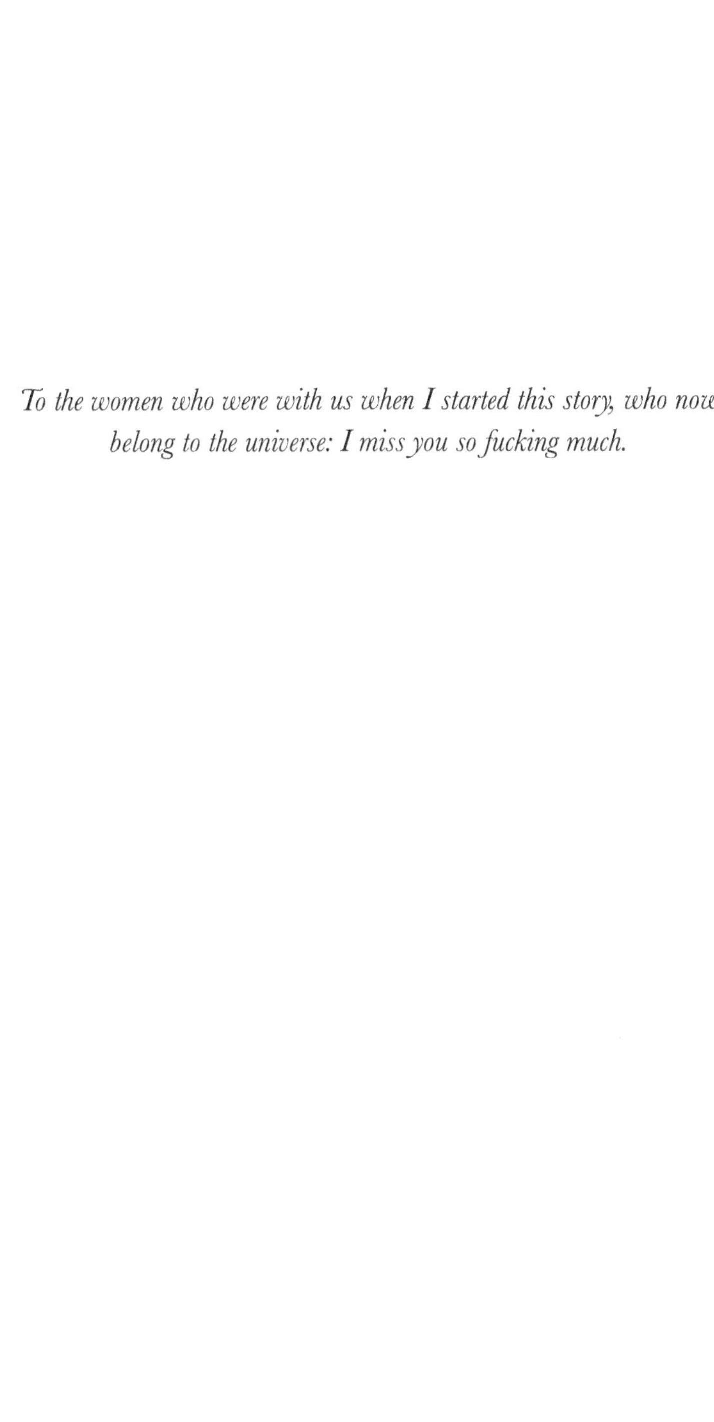

To the women who were with us when I started this story, who now belong to the universe: I miss you so fucking much.

Chapter One

Show me a pure bride, and I'll show you a damn liar.

No one waited until marriage to have sex anymore, so the white dress was moot.

Weddings were a waste of money, and I didn't understand why anyone would want one.

The saleswoman came over, pulling me out of my thoughts. "Would you like a glass of champagne while you wait?"

I started to say, "No thank you," but before I could finish, Valerie clapped her hands. She was the wild half of my two platonic soulmates, so her excitement usually meant danger was afoot.

I was the driver for today's carpool of insanity, and we were at the third dress shop on the itinerary. It was feeling more like a pub crawl than wedding dress shopping.

"Sorry, Blake's being a total grouch today. She's not usually like this." She gave me a look that said "*What's with you?*" before answering the saleswoman's question. "I'll take one for me and one for the bride, please."

The woman nodded her head, smiling from ear to ear. "I'll get right on that," she said and disappeared down the hall.

I picked up a dress catalog lying on the table between our fancy white chairs and flipped through it. "I just don't get it. Why would anyone want to pay $300 a person to eat overcooked chicken while listening to bad music being played from tinny speakers?"

Val shifted in her chair, twisting to face me. She was clearly over my bad attitude. "Receptions don't have to cost that much, you know. You're just biased because you run an overpriced wedding venue."

I rolled my eyes. "It's not just a wedding venue. It's a resort."

"Yeah, where people visit so they can get married." She paused and did that thing where she squinted her eyes, allowing her to read my thoughts. "What's this really about?"

The saleswoman came back, handing one glass to Val and setting another on the table. "I just snuck a peek at Lina—"

I interrupted her. "It's pronounced Lynn-a, not Lean-a." And the girl's face went totally red.

Fuck. I really was being an asshole today. "Sorry. That was rude of me. I shouldn't have cut you off like that."

She smiled. "No, I'm just embarrassed because I've been calling her the wrong name since you all walked in." It was so like Lina not to correct someone for saying her name incorrectly. Her full first name was Magdalina, but only her closest friends knew that. Her future husband and his friends called her Maggie because of some inside joke or whatever, but other than that, she was just our Lina. The saleswoman turned around, looking toward the hallway my other platonic soulmate had disappeared down ten minutes before. "Anyway, Lina looks really beautiful right now."

Valerie leaned forward, taking the attention off me. "Is she trying on the mermaid cut or the fluffy ballgown?" We had given Lina an enormous pile of dresses to try on before sitting down in the mirrored reveal room, but she wouldn't tell us which one she liked the most.

She gave us a conspiratorial smile. "You'll just have to wait and see."

The saleswoman left again, probably to go assist Lina, and Val snatched the catalog out of my hand. "So tell me again why you hate weddings so much?"

"I just don't see the point. You're going to spend your life savings on one party? for what? Cheaper health insurance rates? I can take care of my own health insurance, thank you very much." Lina's tinkling laugh sounded down the hall, followed by a rustling sound. I pointed toward her, as if we could see her from where we sat. "She and Reece are so happy. You and Joey are so happy. Why can't people just be happy without the mess?"

Valerie flipped through the catalog without speaking for a few moments. "If Joey asked me, I would marry him tomorrow, even though it would cause my insurance rates to go up." She looked down the hall. "And I know Reece just asked Lina a few weeks ago, and while some people may think they are speed-running to the altar, I think it's romantic."

I laid my head against the back of my chair,

wondering if I was just born wrong. Even as a little girl, I had never wanted to play bride. It just didn't seem fun to me. I hadn't wanted to share my toys then, and I didn't want to share my money now.

"When's the last time you got laid?"

Her question caused me to sit up in my seat. "Valerie! That's not a conversation for Lina's dress shopping."

She put the catalog on the table and took a long drink from her glass. "Answer the question, Blake." I usually had to be very drunk before I spilled the tea on any personal bedroom exploits, and she knew that. The fact that she was asking so blatantly meant she knew something was up.

I knew exactly how long it had been. And who it had been with. But I didn't want to tell her. It would just lead to more questions I wasn't willing to answer yet.

"How about this one?" Lina floated around the corner in the most beautiful dress I'd ever seen, saving me from having to answer Valerie's awful question.

She looked like a princess in her strapless mermaid-tail gown, covered in pearls. With her long black hair contrasting the white dress, I realized that our girl-tribe was exactly where we needed to be.

I stood up, all the air having left my lungs. "I think it might be the one."

Lina's eyes filled with tears as Val stood with me, wrapping her arms around Lina. We enveloped our friend in a hug, excited that she had found her perfect dress after the whirlwind of a year she'd had.

As much as I wanted to keep my walls up, her excitement was spreading into me. I'd been in loving relationships before, all of them ending with my heart being decimated. While I was unbelievably happy for her and Reece, I knew it was a path that wasn't paved for me.

Lina pulled away from us. "I'm so glad the two of you are going to be my bridesmaids." Her eyes spilled over, a line of mascara blurring down her cheek. "I wish my mom and Ester were here, too."

I smiled at her, squeezing her tightly once more before stepping back. "They would have been, if you hadn't sprung this trip home right in the middle of their cruise. Your mom will be just as excited to see this dress when she's back as she would be right now, and Ester will be here for the wedding before we know it."

Lina had called us a few weeks ago from France, telling us that Reece proposed and they wanted to get married as soon as possible. They had to do most of their planning on the road, but they wanted to have the small ceremony here in Santa Barbara at the end of April— early May at the latest.

This gave us about two and a half months to help them plan the best wedding a couple of traveling artists could afford. With all our resources combined, the short timeline was manageable, even though I didn't understand why anyone would want to get married in the first place.

"I know, but I'm just so glad that the two of you are here. I know you're so busy with work." She squeezed us even tighter. "I'm thankful you agreed to be co-maids of honor."

Val smiled. "You know we wouldn't miss it for the world."

Lina excused herself to change back into her clothes, and Val and I took the opportunity to sit back down on the chairs flanking the little stage.

Val turned to me, taking another sip of champagne. "So I was thinking. How about you plan the bachelorette party, and I'll do the rehearsal dinner? Divide and conquer, you know?"

I sighed. "The bachelorette party is way more your sort of thing than mine. Can't I just do the rehearsal dinner?"

"My new store is scheduled to open April 1st." She had joked when she was planning the grand opening of her second record store that if she couldn't open on a Friday the 13th, April Fool's Day would be the next best choice. "No offense, but a rehearsal dinner just means getting a headcount and making reservations. A bachelorette party takes a lot more planning and, as much as I love you," she sent a sweet look in Lina's direction, "I just don't have the mental capacity to take it on right now."

Lina skipped back into the room with the most beautiful smile I'd ever seen plastered on her face. "We have about an hour to look at the bridesmaids' dresses before meeting the boys for dinner. Want to see what I had in mind?"

I knew I couldn't let either of them down, even though I was knee-deep in renovations at the resort and I panicked that the restaurant wouldn't be reopened for this summer's wedding season. I also had very limited mental capacity, but I knew if I said a word about it, it would crush one or both of them.

Or worse, they'd make me talk about it. Which wasn't something I was willing to do on Lina's happy day.

I tried to make my smile reach my eyes when I looked at Val. "Okay, I'll do it. I'll plan the party, and you take on the rehearsal dinner."

We found our seats at a cozy Thai restaurant and started reading through the menus. Val sat on one side of the table, Lina and Reece on the other. I assumed Joey was running late, so I sat at the end of the table. I wasn't super excited to be the filling in a happy couple Oreo, but here I was.

Lina used to work at The Pacifica with me as our photographer. She'd left last summer to go freelance, and her fiancé Reece, who was my former boss, had left the hotel industry to manage a couple of bands that were currently on tour in Europe.

One reason they wanted to get married so soon was to work around their packed schedule. Neither of them had a lot of downtime for the next two years, and they didn't want to cancel any events. But they were living their dream traveling the world together, and I couldn't be happier for them . . . even if it had taken me a little while to warm up to him.

"So, we were thinking . . ." Lina began, but before she could finish her sentence, the door swung open, and all the air escaped my lungs. When Lina mentioned we were meeting the guys for dinner, I hadn't thought about there being a third one in this friendship circle.

The most aggravating man I had ever met strode through the door like he owned the place. If someone had told me he was coming, I would have faked an illness or something. Hell, I would have injured myself on purpose.

Reece called out, "There's my best man!"

Sal made it to the table in three steps and leaned down, kissing Lina on the cheek. I broke out into a cold sweat and started thinking of reasons I could get up and leave.

"Sorry I'm late." His voice was smooth, like dark chocolate.

It was a good thing I was more of a milk chocolate kind of girl.

He stood to his full height, shaking Reece's hand. "There was an issue with the plumbing at our Carpinteria location I had to take care of. Then it took me forever to find a parking spot." He sat in the empty chair next to Valerie, and I swore he scooted it my way. His knee pressed into mine, and every alarm in my brain went on red alert. If I hadn't been in the mood to be nice earlier, I definitely wasn't now.

He wrapped an arm around Val, giving her a side hug. "It's nice to see my friends so happy."

I hadn't spoken to him in months. I'd seen him at a few events here and there, but until now, I had been quite successful at avoiding him completely.

He picked up his menu and turned toward Val. He somehow did this without moving his torturous leg away from mine. "How is the new store coming along?"

I sucked in a breath. This man drove me insane, and it was clear that he was taking over my best friendships.

My traitorous eyes scanned over his body as he infiltrated my personal life. The way his body took up space was too much—his wide shoulders and thick, muscular thighs had me worried that the flimsy metal chair he sat in wouldn't hold. His black T-shirt and black slacks made him look every bit the villain he was in my heart.

Valerie smiled back at him. "It's going really well. Thanks for your help with all those crates the other day. With Joey in and out of town lately, I don't know how I would have moved everything without you."

He said something, but I tuned it out, watching the graceful way he moved as he turned the page in his menu. As he ran his fingers through his jet black hair, which was cropped short on the sides and long on the top, I wondered if he would let me spike it up like a punk-rocker. It was slicked back with product right now, but I imagined sliding my fingers through it.

The thought of it grossed me out. I did not want to touch him, let alone caress his hair.

He shifted in his seat, pressing his leg against mine even more, and I realized he knew I had been staring at him this whole time. I looked down at my menu, remembering what he had done. Why I hated him.

As the emotions flooded back into me, having him sitting so close ruined my appetite. I wanted to scream. To slap him for having the audacity to be here like nothing had happened.

But nothing had happened on his side. I was the one who had been an idiot.

Sal sat his menu down and looked at Reece. "So, what's first on the best man to-do list?"

Dammit. I had spaced it when Reece mentioned it a few minutes ago.

As Lina's co-maid of honor with Valerie, I was going to have to stand across from Sal at the altar of this wedding, since I knew Reece had already asked Joey to be a groomsman.

Every seat of the table had been taken, and I wondered where that other groomsman was. "Where's Joey? I thought he was having dinner with us tonight?" He was supposed to be sitting in the seat next to me instead of the world's largest jerk.

Valerie smiled. "Oh, he got caught up at rehearsal. The band is working on some new stuff, and you know how they get when they're in the zone." She checked her watch. "He should be around in a couple hours, though."

Reece asked her more about Joey's band, and the two of them chatted about the indie music industry for a few minutes. I shifted away from Sal, moving my chair a few inches so that our legs were no longer touching. He hadn't as much as nodded in my direction yet, so I spoke over the conversation flowing before me. "Anyway, Lina, you were about to tell us something."

Lina's smile brightened the room. "Oh yeah. So, Reece and I were wondering, what if we do one party for all of us instead of separate bachelor and bachelorette parties? We don't want to do anything wild, since we're basically living as married people already, and we think it would be easier for everyone."

Reece added on, "Sal already said he would do the bachelor party, so I was thinking he could just jump in and help with whatever you girls wanted to do."

I shot a sideways glance at Val, wondering if I could convince her to switch responsibilities. I pointed to Sal with my thumb. "Is that really the best idea? Do we not remember the disaster that happened the last time he planned a party?"

Sal leaned forward, not looking at me, but at Reece and Lina. "None of that was my fault."

I faced him, trying to ignore how beautiful his naturally tan skin was. As well as those long legs, which were impossible to ignore under the table. "Look, Salamander. They almost broke up at your birthday party. Do you really want to ruin their wedding, too?"

He scoffed, finally meeting my eyes. "Salamander? You know, I could come up with a hell of a lot of things to call you, too, Blake Thomas."

I stared him down, thinking of a reply. He held my eye contact, and all I could think about was how much I hated the green flecks that sprinkled through his irises. Those stupid hazel eyes with their creamy browns and greens that swirled together like a frickin' galaxy.

My eyes drifted downward to his full mouth. As if he noticed the shift in my attention, he pulled in his bottom lip, dragging his teeth against it. I felt the heat of what could have been pool in my belly. Lower, even. But then I remembered how poisonous that mouth was.

Reece coughed loudly, and suddenly I remembered the table was filled with people. People who were under the impression that I didn't hate the groom's best friend with every speck of energy in my entire body. Val leaned toward Lina and whispered loudly, "Is there something going on between those two that I'm missing here?"

Before Sal could embarrass me, I said, "No. We're fine." I gave a fake smile. "A joint party sounds lovely. I'm sure we'll be able to work together to plan something really fun."

Maybe we could go axe throwing and I could toss the blade somewhere between his neck tattoos and his stupid little mohawk.

The rest of the meal went smoothly, and I came up with multiple ideas that could lead to an accidental dismemberment of the man sitting way too close to me.

Go kart racing? Deep sea fishing? There had to be something.

Before I knew it, we were paying for our meals and pushing in our chairs. Reece wrapped his arm around Lina's shoulder as we walked out of the restaurant. "Are you guys ready to head to the show?"

Val bounced on her toes, "Hell yeah. The opening band is going to meet up with Joey's band on his tour this summer, and I want to learn their songs before I join them for a couple of weeks."

Sal's head tilted to the side. "Ooh, what band?" and my stomach sank. I was really looking forward to some live music therapy tonight, but I really didn't want to go if he was coming, too.

Reece filled him in as we walked down the street to the venue. I wrapped my arms around myself, wondering if I should have worn a sweater, but I knew I would have regretted it when we got inside.

Living in Santa Barbara was magical, with the nightlife of restaurants and live music all within walking distance. Even in early February, when the air was freezing cold, there was always something fun to do as a group.

Of course, Sal decided to tag along, ruining the whole evening. I glanced up at him. "It's a Friday night. Don't you have dinner service to take care of, or like a room full of prostitutes to see to?"

He looked over his shoulder at me, about to respond, but Lina twined her arm through mine. "You know what's going to be really cute? The two of you paired up together at the wedding." My eyebrows bunched as I tried to track where she was going with this conversation. "Since both you and Sal are single, it will be you both, close enough to cuddle."

A shudder rolled through my body. I caught Sal's eye still lingering on me, but it made me want to throw up. I told Lina, "I'm sure I'll have a date by then. I'll walk down the aisle with him for you, but as for dinner, I'm going to need a plus-one."

My phone vibrated in my pocket, and I had the dreadful feeling it was work. I pulled it out, and my shoulders relaxed when I saw it was just a notification from my favorite treasure-hunting app. There was something special nearby, but now wasn't the time to look for it. I tucked the phone back in my pocket, hoping no one had seen my screen.

I wasn't ashamed of my geocaching hobby by any means, but Lina and Val didn't find it as exciting as I did. They had tagged along with me a few times, but neither of them had the burning urge to find all the geocaches in the city. And tonight was about Lina and Reece—about the group being together for the first time in months.

Sal cleared his throat before telling Lina, "You're acting like I don't have a date lined up already."

Reece gave him a confused look. "Wait, you do?"

"Please, I already have like three girls I'm thinking about . . . just gotta whittle it down to the one worth bringing to the party."

Ugh, this guy.

We made it into the venue and found a spot to stand near the back as the opening band set up their instruments. The house lights were already down, casting us in darkness. The only light came from the neon beer signs behind the bar that wrapped around two of the three walls. There was already a crowd forming by the stage, even though the bands playing tonight weren't exactly world renowned yet. I had a feeling it was going to get even more packed in here as the night went on.

Valerie kissed our cheeks before disappearing into the crowd to say hi to some friends. I found myself standing next to Sal as Lina and Reece lost themselves in a discussion about lord knows what, already dancing slowly to the preshow music. The way he pressed his forehead to hers as they spoke made me feel like I was witnessing something way more intimate than a regular conversation.

"So," I jumped as Sal's voice filled the space around me. "What are we going to do for the stag party? Do you have any ideas yet?" I took a small step away from him, desperate to be anywhere but here.

I had no ideas other than wanting to plan something that would accidentally maim him permanently. "Are you sure we should plan something together? I was under the impression that Lina didn't get along with a lot of Reece's friends. You know, after we had to clean her up because they tortured her at that nightclub."

"Are you seriously going to hold that one event against me forever?"

I rolled my eyes before replying. "You know exactly what I'm holding against you. And it's not some stupid party."

His lips pressed together tightly as he folded his arms across his chest. The cocky way he leaned back promised that whatever he was going to say was just going to piss me off more.

The crowd erupted into cheers as the opening band began to play, muffling whatever asinine thing came out of Sal's mouth. I didn't ask him to repeat himself as I turned away and gave my attention to the people on the stage.

They played three songs before I decided it was time to go. My two best friends were living their best lives, and I was stuck standing awkwardly with the one man I wouldn't want to dance with if he were the last man on earth.

I needed to leave, but I felt guilty, having driven the girls here. After the next song ended, I tapped Reece on the shoulder. "Hey, I've got a headache and need to get out of here. Can you make sure everyone gets home okay?"

He looked over at Sal, and I could have sworn they had one of those weird silent conversations between them. Then he looked back at me, "Yeah, between Sal and I, we'll make sure everyone gets where they need to be."

I walked out, thankful for the cool air rushing over me. I didn't want to spend another moment with that tattooed jackass. Planning a party with him was going to be torture.

I pulled out my phone when I made it to the parking lot we had crossed earlier, opening the geocaching app. My favorite hobby was something not many people knew about. In fact, I hadn't known there were containers filled with logs and trinkets all over the world until I met my college roommate freshman year. She was obsessed, and it quickly rubbed off on me.

We were a secret community of people who hid treasures all over the world and tagged where we placed them in the app. Then, like-minded people had the opportunity to find these treasures and log when they found them. Some people left trinkets behind, or traded what they found in the treasure box with what they brought with them. Most of these containers had been hidden in places many people passed every day, so an additional challenge was making sure people who didn't know about geocaching—Muggles as we lovingly called them—didn't see what we were doing and accidentally throw away or vandalize what we were looking for.

Most of the time I geocached, I had nothing on me, so I usually just signed the log and went on with my day, but there were a few in town that were my favorites. There was one, up in the hills, that was an old wine crate attached to a Little Free Library, and I couldn't help but check on it every few months . . . for the books and the goodies.

I checked the map to make sure I was in the right location and started hunting. The app said it was micro-sized, meaning it was going to be small and probably well-hidden, so I scanned the ground by the brick wall at the back of the parking lot. I used the flashlight on my phone to try to find something out of the ordinary.

"Is there a reason you're lurking around in the parking lot by yourself?" I screamed and immediately hated that I recognized Sal's voice.

I spun around and pointed at him angrily. "You should know better than to sneak up on women in dark parking lots. You could get yourself killed." My heart threatened to beat out of my chest, but at least I knew he wasn't mugging me.

"Would that upset you?" He stepped closer, and I could smell the sandalwood coming off him that I used to adore.

I decided to counter his question with one of my own. "Aren't you supposed to be inside, waiting to take one of the girls home?"

He looked off toward the venue, and my eyes traced the muscular lines of his neck, barely visible in the streetlight. "Val's going to ride home with me, but I needed some air first."

I didn't believe him. Why should I, since he had never been truthful with me before? "Why are you really here?"

He held his hands up. "Look, you can choose to trust me or not. I'm just out here because it was too stuffy inside." The man was known for the hours he spent inside of busy kitchens before going out dancing in nightclubs, grinding against strangers until the sun came up. I knew he was up to something. "What are you doing over here? Did you park nearby?"

Unable to explain why I was standing here without going into way too much of my personal life, I came up with a quick story. "I'm actually on the other side of this building, but I thought there was an alleyway." I shrugged. "But now that I see it's not connected, I'm headed back the other way."

"Can I walk you?"

My heart fluttered at his request, but then I remembered that I didn't trust him. Not one bit. "That's nice of you, but I know the last thing you want to do is spend any more time with me than you have to." I turned around and started walking to the sidewalk that would lead me to my car.

"Blake, wait up." I heard his boots smacking the asphalt of the parking lot and stopped.

"It's been a really long day, and my limit for bullshit has been met. Can you please just go back inside and make sure my friend gets home safely?"

His mouth opened like he wanted to say something,

but he closed it almost immediately. "Yeah, I can do that. Get home safely, too, Blake."

He turned around and walked toward the concert hall, and I walked to my car, wishing he had at least approached me after I had found the hidden treasure. Guess I'd have to come back another time and see if I could find it, preferably during the day.

Chapter Two

I plopped into my oversized leather chair, the only thing in my office I adored, and took a deep breath. I had moved here from my old office six months ago when I became the general manager, but I hadn't had the motivation to decorate it. To make it my own.

I scanned the bare white walls, wondering if maybe a coat of cerulean paint on the opposite wall would make it feel a little more like home. I had already added some blue chairs and a fuzzy rug. Bright colors always perked me up, but for some reason, it still felt like someone else's place.

I wiggled my computer mouse, waking up the screen. It was only ten a.m. this Monday morning, but the day had already lasted a thousand years. Between the renovations all over the resort and the cantankerous guests that checked in this morning, I was ready for a vacation. Knowing my friends were in town for the week and I was stuck at the office didn't help either.

The wallpaper on my computer was a shot of Lina,

Val, and me from last summer. We had planned a picnic on the beach, but didn't account for how windy it would be. The meal was a bust, but we had laughed until our ribs ached. We asked a stranger walking his dog to take our picture, and it had become my favorite one of the three of us. We were windblown and not entirely in focus —my long chestnut hair blocked most of my face—but our smiles were infectious. Just the kind of joy I needed to see every time I sat down to get work done.

There was a knock at my door, so I answered, "Come in."

Lizette entered, looking perfectly polished as usual, wearing her black power suit and bloodred lipstick. She ran the company that owned our resort—The Howell Group—and she was one hell of a ball-buster. She sat in one of the velvety barrel chairs facing my desk and practically melted into it.

When I had met her last year, after her corporation took over The Pacifica, I thought she was going to make my life miserable.

I had been second in command here for longer than I would have preferred and hated that our quaint beach resort had been purchased by a company with a habit of squeezing the personality out of everything they acquired. But as I got to know and work with their employees, I learned it wasn't an evil corporation hell-bent on world domination.

Especially now that Lizette was in charge. I knew I was in good hands with her. She had a keen eye for business and didn't pussyfoot around.

We'd grown close these last several months, and I'd

learned that there was a storm inside of her that she was keeping under tight wraps. We were friends now, and my office was the only place on our property she would drop her shields and just be Lizette.

She hadn't said a word, just sat there decompressing for a couple of breaths. I started to joke that I loved the opportunity of running this place, but I wanted to quit and go live in the hills somewhere, but she spoke before I could. "I have an offer for you, but I know how you are, so you're not allowed to answer me without sleeping on it."

She had the same smooth brown skin and black hair as my best friend's future husband. Their brown eyes and perfectly straight noses were carbon copies of each other. This made our friendship somewhat awkward. Especially when she asked me to keep secrets from her brother. Secrets like her ongoing divorce. "Is this going to be one of those offers I can't refuse?" I didn't know what she had in mind. There were many things I had learned about her that she didn't want Reece to know, so my thoughts started racing.

She sat up straight, going from friend Lizette to work Lizette in half a second. "I want to offer you a job at The Howell Group. I've seen what you've done with this property, and I think the company would be lucky to have you supervising multiple properties instead of just this one."

I didn't know what to say, so I picked up my favorite purple pen and spun it around in my hands. "What exactly does this job entail?"

"You'd oversee the general managers from resorts

across the country. Slightly more hours than what you put in now, but the raise would be substantial. You would have to travel from time to time to the East Coast offices, too, but I think you would be great at it."

I thought about the dream I'd had since my sophomore year in college. The one that had called to me during that first hospitality class. The one I didn't share with anyone, just in case it never came true.

Would this be a bridge to get to that dream, or a barrier?

"I'm definitely going to have to sleep on it."

She smiled, the kind she never gave out at work. "See? I knew you would say that. The board doesn't meet again until next month, so you have time to think it over. And you know how quickly the board makes decisions, so really we're looking at three months before your start date." She clutched the edge of my desk. "If you want the promotion, I mean."

"And what if I don't want it?"

She tapped her perfectly manicured fingers against the mahogany wood. "We'll talk about that when we get there."

"You're not going to fire me, are you?" This place stressed me out a lot sometimes, but I wasn't ready to leave The Pacifica . . . . I didn't even have the guts to admit my dream out loud.

She laughed, a sound that was rare coming from her. "Oh, hell no. I'm never going to let you go."

I blew out a breath, thanking whatever deity in the universe that was looking out for me. The only option was to move up, I decided.

We chatted for a few more minutes, and I let her know how the renovations were going. None of this was news to her, since I had sent a detailed report to her yesterday, but it was nice to see her for longer than a few minutes at a time. She checked her watch and jumped out of her chair. "Shit, I have a meeting across town in twenty. Happy hour soon?"

I smiled and agreed to get together before too long. I could see her put her business face on like a shield before she strode out of the room like she owned the place. Which she did, I guess.

I laid back in my chair again and closed my eyes. I really enjoyed running the resort, even with all the added stress, but would I like to run more than one at a time? Did I really want more hours than I already put into this place?

Was I giving up on my dream? Was it a dream that needed to be let go?

I was thinking about what I would do with a raise when my assistant's voice blared through the earpiece in my headset, jolting me back to reality. Of course, sitting for over ten seconds was a luxury I couldn't have. "Blake, you have a call on line two."

I told Paige I copied before I took the call. "This is Blake. How can I help you?"

The overly cheery voice on the other line let me know I was about to be dealt a blow I wasn't ready for. "Hey, girl. Happy Day Before Valentine's Day! I have big news. Are you sitting down?"

I was, obviously, but I wanted to tell my roommate—my landlord to be more specific—that now wasn't a good time. Like an idiot, I told her the truth. "I'm ready, Chelsea. What is it?"

"We sold the house."

"The house we live in? I didn't know it was on the market." My stomach sank.

"Well, it wasn't." Her words spilled out of her, almost too fast for me to comprehend. "But we got a letter in the mail last week from an investor. At first, we thought it was a scam, but after really thinking about it, Connor and I decided to call the number and see what they said."

"So you sold the house to someone sight unseen?"

"Blake, you are going to flip when you find out how much they offered us." She paused, and I knew she wanted me to ask her how much, but I didn't want to give in to her game. "One point six million. Cash. We're going to be able to buy our dream house in Sedona and still have like three hundred grand in the bank. It's like a Valentine's Day miracle!"

"Oh wow, that's really great for the two of you." I didn't think there was such a thing as a Valentine's Day miracle, much less a reason for celebrating some random day in February, but I had bigger things to think about. What did this sale mean for me, the idiot who rented the front bedroom in their suburban tract-house? "Will I be able to keep renting from the new owners?"

"I asked, and they said that after they assess the property for repairs, you're welcome to complete a rental application, but their company already has a waiting list, so it's not guaranteed." There wasn't a hint of apology in her voice.

Great. I loved that the place I'd already signed a lease

for was no longer guaranteed. Happy National Greeting Card Day to me, indeed!

"So how long until closing?"

I heard her suck in a breath between her teeth, and I knew I should have never trusted this woman or her idiotic husband when I moved into their house four years ago. "That's the thing I wanted to talk to you about. Because it's cash, the buyers want to close in fourteen days. But we were hoping you could move your things a little sooner, so we could shampoo the carpets and stuff."

I stood, eager to shake out the anger flowing through my veins. "You've got to be fucking kidding me." I wasn't one to raise my voice, and I'd never lost my temper on Chelsea before, but this called for it. "California law says that you have to give me a sixty-day notice. This is not okay."

"We know. And we want to help you out, we do. But we can't turn down this offer. This is our dream."

I had dreams, too. Not living on the street, for one. And not using the money I had squirreled away between savings and investments for my own hotel one day. Sure, I had about a hundred thousand dollars, but it was tied up in stocks and bonds, not something I could just use right away. I wanted to tell her just that, but I was too mad to respond.

"We want to make it up to you. Since we can't give you sixty days, we wanted to pay for your first and last month for your new place. We'll even pay for a company to pack and move your stuff."

My head was spinning. Just before I told her to take her rent money and shove it up her ass, my earpiece went off again. "Blake, Mr. Harris is complaining about the hot tub again. Can you come to the lobby and talk to him?"

I growled into the phone. "I have to go. I need to go take care of a very needy guest."

"Oh Blake, thank you so much for understanding. We're just so excited—" I hung up before I had to endure the sound of her voice for another second.

The next time I spoke with her, I would tell her that I wasn't planning on being understanding and that the only thing that excited me about this was the possibility of moving far, far away from her.

I stood from my desk and smoothed out my yellow skirt. I was a sucker for a blazer and a pencil skirt, but I couldn't be the kind of executive that wore black every day like Lizette. Bright colors were my jam. Probably to offset the drab I always felt with plain brown hair and unremarkable brown eyes. I was average, in every sense of the word.

I stomped down the hallway and came through the door behind the check-in desk, wondering what issue I was about to deal with. Pulling my shoulders back and putting on my best pretend smile, I waved at Mr. Harris, who wore a pair of white swim trunks that stuck to his legs in the worst possible way. Watching his shorts drip across the tile floor made me want to burn the entire resort to the ground.

He told me, in his vast knowledge of hot tub maintenance, that we should have the temperature set between 101 and 102 degrees, but according to his highly sensitive skin, the temp in our tub was at least 104 right now, which was unacceptable.

I slammed my fingers into random keys on the nearest keyboard, telling him I was putting a ticket in right away because I agreed with him completely. All of this was unacceptable. But really, I just wanted him and his tiny soaking-wet bathing suit to go away.

Mr. Harris thanked me, shook my hand, and headed back out to the pool. I knew it was unprofessional, but as soon as he was gone, I laid my head down on the counter, groaning. "Can someone just put me out of my misery?"

"But misery looks so cute on you."

I stood and made eye contact with the man on the other side of the counter. I hadn't thought I could have been any angrier than I had been when Chelsea called me, but I was wrong.

"Nope." I waved my hands in surrender. "Not today. I can't do it." The air in the room felt thicker. I looked around, wondering if maybe the heat had been cranked up because I was sweating through my blazer.

Sal shot me a smile that probably caused most women to throw themselves at him, but I was not falling for his game. "I just came by to talk. I even brought you a peace offering." He held a coffee in each hand, placing one on the counter in front of me. Then he narrowed his eyes at me. "Then again, judging by your reaction, you probably don't need any more caffeine."

I spun on my heels and walked down the hallway, back to my office, but he called after me, "We only have like a month to plan this party. We need to get started if we want it to be as good as they deserve."

I paced the floor, my fingers tingling. I gasped for air, but I couldn't get enough in. My entire world was changing drastically. Falling apart. No. Falling apart wasn't right—it was crushing me like a trash compactor.

I felt a sharp pain in my chest. Was this what a heart attack felt like? I wanted to throw up, but I couldn't remember where the trash can was. My vision went blurry. I couldn't focus on anything. I must have sunk to the floor of my office since the palms of my hands grazed the fluffy carpeted rug.

"Whoa, Blake, let's breathe." Sal put the coffee cups on my desk before he crouched down in front of me and put his hand on my back. How was he in my office?

"Breathe." His stern command switched something in my brain, and I was able to take air in. "That's it. You're doing great. Keep breathing with me."

My eyes locked on his as we slowly breathed together. Every inhale he took in, I did, too. With every exhale, I followed.

After a few minutes, my heart returned to its normal pace.

I was beyond embarrassed that he had seen me like this. Mortified was not strong enough of a word. "Who let you in here?"

He flashed that ridiculous smile. "No one did. I saw you spiraling out of control and jumped over the concierge desk."

"You just jumped over? And no one stopped you?" I was going to have a long talk with security later.

"Maybe they knew I rushed back here to help?"

I groaned, but he held his free hand up, reminding me

that his other hand was still rubbing circles across my back. Against my better judgment, I melted into his touch, letting his calm energy regulate mine. "Hey, I came here to talk about wedding stuff, but I can see you have a lot on your plate. I can plan the party myself if that helps." His voice quelled the storm inside of me.

The bachelorette party hadn't even been on my radar until he walked into the lobby and brought it up. But I remembered how upset Lina was after his birthday last year, and I wanted to have some control over the guest list. "I can handle it." I stood, slightly embarrassed that I had let him touch me for so long, shaking his hand off me.

He stood, looking down at me skeptically. "How often do you get panic attacks?"

"Look, Salami, I appreciate the help, but we aren't friends, and I'm not going to talk about personal stuff with you."

He ignored the dig and moved from the floor to the chair Lizette had been in just minutes before. I wanted to laugh at how silly he looked sitting in the barrel chair, his leather jacket and tattoos contrasting the feminine blue velvet. "We could be friends, you know. All you have to do is tell me what's bugging you. I can make it right."

I got up from the floor and, for some reason, I sat in the chair next to him. I glared at him as I asked, "Why do you want to know?"

"Because our best friends are getting married, so we're going to be family."

"You're not my family."

He huffed out a sigh. "You know what I mean,

Blake." He stood, picking up one of the coffee cups. "I just wanted to be nice, but I see you're not interested."

I reached up, grabbing his wrist, but regretted the contact instantly. It reminded me of the time before.

The time I was trying to forget.

"Wait. I'm sorry." I tucked my hands into my lap, trying to ignore how warm his skin felt against mine. "My landlord evicted me five minutes before you walked in. They want me out in a week, and I don't know what I'm going to do."

He sat down again, and his eyebrows bunched together. "That's against the law. They have to give you notice."

"I know. And usually, I would fight it. But my roommates have been awful since the day I moved in. It's hard right now, but being rid of them might be a small blessing."

"Isn't Reece and Maggie's place empty right now?"

I shook my head, hating that he was close enough with my best friend to call her by that cutesy nickname. "It was, but *Lina* and Reece just leased it to a family who signed a two-year contract." I couldn't help but emphasize how he should be saying her name. "The new people started moving things in last weekend, which is why they're staying in a rental while they're here."

"Hmm." Two deep lines appeared in the skin between his eyebrows as he tried to solve my problem. "What about your curly-haired friend? Didn't *Lina* used to live with her?" I tried to hide my irritation. Not only did he know Val well enough to remember her name, since he had apparently been helping her with her new store, but the patronizing way he said Lina's name just pissed me off.

"Valerie? She rented the spare room to one of her employees." I shrugged. "I guess I could see if I could stay on her couch until I find a place."

"Stay with me." When he saw the shocked look on my face, he added, "Not like, *with* me. Come stay at my house."

My eyebrow shot up skeptically. "No offense, but I'd rather sleep on a couch than in some biker-bar bachelor pad." A shiver ran through me, thinking about beer bottles scattered over coffee tables and socks hanging from doorknobs.

He just smiled. "Well, the offer won't expire. If you don't find anything in a few days, let me know. You don't have to stay forever."

My earpiece went off before I could tell him thanks, but no thanks. "A guest just reported an intoxicated person sleeping on the stairs at the top of the third floor."

I held up my finger so Sal didn't think I was talking to myself. "Security. Did you copy?" I waited ten seconds but didn't hear a reply. I hit the button on my radio again. "Security?" Again, no reply.

I stood and motioned toward the door. "I'm sorry, but I have to go handle something."

He got up, stepping toward the doorway. "Is it serious? I can come help."

I waved him off. "Nah, nothing I'm not used to. Thanks for your help earlier. I'm sorry you had to see me like that." I was appalled that he had been the one to find me in a panic, but I was glad he knew just how to get me out of my head.

He took half a step toward me. "I get them, too, Blake. If you ever need to talk—"

"Thank you, but I'll be fine." I stepped into the hallway. "If you'll excuse me, I really have to go check on this issue." The concern on his face pulled at my heartstrings, so I added, "We'll get together to talk about the party soon, though, okay?" I hadn't had a panic attack that bad in a long time, and the sooner I could forget about it, the better. I needed to get a hold of my emotions.

He nodded, giving me a small smile. I hated that it made me miss his lady-killer grin. "Yeah, I'll see you later."

I made my way up the back staircase, glad I had a drunk guest to distract me from the whiplash of being offered a job that might help me afford what I really wanted while also not knowing where I was going to sleep at night.

Chapter Three

I stood at the front door of the cute beach bungalow Lina and Reece were staying in. It had been two days since my roommates set the ticking time bomb, and I hadn't been able to secure a new place to live yet.

Not anywhere that I wouldn't want to move out of immediately, anyway.

Finding a house or apartment without a waiting period for the landlord to run my credit and check my references had been impossible anywhere in the neighborhoods I wanted to live in Santa Barbara.

I decided that tomorrow, I would set my sights on areas a little further out of town. Ones with short leases, so I wouldn't have to commute to the resort for long.

Luckily, my roommates had gone on a Valentine's Day vacation to celebrate their sudden income as soon as they broke the news to me, so I hadn't had the pleasure of running into them at home yet. It was for the best. I needed some time to cool down so I could talk to them without my emotions taking control. The last thing I wanted was to have a panic attack in front of them.

But that didn't mean I hadn't come up with replies to every single scenario I could possibly imagine. It had been an obsession the last two days—Hyperfocusing on what I would say when I finally looked them in the eyes and told them to fuck themselves.

I had so much to do, though, so I needed to shift my focus. Most importantly, I had to pack. To organize my items based on how badly I needed them, and which things could live in storage for who knew how long.

As much as I wanted to hang out with my friends tonight, I knew I needed to make this a quick visit so I could be on my way. I had to go buy boxes and tape and—

"They won't know you're out here unless you knock, you know?"

The sound of his voice startled me. I had gotten so deep in my thoughts that I forgot where I was. I spun around, facing him. My bad mood turned even worse. "Why are you always around? Like a barnacle I can't scrape off."

He reached over my head, no doubt to let me know just how much larger he was than me, and knocked on the door. "Or, you know, a reliable friend."

"Don't you have multiple businesses you run? Why aren't you at one of them?"

"Don't you run a resort? Why aren't you there?"

Before I could give him some smart-ass retort, the door swung open and Lina burst over the threshold. "Blake, you're here!" After she hugged me, she practically threw herself into Sal's arms. "Aww, you made it, too! We were worried you were going to get stuck at the restaurant."

She looked between us, and her brows bunched together. "Did you drive together?"

I yelled, "No!" before biting my bottom lip, embarrassed at how loudly I had answered. I hated how I let this man get under my skin.

Lina looked at me like she had a whole lot of questions to ask me, but Sal tucked her in under his arm and walked them both into the house, leaving me standing on the doorstep. He was mumbling something about me not being able to handle his motorcycle when I lost sight of them.

As soon as I took a step inside, Val's warm, smiling face greeted me, welcoming me into the rental house.

Lina and Valerie had been best friends since high school. And when Lina had taken a job at The Pacifica as our house photographer four years ago, the two of them had quickly absorbed me into their group. I was glad they were doing amazing things, and they weren't leaving me in the dust.

But sometimes, like tonight, I felt more alone than ever before.

The smell of pizza filled the air, and I came around the corner to find the whole crew digging into boxes covering the kitchen island. Lina, Reece, Val's boyfriend Joey, and of course Sal were engaged in conversation.

I really needed to bring a date to the next one of these hangouts. I didn't like being partnered up with him, especially after what had happened between the two of us.

I filled a plate with a couple of slices of pepperoni and followed the group to the living room. Everyone settled on the floor in front of the TV, even though there was a perfectly good glass-topped dining room table in the other room. The house was a vast difference from Lina's usual bohemian style, with its dark slate flooring, glittery quartz countertops and white cabinets.

I, on the other hand, would love to live in a house so clean and modern. Not that I had a choice about that right now, though.

Valerie's explosive laugh jolted me out of my thoughts. She had her head thrown back, and Joey had his arms around her waist, tickling her.

In an attempt to join the group, I asked, "So, Lina, when are you guys coming back next?"

She smiled and answered, "I'll be home for a few days in three weeks, just long enough to do a final dress fitting and to finalize the venue." She looked at her fiancé with hearts in her eyes. "Reece can't get away from work, so he's going to have to stay up late and FaceTime me." She took a sip of her drink before going on. "Then we have another few weeks on the road, and then we'll be back for the wedding."

Sal asked, "Do you have a date set for sure yet?"

Reece answered, "We're shooting for the second or third week of April. Getting married on short notice in a town known for its weddings means we have to hope somewhere we like has a cancelation."

"I know it might not be your favorite place, but I'm

sure I could move things around at The Pacifica. Say the word and I'll get you booked for whatever you want."

Lina let out a long breath. "As much as we would love that, we couldn't afford it. All of our money is tied up in our business right now." Then she looked at Reece again, like he had hung the moon. "Plus, we don't need anything fancy. Just a priest and a dance floor."

Valerie asked, "Are you going to be renting another house? This one has an amazing view." She pointed to the big picture window in front of us, facing the ocean.

Lina had just taken a big bite of pizza, so Reece laughed before answering. "Actually, we'll be renting this house again. The owner is giving us a good rate for booking multiple times in advance." He had a weird smile on his face I couldn't discern.

I looked around the house, thinking how beautiful it was. I would be lucky to ever afford something so perfect. Sal nudged me in the side with his elbow. "Speaking of houses . . . . How is your search coming along?""

"Umm." I sat my plate down on the carpet and pushed it away from me, my appetite suddenly gone.

Val tilted her head to the side. "House search?"

If looks could kill, I knew just who I would like to murder right now. "Thanks for asking, Salad-Spinner, but I hadn't actually told anyone else about my housing situation."

He raised his perfectly sculpted eyebrow at me. "Well, that's dumb. I thought you girls told each other everything."

Lina put her hand on my shoulder. "What's he talking about, Blake?"

I let out a sigh, regretting coming over here tonight. "Chelsea and Connor sold the house for cash and told the seller we'd be out in two weeks. So I have . . ." I pretended to look at my watch. "Like ten days to move."

Valerie leaned forward. "What the hell! That can't be legal!"

"I know, that's what I said. But I hate them and really don't want to spend another sixty days with them."

"I'm sorry we just signed the lease with our renters, or you could stay in our house," Reece said. "I can ask Izzy if the company has any properties you could stay in."

Reece hadn't spoken to his sister since he left Santa Barbara, so I knew what a sacrifice his offer was. And as much as I wanted Lizette and Reece to repair their relationship, I didn't want to be in the middle of it if it didn't go well. "Thanks, but I'll be okay. I have a few leads, but I'll ask her myself if it gets bad enough."

This time, Joey spoke up. He wasn't a man of many words, so when he said something, it was usually well thought out. "I know it's not much, but if you need to crash on our couch, you can. For however long you need." Then he paused, his eyebrows furrowing together as he pointed toward my arch nemesis. "Wait, why don't you move in with Sal? He's got a great house."

As our eyes turned to Sal, he stuffed a slice of pizza into his mouth, stopping him from answering. But he nodded his head.

The panicked feeling that had rushed through me at the office earlier this week pumped through my veins. The room tilted, and I found it hard to breathe again. I shoved my plate into the center of our little circle and stood. "I'm sorry, but I need some air."

I swung open the back door and stepped out onto the porch. My fingers were starting to tingle again, just like they had before.

As I inhaled and exhaled slowly, my two best friends came through the doorway behind me. Lina closed the door to give us some privacy, and Valerie put her hand on my back.

"Sorry. I don't know what came over me." The panic ebbed, but they knew everything wasn't okay.

"Blake, talk to us," Lina said quietly.

Valerie stepped back from me, giving me some space, but still looked concerned. "Why didn't you tell us you were looking for somewhere to live?"

"I didn't want to make a big deal out of it. You both have a lot going on. I'll find a place."

Lina added, "Now I feel like a jackass talking about all this wedding stuff while you have actual problems going on."

I reached for her hands. "No, I'm the jackass. I didn't want to get in the way of either of your plans. The wedding and the new store are way more important than this . . . speed bump."

"Is your mom helping you look?" I knew Val was trying to be resourceful, but I didn't want to think about inviting more people to worry about me.

"I haven't told her, either. Her real estate office is all the way back in Bakersfield. I'm not going to make her drive for two hours to find me a house."

What I didn't say was that when we were growing up, there wasn't a lot of money and my parents had to work a lot to get where they are now. Asking for help just added one more thing for them to take care of. I couldn't shake the feeling that even though my parents were successful now, I didn't want to add to their plates, either.

Lina interjected. "Reece's real estate agent was based out of Malibu when he bought my mom's house. Your mom could find something for you without leaving her office."

"I just don't want to bother her, you know?" She looked at me as if she didn't believe me, so I frantically thought of a way to change the subject.

Val pointed through the window to our group of men, still sitting on the floor, and based on how quickly they turned away from us when we looked over, I could guarantee they were talking about us. "Why not stay at Sal's house? We went to a party there a month ago, and it's really nice. Like gorgeous."

"No offense, but I would rather sleep in my childhood bedroom and commute than live with him."

Lina's eyebrows bunched together. "What aren't you telling us?"

My thoughts flashed back to that night eight months ago. His hands on my hips. His breath on my neck.

I rubbed my hands on my thighs, desperate to erase the memory. "I just don't like him, okay?"

Val asked, "The other night at dinner, things between the two of you were weird. Did he do something? Did he hurt you?" She glared at him through the window.

Oh, he hurt me, alright. But not in the way they were thinking. He crushed my heart into a million pieces, but if I told them the truth, they would try to fix things, and I'd honestly rather forget any of it ever happened.

Lina was only in town for one more night, and I didn't want to sour her visit with my issues. Instead, I grasped at straws for a reason I could use instead. "Do neither of you remember the reason Lina and Reece broke up last year?"

Lina rolled her eyes at me. "We didn't break up. We took a pause."

I rolled my eyes back at her. "You threw away all of your bedsheets. It was a breakup."

"You're avoiding the question, Blake." Val's voice had an unusual edge to it.

My eyes met Sal's through the window. He was too far away for me to see the detail in his face, but the intoxicating pattern of the freckles across his nose was seared into my memory forever. I wasn't ready to tell them what had happened.

I pulled my eyes away from him, focusing back on Val. I tried to think of an excuse, but her mouth opened like she was about to say something. She tilted her head, closed her mouth, and started to speak again.

I laughed at her facial expressions. "The fact that you're second-guessing what you're about to say is disturbing. Spit it out."

She looked sideways at Lina for a second before finally saying, "Is it because he makes you feel the way Chris did in the beginning and you're afraid he's going to cheat on you or break your heart?"

My laugh was incredulous. "This is not about Chris." My ex-boyfriend—who could not keep his dick to himself for almost the entire two years we spent together—had not been a thought in my mind for a long time. "I'm not even mad at him anymore."

Lina and Val folded their arms over their chests like twin crime scene investigators.

Eager to talk about anything other than why I couldn't stand Sal, I was willing to admit something else I had been keeping to myself. "I did a little bit of internet stalking a few months ago, and he and Maxine are married now. They seem really happy, with a baby on the way, even. It really doesn't bother me anymore."

It was a sentence I could finally say truthfully, which I hadn't been able to until just now. Chris had started sleeping with Maxine three months after he started dating me. He had sworn they were just friends, but the signs were there. It just took the better part of a year and a half for me to see the glaring red flags.

It hurt when I found out, not only because the person I had thought I loved was unfaithful, but also because Maxine had been a good friend of mine. We had happy hour together once a month the entire time she was fucking my boyfriend. Awkward.

I shook off the anger bubbling up. "If I had to suffer a little so that the two of them could have their happily ever after, I'm okay with it. Sure, they went at it horribly, but they found true love, and I realized months ago that it was their problem, not mine."

"That's exactly my point." Val said. "I think you've been keeping anyone who might actually mean anything to you at arm's length so they don't do you dirty like Chris did."

Lina put her hand on my shoulder gently. "We just want you to move on when you're ready."

My eyes rolled at her practically on their own. "I have been ready! I've been dating idiots from the dating apps for over a year. They're just not the right fit."

"Which brings us back to Sal." Val whispered.

"Nope. Absolutely not. He's not it, so don't even start." I thought about what he had done to me last summer. Or not done, I guess. "Sal's playboy attitude and drug-abusing friends are the reason the two of you *paused*." I repeated her own word, to show her how ridiculous it was.

Lina put her hand on her hip. "Well, that's bullshit. It wasn't his fault, and you know it."

I turned my glare on her, determined to keep my secret to myself. "I'm allowed to feel the way I do, you know."

Val leaned against the balcony railing. "I agree. You're allowed to feel the way you do, but we can't go in there and kick his ass for you if you don't tell us the real reason you don't like him."

All three of us turned back toward the window, where Sal was telling an engaging story, full of arm motions and facial expressions.

"I just hate him. Believe me."

"But where are you going to live?" Lina's voice had become quiet and concerned.

"I'll figure something out. I'm taking some time off next week to pack, and I'll make a few more phone calls to see what I can find in between trips to my storage unit."

Val nodded toward the boys. "I'm going to believe you for now, but I still think you're full of shit. Promise me if nothing comes up, you'll at least take his offer until you can get in somewhere else."

I nodded, even though I had no intention of moving in with him. Lina reached for the door. "We should go back inside. One of them is going to come get us soon. I can feel it."

As we walked through the doorway, the boys were engrossed in conversation. Sal's booming voice echoed across the room. "Well, I can't fucking stand her, either, so it doesn't matter."

Reece responded, "That goes against everything you've ever told me about—"

All three sets of eyes locked on us, and the men went suspiciously silent. Joey smiled and gave a little wave. "Welcome back, ladies. Everything okay?"

Valerie snuggled up next to him on the floor and shot him a look, which I interpreted as, *"Blake is being unreasonable, and we will come up with a plot to crack her open as soon as we leave tonight."*

His sweet kiss seemed to be a silent agreement, and I knew the clock was ticking for me to find my own place, even more now than before.

The rest of the night went by quickly. The group fell into the usual banter, sharing jokes, movie and music trivia, until we were all too tired to comprehend anything any longer.

We poured out into the driveway as a group. I waved

to Val and Joey as they drove off, and Sal came to stand next to me.

He gave me a nod and mumbled, "The offer stands, Blake." But now that I knew he hated me as much as I hated him, I didn't even respond.

Without another word, he put on his helmet and walked to his bike. I barely noticed those long, muscular legs swinging over his motorcycle, or how his strong shoulders moved when he started the engine. The smell of exhaust as he drove away also did not make my girly bits tingle. Not even a little.

That guy was nothing but trouble.

Lina's arms wrapped around me warmly as she said goodbye one more time. "I understand that you don't want to stay with him, but his house is big, and he works all the time."

Reece added, "You'd probably never see him."

I tried to give them a smile, but I couldn't make it meet my eyes. "I'm glad you're looking out for me, but I can handle this."

Reece tucked Lina under his arm. "I know you've got this, but let me call my sister. There's probably a corporate rental you can stay in for the time being." He paused, probably noticing my grimace. He looked down at his future wife, something unspoken happening between them before he looked back up at me. "But please, don't let Sal be your last resort. He's a good guy."

I hadn't fully been Team Reece until a few months ago, when I knew for sure he wasn't going to destroy my best friend's heart. But I had to admit, he was kind and helpful and sweet. I really wanted to trust him about this, too.

I smiled for real this time. "I'll think about staying with Sal. But only if there are no other options."

The day Chelsea wanted me out was finally here. I turned on my blinker, about to turn into my storage facility for the fourth time today. I knew that legally, if I needed a few more days, she wouldn't be able to stop me, but I was looking forward to never seeing her face again.

When I had finally had a chance to talk to my now-former roommates a few days ago, they went back on their offer for a moving company, but promised they would help with at least a security deposit on a new place. Which meant that I really couldn't rely on them for anything.

So here I was, dropping off the last of my belongings with a plan to stay at a cheap motel until something else presented itself. Val and Lina had spent the last week relentlessly sending me properties in the area, but unfortunately, there hadn't been a single place that was willing to let a tenant move in immediately.

I thought about staying at The Pacifica, but I really didn't want to deal with nosy staff members. I hoped that wherever I slept tonight didn't have bedbugs.

My phone rang, and I cringed. I had taken yesterday and today off to get my things organized and packed, and I was worried it was Paige calling about a problem no one at the resort could solve without me, which was getting old.

I glanced down at the screen in the middle of my dashboard as I made the turn and saw that it was not work at all, thank goodness. I hit the button on the dash, answering the call, before leaning out my window to punch in the code to open the security gate. "Hello?"

"Hey twerp. What are you up to?" My older brother's voice came through the phone, giving me mixed emotions. I usually told him all the drama going on in my life, but I didn't want him to tell Mom what I was currently handling on my own, because it wasn't going well.

"Nothing much, Jake." I lied. "How about you?" Our parents weren't cruel people. In fact, I didn't think I'd ever seen them fight before. However, the meanest thing they ever did was give their children names that rhyme. The second meanest thing was giving their daughter a masculine name. Everyone always assumed I was Jake's little brother, especially when I went through my pixie cut stage before my boobs came in during high school. I shook my head, trying to forget those years completely.

"Well, Sophie and I have news, and I wanted to tell you before Mom called you and talked your ear off about it."

I parked the car in front of my little storage garage. "Ooh, do tell!"

"We're having another baby!"

"Aww, Jakey, that's amazing. I'm so happy for you." When he didn't say anything, I asked, "How are the other two taking it?"

He laughed at the question. "Well, Annie is ecstatic about being an older sister, but Phillip hasn't come out of his room since we told him. He's upset that the boy to girl ratio might be thrown off, and he doesn't want to wait four more weeks to find out."

We talked for a few more minutes about their growing family before a crashing noise in the background caused him to hang up quickly with a promise that he would call me back soon and a warning that Mom was probably going to call.

I hopped out of the car, opening the back hatch of my Subaru Forrester before rolling up the door of my storage unit.

I had tried to pack everything based on when I might need it. My first trip here today had been stuff that I probably wouldn't unpack again . . . old yearbooks, clothes, and toys from my childhood that I wasn't willing to donate. This trip was stuff I wouldn't need right away but wanted access to, just in case—pots and pans, cocktail dresses, and two gigantic boxes of blankets and throw pillows.

It was freezing outside, but I was drenched in sweat several minutes later as I pulled the last box out of my car and laid it on the ground in my unit. Out of breath, I sat on one of the sturdier boxes.

It sure would have been nice to have some help moving all this stuff, but I knew how busy all of my friends were, and I worried I was bothering them with all the time they'd already used helping me look for houses. This would be a great time to have a boyfriend. Maybe one with a truck.

Sure, I could have hired movers, but the thought of using any of my savings for this situation that was out of my control drove me insane. Looking back, I probably could have gotten help, but the principle of doing it my damn self was more important than anything at this point.

I'd spent my whole adult life supporting myself. Putting people out because of my needs was not something I did. If I couldn't do it myself, I didn't do it at all.

But having a cute guy to help me move would have been really nice.

I pulled out my phone and opened up the dating app I had been browsing the last month or so. This one was new, and the ads said it guaranteed a happily ever after. It was probably full of shit, but I was willing to give it a try.

I swiped through a few profiles, finding a couple of guys that I thought were cute, and sent them messages introducing myself. Maybe one of them would turn into a whirlwind romance, and I would move in with him and all my worries would disappear.

Ugh, I really needed to get laid.

I hadn't reached out to my hookup guy in forever, so I decided to send him a booty-text. I pulled him up in my contacts—of course he was saved under "Hottie Hookup" instead of his real name, Grant—and sent him a message: *Hey you, sorry it's been a while. I've been slammed at work. Wanna get together this weekend?*

Hopefully he understood that the slamming I really wanted was against a headboard somewhere.

I scrolled through our texts, trying to remember the

last time we had gotten together, and I realized that it had been last June. Wow, work really had kept me too busy.

I started thinking about June and realized that I hadn't seen him since before that night with . . . . I stopped my thoughts before going down a spiral I didn't want to ride.

My phone rang in my hand. My mom was on the other line, just like Jake had predicted. "Hi Mom."

"My goodness, Blake, have you heard?"

"I'm assuming you're talking about Jake's news?"

"Isn't it wonderful? Babies are such a blessing." The excitement in my mom's voice was contagious, and I found myself smiling.

"Three kids is definitely going to be an adventure for them." She said something else, but a motorcycle drove past, its sound echoing through the metal cubicle I sat in. I stood up and peered out the door, watching the rider stop about ten spaces down from me.

"Are you going to answer me or not?"

"Sorry, I didn't hear the question."

"Sure you didn't." She laughed, not believing me. "I said, when are you going to give me grandbabies?"

My mother's thirst for grandchildren was unquenchable. "You know my stance on babies, mom. I'm so happy that Jake and Sophie have them so you and Dad can get your fill. But as for me, it's not going to happen."

"I know, sweetheart, I just hope that one day you'll change your mind." She usually didn't pester me in the kid department, and I knew she was coming from a place of love. But I just didn't have the maternal urge, and I doubted that I ever would.

I propped the phone against my ear with my shoulder and made sure everything was in its rightful place. As I stepped out and rolled the door closed, she asked, "How are your roommates?"

It was odd that she brought them up, because she knew I thought they were the most annoying humans on the planet. "They're okay, I guess."

She made a squeaky noise before blurting out, "I have to tell you that I know about your living situation."

My heart stopped. "What? Did Val tell you?"

She let out a long breath. "No. You're going to accuse me of being a stalker, I'm sure, but I was looking at houses in your area for a client yesterday, and I saw your house was pending. Were you going to tell me you were moving?" She sounded a little hurt, which made me feel guilty. I had kept it from her to not add to her stress, but no matter what, I was a burden.

I reached up, closing the hatch on my car, and propped myself on the back bumper. "It happened so quickly. I haven't had a chance to think about it, really. I was going to tell you once I found a new place."

"I can help you, you know. I wasn't voted Bakersfield's best real estate agent three years in a row for nothing."

"I know you can help, Mom, and I promise to call you if I can't find a place." Luckily, she didn't see my fingers crossed behind my back. I didn't want to be the woman who left her hometown to become successful, only to beg for her mommy's help.

The sound of a motorcycle reverberated down the

alley again, and I looked up as it stopped in front of me. I didn't recognize him until he lifted his helmet's reflective visor. Every muscle in my body went tight, and I suddenly understood how a gazelle experiencing fight-or-flight reflexes felt.

I didn't hear what my mom said next, but I mumbled, "I've got to call you back later. I love you," before I hung up on her.

He killed the engine on his bike, and I yelled out before he could speak first. "So, you're just following me around now?"

He barked out a laugh, and I was glad he had his helmet on so I couldn't see the way one side of his mouth lifted higher than the other when he smiled. "I own multiple restaurants in Southern California. Excuse me for keeping excess furniture in a storage unit in case something gets broken or stolen."

I looked him up and down, fully aware of his bullshit. "You really expect me to believe that you're picking up furniture while riding that thing?"

In one smooth movement, he took off his helmet and rested it on the gas tank. Then he pulled off his backpack, unzipped it and took out two silver candlesticks. "A set of these were stolen last night from my downtown location. Since I'm working there tonight, I thought I'd grab a replacement before I had to head over and prep for the dinner service. And before you ask, this is the closest unit to my house, which makes it easy for me to stop by on the way to work." I still wasn't sure if I should believe him. It was an awful big coincidence that my only housing option just showed up on two wheels before my mom stepped in and tried to save the day.

He went on, "I can show you my storage unit, if you don't believe me. I have too many things to do every day besides following you around town, saving your ass."

I crossed my arms, trying to keep from slapping him. "Speaking of saving me . . . why did you tell everyone my business the other night?"

He smiled, putting the candlesticks back in his bag. "I assumed you had already told them, since you're best friends and all."

I looked down at my dirty sneakers. "I hadn't had a chance to." His stare bore into me. He didn't believe me. So I let the truth out. "They both have so much going on with the wedding and the new store. I didn't want to give them anything else to worry about."

"From what I know about your friends, they would love to take care of you." I finally looked up at him, and I realized I wasn't going to win this. His voice was barely audible when he said, "Look, it's really important to Reece that you come stay with me until you find a place. He's been bugging me all week about it. You don't have to sign a lease or anything, and you can leave as soon as you find somewhere else." When I still didn't respond, he said louder, "The girls will also kill me if I don't do this for you."

I rubbed my forehead. "Okay fine. I'll go take a look. But only so Lina and Val get off my case. But I would rather live literally anywhere else."

He nodded. "I agree. I'm only doing this because my

best friend wants me to. Otherwise, you could sleep in this storage unit for all I care."

When he didn't move to put his helmet on or start his motorcycle, I threw my hands up. "Well, are you going to take me to this mysterious house of yours or what?"

A smile crept onto his lips, and he slipped his helmet over his head. "Yeah. Get in your car. You can follow me there."

Chapter Four

I followed him through winding roads and up into rolling fields in the hills outside of town. It made a little sense to me why he drove a motorcycle now. I was sure it was fun going up and down switchback roads at the speeds that thing could probably get up to.

When I imagined where Sal lived, I expected him to live closer to downtown or maybe in a condo overlooking the beach. I was surprised that he had a house so far off the beaten track.

I had been in this neighborhood before, though. It was right up the road from my favorite geocache. At least if I stayed here for a little while, I'd be able to visit it more often.

We stopped at a wrought-iron gate, and I watched him type a code into the security box. I made a mental note to ask him for the code as soon as we got inside so I wouldn't get locked out in the two or three weeks I had to stay here.

Once the gate opened, I followed him in, and my jaw

dropped at what was on the other side of the vine-covered walls.

The yard was at least two acres across, the grass greener than any I'd seen before. To the left were horse stables and a sprawling corral.

To the right was a Spanish-style house that could only be described as a mansion. It had to be at least 8,000 square feet.

How did a loud-mouthed, tatted-up man live in a place like this? It looked more like a small resort than a single guy's house.

As we drove closer, I saw that the building was the typical white plaster with dark wood accents, like most houses around Santa Barbara, but what set it apart from all the rest were the giant curved windows on almost every wall. I peeked in the rearview mirror, looking at the rolling hills behind us. The views inside this place must be magical.

Why the hell hadn't Valerie led with this when she told me she'd been here for a party? Gorgeous was an understatement.

I continued following him until he pulled up to a detached garage with enough space for at least eight vehicles. It made me wonder what was inside. He got off the bike but didn't open a garage door, so I parked next to him. When I got out of the car and walked around to him, he had his helmet tucked under his arm and his eyes were scanning the house in front of us. "It's not much, but it's mine."

I laughed and took in the surrounding landscape.

"Why didn't you say something when I accused you of having a dirty little bachelor pad?"

He looked down at me, smiling. "Well, you haven't seen the inside yet. It could very well be littered with beer bottles."

He took off down the cobblestone path and gestured for me to follow him. He unlocked the tall wooden front door and swung his arm in front of him. "After you."

I stepped through the doorway, and my breath left my lungs. The circular entryway had hardwood floors that looked older than the city itself, and a giant bouquet of flowers sat on a round antique table in the center. But the real beauty, the thing that caused my heart to flutter, was the bookshelves that lined the walls. I walked up to one and ran my fingers along the spines.

"I feel like Belle when she moved into the castle."

He laid his helmet on the table and grabbed a book from a shelf on the other side of the room. The paperback in his hands looked worn and well-read. He flipped through the pages and then looked at me, concern in his eyes. "Wait, did you just allude that I'm the beast?"

I shrugged at him, letting him know that he knew what I meant, and reached for a book. "Have you read any of these?"

He put the book back and thumbed over the spines closest to him. "Maybe not all of them, but I would say about 80 percent."

I grabbed a paperback that looked like it had been read a hundred times. The cover featured a shirtless man who was just barely covered by a woman wearing an awful lot of tulle. "Even *The Lady and the Duke*?"

He took two steps toward me and snatched the book out of my hand, hugging it tightly to his chest. "Especially that one. Lady Croxley is a badass."

I burst out a laugh until I realized he was completely serious. "Wait, you like trashy romance novels?"

He gave me a shy smile before slipping the book back on the shelf. "Romance novels aren't trashy. Who's your favorite author?"

"Hmm, that's a hard one." I thought for a few seconds. "Probably Jane Austen."

"Emma or Pride and Prejudice?" He asked with a gleam in his eye.

"What do you mean?"

"Which one do you like better?"

"Oh, that's not fair. They're both amazing." I thought for a second. "Probably Pride and Prejudice, but only if I was forced to choose."

He nodded his head, smiling. "So you're a Mr. Darcy kind of girl?"

"I mean, I wouldn't turn down Mr. Knightly, but yeah, Mr. Darcy is the best." I took one more glance around the room. "How did you get into reading romance?"

"I spent every summer in this house growing up, and my grandparents didn't have television or Internet, so I had to keep myself busy somehow."

He took a step through an archway that led to a massive kitchen, and I followed him. "So this house belongs to your grandparents? Lina told me you cut yourself off from your family when you opened your first restaurant?"

He sat his elbows on the massive island countertop, leaning forward. He let out a deep breath, staring at the granite in front of him. "It's complicated, but yeah, I don't have the support of my family anymore." He shifted his gaze to me. "My grandfather gave this house to me for my twenty-fifth birthday, before any of the shit went down."

Wow, what a birthday gift. I got a necklace with a B on it for my twenty-fifth, and he got an entire villa. "Do you talk to any of them?"

He shook his head. "Just a couple of cousins on my mom's side and my little sister Camilla. Our grandmother was diagnosed with Alzheimer's last year, and Cami takes care of her more than anyone else. She brings her to the house to jog her memory sometimes, but other than that…" He shrugged, letting me guess how bad it had been with his family.

I didn't see my family a lot, but we were close. The thought of not being able to talk to them whenever I wanted made me nauseous.

Sal must have read my mind, because then he quietly said, "I would totally give up the property if it would fix things between us, though."

He stood and gestured to the rest of the vast, open living space. "So this is it." Before I could ask him another question, his phone rang. He unzipped his leather motorcycle jacket and took it out of an inner pocket. His eyes lit up when he saw the screen and mumbled, "I've got to take this. Take a look around."

I knew I shouldn't be listening, but I couldn't stop

myself. I pretended to be looking out the tall windows, but my attention remained fixed on his words.

"Hey, how's your day going?" The pitch of his voice was higher than usual. He must like the person on the other line a lot. "No, right now is fine. I've got a little time before I have to head to the restaurant."

I walked around the open living area, running my fingers across the top of the plush white couch that faced the window overlooking the swimming pool and the grassy hill sloping down to the valley below. The other person must have asked a question and Sal answered, "I should be done around midnight. Unless that's too late?"

I heard him opening cabinets in the kitchen but had to use all my wits to not turn and look at him. Instead, I walked over to the formal dining area and pretended that the dark wood table with seating for twelve was the most interesting table I'd ever seen. He went on, "But can we meet at your place tonight? Reece's friend is staying at mine for a bit, and I don't want it to be weird."

Hmm, now I was Reece's friend. So whoever was on the phone with him was close enough to know his best friend.

The mystery person must be funny, because he started to laugh, and replied, "No, really, though. I can't wait to see you, either." Then he laughed again. Okay, there was definitely an attractive girl on the other line.

I made a lap around the dining room, wondering what kind of girl she was. If she was taller than me . . . thinner . . . blonder. I wondered what she had that I didn't.

"Sorry about that." The proximity of his voice startled me. I hadn't noticed that he had ended the call and walked right up to me. "Why don't I show you to your room?"

"Please don't think you have to reschedule your booty calls because I'm staying here. I'll be gone as soon as I can get a lease somewhere else."

"Excuse me?" Anger flashed in his eyes.

"I'm just saying, don't stop your revolving door of women in here on my account."

The muscles in his shoulders flexed defensively. "My what?"

"Look, I get up early for work, and you're always out late. I probably wouldn't notice your harem of women, anyway."

He rolled his eyes and grumbled, "Follow me," before stomping down the hallway that was off the dining room. "The room you're staying in is at the very end of the other wing from mine."

We passed multiple doors as we walked down the hall. He pointed out where the bathrooms were and how to get to the laundry room from where I was staying, but his voice was clipped and his sentences short. I thought about asking him more about the history of the house, but I had a feeling he wasn't in the mood for chitchat anymore. Part of me regretted what I had said. I didn't mean to piss him off right after he had given me a place to stay, but it was like I couldn't stop myself from antagonizing him every chance I could get.

He swung the door open and directed me to enter the room. It was enormous, but if I were being honest, ugly as hell. The walls were orange, and the queen-sized bed had a canopy with gauzy curtains, matching the wall. I felt like I had stepped inside an orange creamsicle.

"Since you're only staying temporarily, I figured the room farthest from mine would be the most comfortable for you. That way, I don't wake you up when I come home in the middle of the night with a woman under each arm."

I sat on the bed, wondering if I should ask him what nerve I struck, when he leaned against the doorframe. His shirt bunched up and my eyes betrayed me, scanning the tanned skin above his belt buckle. He was surprisingly toned for a man who spent his life surrounded by Italian food.

"I can fuck whoever I want, when I want." His tone was blunt, and it snapped me out of my thoughts.

"I never said you couldn't." My eyes met his, and some of the ice seemed to melt.

"I'm just saying, if I want to bring a woman home, I can and I will. And if you want to have men over." His mouth twisted, like he had bitten into a lemon. "I hope they enjoy your orange bedroom."

With that, he turned and walked down the hallway. He called out behind him, "The gate code is 6969."

I replied too quietly for him to hear. "Of course it is."

After sitting for a few seconds, I stood up and scanned the room.

My phone vibrated in my pocket, so I pulled it out to see who it was.

A spark of excitement jumped through me when I saw that Hottie Hookup had sent me a picture.

But then my stomach dropped even deeper when I

opened it and saw a Barbie-doll-looking blonde with her hand on his chest, a big rock on her finger. His text read: *Hey girl, long time no see. I actually have some really big news! I'm engaged!*

I plopped back down on the fluffy orange bed, feeling more sorry for myself than I ever had before.

I replied: *Oh my gosh, congrats! I'm so happy for you!* before deleting his contact information from my phone.

Guess I didn't even have a random hookup anymore.

Living here was going to be difficult, but not impossible. Sal and I would do our best to avoid each other, and in a few weeks, I'd be moving into a place I really loved. Or even just kind of liked.

I opened up my dating app and started browsing. Maybe I could find someone else to bring to Lina's wedding so I didn't look like a complete loser.

I sent a message to a cute blond with a puppy in his profile picture.

This misery was only temporary. I had to believe that.

The resort had taken up all of my free time lately, so I hadn't had to spend my first week living in Sal's house cooped up in the orange disaster bedroom. Not that I was there much. Wedding season was starting to amp up, and Spring Break vacationers from all over the country were slowly trickling in. With that and our renovations, I wasn't going to have more than one day a week off for a while.

He was also out of the house a lot. I had only seen him twice since I moved in. Both times he didn't so much as grunt a goodbye before he grabbed his riding gear and left. Things were probably really busy at his restaurants, too.

I sat at my desk, flipping my little paper calendar to March before waking up my computer so I could place an order for more towels. Ours were mysteriously disappearing at a higher rate than usual, and I couldn't figure out why.

My office phone rang, pulling me out of my imagined scene of towel burglars terrorizing the city. "Thanks for calling The Pacifica. This is Blake. How may I help you?"

"Hi honey! How's your day going?"

I leaned back in my chair, releasing the tension in my shoulders I didn't know I had been holding. "Hi Mom, what's up?"

"Well, I have some good news and some bad news."

"That sounds exciting." I closed my eyes, wondering what I should be worried about first.

"Well, the rental situation in Santa Barbara is a lot worse than I had initially imagined."

"Uh huh." I kind of figured that, but she was always more positive than I was. I must have gotten my pessimism from Dad.

"The good news is that you're staying with a friend, right?"

"I would call him more of an acquaintance."

"Well, the good news . . ." she began again, a smile in her voice, "Is that you have somewhere nice to stay, so I think we can shift your market from rentals to something you can buy."

I picked up a pen and drew lazy circles on a sticky

note. "The money I have is for . . ." I stopped, not wanting to admit why I'd been saving for the last decade. Why I spent countless hours every month tracking the stock market, ensuring my investments were going to be there when I needed them. "Everything I have is tied up in investments right now. It's not a good time to pull from them."

"Well, yes, I know that, but the rentals in the area you're looking at that are worth your money all have month-long wait lists just to put in a deposit. The move-in dates are all pushed back even farther than that."

I drew a little sad face on my paper. "That's what I found when I was looking, too."

"However," she started, and I could barely breathe, wondering what she was about to say. "Your dad and I have some savings we can share with you to help, but we can't afford a whole down payment. Maybe if we expand the neighborhood or start doing some cold-calls, we can find something you can buy in a few months."

Ugh, a few months at Sal's sounded like a prison sentence, but her offer was really generous. I pretended to be excited. "That's a great idea, Mom. And thanks for the possible loan. I appreciate your help, I really do."

We talked a little about Jake and his wife, how her pregnancy was going and how he was worried about their small house fitting everyone, but then I glanced at the clock and told her I had to get back to work. It was sweet of her to offer me down-payment help, but I didn't think I should take her up on it. If it came down to that, I would just pull my money out of the stock market.

I finished ordering the towels and then hunkered

down to reply to my daily barrage of customer complaint emails. Six emails in, I had given away multiple nights and a handful of vouchers for our restaurant that would hopefully be open again before summer when my door swung open.

I looked up to find Lizette with a frown painted across her face. I smiled up at her, knowing that she probably just needed to see a friendly face. "What's up?"

She sat in one of my blue chairs and rubbed her face with her hands. "My brother called me last week."

"Oh?" I knew he was going to, but I didn't know how much of their estrangement I was supposed to be aware of.

She put her hands in her lap, already looking more relaxed. "He said you were looking for a place to stay and wanted to know if the corporation had any properties you could rent. I did some digging, but we have nothing available."

"I was looking, but I found somewhere. Don't stress."

She leaned forward a little. "Why didn't you think you could come to me?"

"Because I knew you would worry about me more than you need to. I'll find something more permanent soon, I promise." Laughing a little, I tried to shift the conversation off myself since I didn't know if I could actually deliver on my promise. "So, did you guys talk about anything else?"

"I told him I'm trying to give you a position at corporate and you haven't given me an answer yet." Her sly smile told me she wasn't ready to tell him anything about her own life, so mine would have to suffice.

"I'm not sure if I want the responsibility of more than one property."

"Well, think about it. At least I know now that you were dealing with moving when I offered you the job and not completely ignoring me." She stood, putting her hand on the back of the chair. "I only came by to check on the renovations—which seem to be going well, by the way—so I can't stay and chat. But I want you to know that you are my friend first and my coworker second. You can always talk to me."

This was not something she would have said six months ago. She had mentioned she was going to therapy for her divorce, so maybe her icy exterior was finally melting a little. "Thanks, Lizette. I appreciate it."

She smiled. "I'm actually glad you didn't tell me, though. It was a nice surprise hearing from Reece. I think he's finally in a really good place."

I nodded at her, knowing more about him than probably any other man I knew. "He really is."

After she left, I double-checked my calendar, making sure I still had the next day off. I was going to put some thought into the job offer and the prospect of buying my own house. It was time to put myself first for a change.

Chapter Five

I had my AirPods in, listening to a playlist comprising my favorite showtunes and musicals while I finished up some work on my laptop. I still managed to have the day off, but if I didn't go through my emails and facilities requests every day, the enormous pile of work that waited for me tomorrow would be unbearable.

I wondered if it would be better or worse if they stationed me at the corporate office.

Staring at the basket full of dirty clothes in the middle of this borrowed room made me regret leaving most of my stuff in my storage unit. Only having a week's worth of clothing available was proving to be more difficult than I had thought, and I wished I had access to my entire wardrobe.

Maybe I would visit the storage unit this afternoon and grab a few more outfits.

I had the house to myself all day, since Sal always left early and worked until the middle of the night on Saturdays, so I thought I would wash my clothes and watch a few episodes of the dating show Lina and Val had gotten me hooked on last year.

So far, staying at his house wasn't too terrible. I had only seen him twice, and he was headed out the door both times.

I scooped up my basket and left, not wanting to be in this ugly orange room any longer, and walked to the laundry room on Sal's side of the house.

This room was a dream. It had two washers and dryers stacked on top of each other with cabinets on the opposite wall. There was a giant butcher-block table in the middle of the room that would be perfect for folding and organizing my clothes before I had to take them back to the ugliest room in America.

As I put my darks in the top washer and my lights into the bottom, I sent a silent thank-you to Sal's grandmother for designing a house like this. It was genius.

Right before closing the door, I realized I could save another day of laundry by also washing the clothes I was currently wearing.

I hopped on one foot, getting my last sock off, and reached to unhook my bra. Then I remembered I had left the curtains wide open in the living room, and didn't want to accidentally flash a gardener or the pool guy, so I decided to keep it and my panties on until these loads were clean.

A guilty pleasure Zac Efron song shuffled into my ears, and I couldn't help but sing and dance along as I filled the machines with soap and set them to start.

I blared "Just Wanna Be With You" at the top of my lungs and spun around in a circle, but my joy turned into absolute terror as I found myself eye-to-eye with a woman I'd never seen before. She was dressed in a blue and white floral button-up dress and had long black hair. And she stood in the doorway of the laundry room.

I let out a scream and frantically covered my body with my hands.

She gave me a little smirk and asked, "Is that High School Musical?"

I pulled an AirPod out of my ear and asked, "Who are you?"

Her eyebrow rose, and she let out a giggle. "I assumed the first time I found a naked woman dancing around my brother's house, it wouldn't be because she was doing laundry."

I looked around the room, reached for a towel at the top of a folded stack, and wrapped it around myself. I didn't want to have a conversation with her—with anyone, really—while in my unmentionables.

For a split second, I was relieved that this gorgeous woman walking into Sal's house unannounced was his sister and not some booty-call. But then I felt my skin heat. His sister just saw me pretty much naked. I didn't even like undressing in front of myself with the lights on. This was humiliating.

"Who are you talking to, Camilla?" An elderly voice echoed from around the corner. I cringed. This was about to get so ugly.

My new friend Camilla turned to the woman and responded sweetly, "Nonna, Sal's girlfriend is doing their laundry in here. She wasn't expecting us, so let's go out to the stables so she can get . . . ." She looked back at me and winked, "cleaned up."

I opened my mouth to correct her. I was not Sal's girlfriend, and the thought forced a wave of nausea through my body, but before I could speak, I heard the older woman clap her hands. "Oh, my Salvatore finally moved his girlfriend in. Let me come see her!" Her voice was enthusiastic, and I wondered who she thought I was.

Camilla took a step out into the hallway and held her hands up. "No, Nonna, let the girl have a moment. She'll come out and talk to us in a few minutes." She then turned to me and smiled. "It was nice to meet you. We'll see you when you're dressed."

Her words were a kind-hearted order, not a request. Like she was used to getting her way without having to ask. Luckily, her smile told me she was happy to see me, even though I was practically naked in her brother's house, so I just nodded and said, "Sure. I'll come find you in a few," as she spun on her heel, leaving me alone in the laundry room.

I waited several minutes, making sure they had vacated the house before tip-toeing down the hallway to my room. Frantic for something to wear, I pulled open the top drawer of the dresser I'd been keeping my things in and cringed when all I had were a set of pink silk pajamas —that I hadn't realized I had brought to Sal's until I was unpacking my stuff—and a set of flannel pajamas. I let out a breath, grabbed the flannels, and put them on. There was a coffee stain down the front, but it would have to do.

I fixed my hair in the mirror and touched up my

makeup quickly. I usually had a slight wave in my hair, but today it was a little out of control. At least my eyeliner was on point. If I couldn't be dressed appropriately, at least my face would be put together.

I made my way out the back door of the house and down the hill toward the stables. Standing outside the first stall was Sal's sister and the oldest-looking woman I had ever seen in my life. Her hair was as white as snow, cut short in that muffin-top style that all grandmas seem to have. She was hunched over a walker and had on a burgundy sweatsuit featuring a sailboat embroidered on the front. It was adorable, and honestly, a life goal I didn't know I had until just now.

She turned to me and squealed before I could get any closer. For a woman that relied on a walker, she sure was fast. She took off toward me, saying, "Come closer, dear, let me look at you."

Her Italian accent was thick, and I wondered if this was the grandma that Sal had gotten all of his recipes from.

Not that I cared.

As if I had conjured him from the underworld, Sal's motorcycle came flying up the drive. I'd never seen him drive so fast, and my stomach definitely wasn't flipping from worrying about him possibly crashing in front of us.

He slowed down when he came up to the garage, but he didn't park in his usual spot. Instead, he turned and came toward us on the dirt path. He parked the bike about ten feet away from us and leapt off it without shutting down the engine.

Camilla let out a barking laugh as he yanked his

helmet off his head. She took a few steps forward and pulled him into a hug. "I hope you didn't rush home to see us. Nonna was restless today, and I had to get her outside. The house is usually empty on Saturday afternoon, so we didn't think we had to call ahead."

I felt Nonna's hand wrap around my arm warmly as she said, "Salvatore, why didn't you tell us that your girlfriend was so beautiful?"

I fought to keep my body from going stiff as a board. He had mentioned that she had Alzheimer's, and I didn't want to accidentally trigger anything, so I looked to Sal for guidance.

"Can I talk to you for a second . . ." his eyes went from mine to the hand wrapped around my arm before he added, "babe?"

I felt the seconds ticking around us, like time was slowing down until I made a decision. The corner of his lip turned into a frown, and his eyes were pleading. Sure, I didn't like him, but I knew that his family life wasn't exactly a happy one.

I turned to Sal's grandma. "Excuse me, Nonna. I'll be right back."

She smiled warmly at me and released my arm. I followed Sal down the dirt path to stand behind his motorcycle, the sound of its idling muffling our words. He turned so his back faced them, and I wondered if it was to hide what he was about to tell me or if it was to block them from seeing the scathing look I was giving him. Maybe both.

"You have about ten seconds to tell me what's going on before I scream," I told him.

He let out a long breath. "They think we're dating."

"No shit, Sherlock. Care to explain why your sister walked in on me naked and assumed I was your girlfriend?"

His eyes flared wide, and I realized my voice was louder than it should have been. Sal took a step closer to me, holding his hand out to quiet me down. He bit his lip, worry painted across his brow. I started to tell him he couldn't regulate my volume, but I glanced over his shoulder and saw the absolute sweetest look on his grandmother's face.

Dammit. I knew I could hate him for many reasons for the rest of my life, but I could never hurt a face like hers. I knew then and there I had to go along with whatever this asinine plan of his was.

I spoke quietly, my voice traveling just a few inches. "Care to tell me why they think we're together?"

He ran his hands across the top of his mohawk, which was in surprisingly good condition for having just been stuffed into a helmet. "You know that my family and I don't exactly get along." I nodded, waiting for him to go on, but we were interrupted.

"Turn that death machine off and get back over here. I'm an old woman and don't have much time left." There was humor in her voice, but I realized he wouldn't have a chance to tell me his motives.

He shut off the bike and whispered, "Come to the restaurant for dinner and I'll explain everything. I'm at the downtown location tonight."

His grandma bellowed again behind him, and this time, she was standing right behind us. I stumbled forward and so did Sal, her proximity launching us toward each other. "Hurry up, lovebirds, I want to say hello to the horses before I die of old age."

We were a breath apart, and his arm went to my waist like we had done something like this a hundred times. "Is this okay?" He whispered, and I burst into laughter.

This had to be the most absurd situation I had ever been put in. "Yeah, it's okay."

He tugged at the lapel of my pajama shirt with his free hand and smiled. "You look . . . interesting."

I looked down at myself, regretting so many things that had put me on this course. "I didn't know anyone was going to stop by while I was doing laundry."

Camilla interjected with a giggle, "Actually, she was wearing much less when we found her."

Sal's eyes got that sneaky look to them, and his grin crept out. "Oh, really?"

I looked back at his grandmother as a blush grew up around my neck. "I don't want to talk about it."

Sal's grandma smiled at me. "When my husband was alive, we never said hello or goodbye without a kiss. It's how we stayed married for over sixty years."

"That's really sweet," I said, wondering how cute they must have been together.

Then her eyes focused on Sal, and she had more bite in her words when she said, "Are you going to kiss her, boy, or are you not willing to put in the work for a happy relationship?"

I felt time stand still. My heart stopped beating. My lungs stopped requiring oxygen.

"Nonna, we're not that kind of couple," he protested.

She shook her head. "This could be the last time you have a chance to show me how much you love her." She gave him the same smile I had seen him use a hundred times to get what he wanted. There was no saying no to this woman.

Knowing he was just going to stand there protesting until she got suspicious, I stood up on my toes and pressed my lips to his. They were soft and sweet, and I hated that I liked the way they felt against mine.

Our other kisses came to the forefront of my mind. They were rougher, sloppier. I was transported to that night. To the wall he had shoved me up against. I could practically feel his teeth dragging down my neck before he licked the tender skin under my earlobe.

I took a step away and tried to hide the goosebumps on my skin. I rubbed at my lips with my sleeve, wanting to forget the taste of his mouth.

I didn't want to think about kissing him—or the other wonderful things his lips were capable of—any longer. "Sorry, Nonna, he's just so shy." Then I turned to him and flashed my best work smile. He looked absolutely gobsmacked. I didn't think he expected me to jump in like that. Hell, I didn't expect to do it, either. I tried to hide my embarrassment by asking, "So, honey, what are you doing home from work so early?"

"My sister texted me they had stopped by and had run into you, so I rushed here to . . . um . . . say hello. I can't stay long, though. I have to get back for dinner service."

Camilla asked, "What, you don't trust us being alone

with her? You've been talking about her for months, and we've been dying to meet her."

Months?

None of this made any sense. Did Sal have a secret girlfriend I didn't know about? And now his family thinks I'm her?

I smacked him on the shoulder playfully, but I really wanted to yell at him. That would have to come later. "Hun, you didn't tell me they knew about us."

His smile faltered, but I thought I was the only one who noticed it. Instead of responding to what I had said, he asked, "So. Flannel pajamas?"

"The only other clean outfit I had was too risqué for Nonna to see." The thought of the silk number I'd found in my drawer made me blush again, but I was glad I had chosen this outfit. Especially since I saw a blush crawl up Sal's tattooed neck, too.

"Anyway, we're here so Nonna and I can visit the horses. Shall we?" Camilla pushed open the large barn doors, revealing the stables I hadn't had the guts to step inside yet.

She guided Nonna in, and Sal gestured for me to enter in front of him. "I haven't had a chance to visit Sal's horses much." Really, I hadn't seen them up close at all, but if we were going to stick to this lie, I couldn't tell this truth, either.

Camilla spun around and gasped, putting her hand to her chest dramatically. "His horses?" Then she looked at him. "What other lies have you been telling her, Salvatore?"

I looked between the two of them, and their

expressions mirrored one another as they stared each other down. There was a definite sibling rivalry begging to be unpacked here.

Sal surprised me by wrapping his arm around my waist and pulling me close to him. "Look, Cami, I've told her a dozen times that Snip and Rhea are yours, but she keeps calling them mine."

Okay, so here was information that would have been helpful earlier. "Sorry, Camilla, I'm just so nervous that I misspoke. I meant I haven't had a lot of time to come visit your horses."

Camilla's facial features changed instantly, and she stepped closer to me, grabbing me by the hands. "No worries, I was just messing with Sal. You know how it is with brothers."

I started to agree with her, to tell her about my relationship with Jake, but Nonna interrupted us. "What's your name again, *cara*?" She asked before leaning into the first stall and rubbing the nose of a sweet brown horse.

"Blake," I answered.

"Oh yes, that's it. I remember now." She turned back to the horse and ran her knuckles up and down his forehead.

I sent a glance Sal's way, wondering if he had already told his grandmother that I was his girlfriend or if she was just faking it, trying to hide her dementia. When my grandma was battling it before she passed away, there were a lot of things we just went with.

She continued talking to the horse like it was an old friend, and Camilla turned all of her attention to me. "So, Sal's got you convinced my horses are his. He also has you somehow believing that he's sweet, otherwise you wouldn't be staying with him. What other fibs do you think he's told you?"

"Watch yourself, Camilla." Sal said from behind me. There hadn't been tension in the room before, but now I could feel it all around me. There were many things they were keeping from each other, and I felt there were a lot of things they were keeping from me, too.

She smiled sweetly at him. "Sorry, big bro. You know I like to tease."

Sal gripped my shoulder, squeezing slightly. "Sorry about my little sister. For someone who's about to turn thirty, she acts a lot like a teenager." His voice was like ice.

I was about to comment that Camilla and I were the same age when she replied, "I learned it from you. What with your two more years of experience on this earth and twice as many wild stories?" She looked proud, like she knew she had gotten under his skin.

"You know," I blurted out, eager to ease the energy in the room a little. "I really love watching the sunset from the big picture windows in the living room."

Camilla's smile turned wistful. "That really is one of the best parts of the house. Wait 'till it warms up outside. You get the same view from the swimming pool. That's probably my favorite spot on the property."

I gave her a fake cringe and made sure their grandmother wasn't paying attention to us. "Anything's better than the orange bedroom at the end of the hall, huh?"

Camilla suddenly looked appalled. She was great at playing melodramatic. "That was my room, thank you very much. I worked really hard on color coordinating everything in there." She put her hand on her chest, the same dramatic way she had earlier. "It took me years to make it look that good!"

I was instantly horrified that I'd put my foot in my mouth. "I'm sorry, I was just kidding."

When she started laughing, I looked back and forth between her and Sal, and after a few seconds, both of them were cracking up at my expense.

"It's okay." She finally admitted. "Now that I'm an adult, I also hate it in there. I don't know why he hasn't redecorated."

"I like keeping it that way to remember your teenage years. When you were so nice and kind." He shrugged and gave her the cutest smile.

Wait, no, that smile wasn't cute. I had forgotten myself for a minute. I didn't like him. Not even a little bit.

He nudged her with his shoulder. "Plus, I can't change a thing until I show your future husband how you're going to decorate his house, too. When you finally meet him one day, anyway."

The two of them went back and forth about her dating life and whether her future spouse would move in with her, not the other way around. I realized that this was the way they communicated—bickering back and forth but enjoying every minute of it.

I wandered away from the conversation and instead walked toward Nonna. She was still talking to the horses, but when she saw me come near, she motioned for me to come stand close to her.

I sidled against her, and she wrapped her arm around

mine. "Come, walk me to the field. I don't want to rely on that damn thing any longer." She pretended to spit on her walker, and I helped her walk through the stable to the paddock on the other end.

She asked me about myself, and I answered her as honestly as I could. I told her how I grew up in Bakersfield but came out here to work in hospitality, since the hotels here were glamorous but also kind of private. I tried to steer clear of any relationship questions, since I had no idea what stories Sal had told her. Or why he had told her about a fake girlfriend in the first place.

When she asked how I met him, I told her we had met through mutual friends before changing the conversation to the property we were walking across. She told me all about how her late husband bought it right after they married and just knew it was meant for their family. They gave it to Sal when it got too hard for them to maintain, hoping his family would take it over. She was grumbling about him not having children yet when Sal and Camilla met up with us.

We continued to talk for about an hour until Nonna was visibly exhausted. Sal took her under his arm and guided her up the hill to Camilla's car, and I fell into step next to her. "You two make a good team. I can see what he sees in you."

I tried to brush it off, not wanting to lie more than absolutely necessary, but she went on. "No, I've seen my brother deal with a lot of relationship bullshit over the years, and this is the first time I've seen him interact with a woman that didn't just want him for his money or his connections. His shoulders are relaxed when he stands next to you." She pointed at him a few feet ahead of us. "Look at that spring in his step."

I had to admit, he did look happy, but I was sure it was because his family was here. Maybe this was a sign that whatever was going on between them was about to be over. I knew one thing: it wasn't because of me. He didn't even like me. He had made that clear many times.

He loaded his grandmother and sister into their car and waved them off. Just as soon as they left down the drive, he looked down at his watch. "Holy shit, I didn't realize how long I'd been here. I've got to jet."

He grabbed his helmet and straddled his bike. The engine roared to life, and he slipped the helmet on his head in one fluid movement. "Come see me tonight."

I started to protest, holding up my hand, but he yelled over the idling motor, "At the very least, I owe you a meal after you jumped in for me like that today. Just come eat."

I knew I would have to talk to him about this situation eventually, and I really didn't want to spend any money on takeout tonight. "Fine. I'll see you at eight."

He nodded, flipped down his visor, and drove off.

Somehow I got the impression that today would not be the last time that I would have to pretend to be Sal's girlfriend, and I didn't know how I felt about it. The kiss had brought up too many emotions that I hadn't known were still boiling inside of me. I hated thinking about his skin against mine, his arms holding me tightly.

Chapter Six

Wondering why I had even agreed to come here, I pushed open the door of Sal's downtown restaurant and stepped inside. This one was smaller than the other two, but it was just as packed as the other locations always were.

I had been to all three over the course of the last year with Lina and Valerie, but I had to admit, this one was my favorite. The other two restaurants were decorated like old school Italian places, where the tables were full of large family gatherings and plenty of loud, boisterous laughter.

This one was modern and chic, despite the traditional Italian foods on the menu. Black glass tables, stainless steel light fixtures, and lo-fi music playing from hidden speakers in the exposed ceilings made this place feel hip without being phony. Even the white neon "Sal's Place" sign that hung over the hostess stand looked perfect. The best part, though, was the smell wafting out of the kitchen. I could almost taste the rich sauces that were simmering on the other side of the wall. There was no argument—Sal was one hell of a chef.

I hadn't noticed that the group in front of me had finished requesting a table until the hostess, dressed in a simple black dress, pulled my attention from the decor. "Do you have a reservation?"

Smiling at her, I admitted, "I'm not sure. I told Sal I'd be here at eight."

She gave me a knowing smile, and I wondered if she thought I was dating her boss, too. "Blake, right?" I nodded, and she waved for me to follow. "Your table's this way."

I looked over my shoulder at the people waiting to be seated and felt a little guilty as I followed her to a quiet table in the back corner.

A few moments later, a waitress, also in a plain black dress—although this one was cut low and had cute spaghetti straps—came to take my drink order and handed me a menu. She had the same suspicious smile on her face as the hostess, and I fought the urge to ask her what Sal had told his staff about me.

I put in my order and played with my straw wrapper. The candlesticks at my table, at every table, matched the ones Sal had brought from his storage unit several days ago. I guess he was telling the truth, then. As I waited for my food, I swore a few other employees passed by my table just to take a look at me.

My gaze was in my lap, staring at the paper I had folded into a bunch of little squares when a plate was placed gently on the table in front of me. I looked up and met Sal's eyes, and my lips betrayed me, spreading into a wide smile.

"I wasn't sure you were going to make it tonight." He said as he slipped into the seat across from mine.

I forced my smile to disappear, saying, "I'm not one to turn down free food." He laughed a little, and I caught two waitresses watching us, whispering together on the other side of the restaurant. "What did you tell the staff about me? I feel like I'm in a fishbowl."

He spun around, and caught them looking just as I reached for him, whispering loudly, "No, don't look!"

I couldn't see the look on Sal's face, but the women giggled and hurried away from each other before he turned his attention back to me. "I just told them to set this table up for you and keep it reserved all night in case you came."

"That's it?" I raised an eyebrow at him, wondering how deep his plan went.

"What did you want me to say? My annoying roommate is coming in. Please stare at her until she feels so uncomfortable that she leaves and never comes back?"

"I'm not annoying."

He didn't reply, but he gave me a look that had, "*Yes you are,*" written all over it.

"So, why am I your girlfriend?"

He laughed, like I had told a joke instead of asking him a legitimate question. He pointed to my plate. "Eat."

I picked up my fork, stabbing a ravioli, but paused. "Are you going to just sit here and watch me?"

He laughed again, and I wondered if the fumes in the

kitchen had made him delirious. "Would it make you more comfortable if I ate, too?"

I took a bite of the ravioli and couldn't stop the joyous hum that came out involuntarily at the taste. This might be my new favorite food.

I looked back up at him and caught a hungry look in his eyes. He wanted something, but I didn't think it was the carbs on my fork. He spun around in his chair, waving a waitress over. The woman from earlier—with spaghetti straps barely holding in her bust—stepped up a few seconds later and Sal grunted out, "Will you bring a side of bread to the table?"

She looked confused, but nodded before disappearing into the kitchen. She was back a minute later, handing him a plate with a loaf of homemade bread and a pat of butter. "Anything else, chef?"

He sat the plate down in front of him. "No, Marianna. This is perfect."

She turned her smile to me. "Do you need anything else, Blake? More water maybe?" I blushed a little when she said my name. There was no reason she would know it unless they were all talking about me.

"No, I have everything I need right here. Thank you." She nodded before rushing off to the kitchen. She was probably excited to gossip about whatever she thought was happening between Sal and me.

I pointed at his bread with my fork. "Eat." And then I finished the bite of the greatest damn ravioli I'd ever eaten.

He tore into his bread and stuffed a bite into his mouth. After chewing a little, he finally said, "You don't have to stay in the orange room anymore if you don't want. There are plenty of rooms you could choose from."

I took another bite, wondering which room I would pick. I had done some snooping the other day, and there were a few great choices. Ones with more subdued tones and softer-looking linens.

But the ugly orange room had the best view in the house. I could see the rolling grassy fields. The view from the bed went all the way to the coast. "No thanks, I don't plan on being around for more than a few more weeks. I'm fine where I am."

He leaned in a little. "We could paint it, if you wanted to."

I was a little confused. "Paint what?"

"The orange room. If you like it, we could paint the walls. Swap some furniture out, too."

I stuck my fork through another perfectly crafted piece of pasta. "I'm not staying, Salami."

He stuffed another chunk of bread in his mouth, but he looked like he was contemplating something.

"Why do I get the feeling I'm about to get roped into something else?" I asked before taking another bite.

"So, you know my parents and I are . . . estranged, right?" I nodded, still chewing my food. "Well, it all started because I wanted to open a restaurant instead of staying at their company. Commercial real estate wasn't my dream. Anyway, my dad and I got in this big fight because my parents thought I just wanted the nightlife party aspect of a restaurant, not the responsibilities."

I looked around the room, knowing this restaurant was successful, and so were his other two. Maybe he was more responsible than I had given him credit for. I couldn't imagine not having my parents to rely on. For them to not take me seriously. "So why don't you just invite them here and show them what you've built?"

He cringed a little. "It's deeper than that."

"How deep?"

"My father said that until I found a wife and began a family, I wouldn't understand the sacrifices he made for us, so I had no place in the family."

"That seems harsh." I wondered what kind of man would cut his son off because he didn't want to work for the family company.

He tore a couple more pieces of bread from the small loaf but didn't eat them. "Then he accused me of disrespecting hundreds of years of family history when I told him I had no plans of ever getting married or having children."

"Well, marriage is overrated, and children are sticky."

His face lit up a little. "I know! I tried to tell him that! But he said that one day I'd meet the right woman and my feelings would change. He went on and on about the importance of passing along the family name." He paused, concentrating on squishing the little bread pieces between his fingers. "But it hasn't happened, and I don't think it's going to." His hazel eyes met mine, reminding me just how striking they were. "I know what I want out of life, and it's not a white picket fence, you know?"

This conversation scared me a little because I did know. It was exactly how I felt, too. "So what does this have to do with me being your pretend girlfriend?"

"Camilla is throwing a party for my parent's fortieth wedding anniversary, and I really want to go."

"You want to go to a party for people who basically disowned you? Why?"

He sighed, rubbing his chin. After a minute, he quietly admitted, "Because I love them. I miss them." His eyes met mine, and I could see the pain and turmoil bubbling below the surface. "It's been six years since I've seen my mom or dad. And like Nonna said, they're not getting any younger. I'm sick of missing out on their lives."

"So why not just call them and tell them that?"

He shook his head. "I've tried calling. They don't answer. I even tried knocking on their front door, and they pretended they weren't home." He finally put his squashed little bread pieces in his mouth and ate them. "But I was thinking . . . if they think I'm in a committed relationship and I'm trying to settle down, maybe I'll get an invite to the party." His eyes locked with mine again. "I know it's stupid. I was just going to ask whoever I find to come with me to Reece's wedding to come to this, too. But then you were home when Cami and Nonna showed up, and the opportunity just kind of fell together."

I narrowed my gaze at him. "Didn't you say you had a few choices lined up to bring to the wedding? Why not one of them?"

His face turned shy. "I'm surprised you didn't see right through me. I didn't want to be the only person in the group without a date, so I lied."

I almost told him I had been worried about the same thing, but I wasn't willing to let that truth out just yet.

My eyes scanned to the small group of servers that looked like they were desperately trying to read our lips from the hostess stand. "Why not ask one of them?"

He turned in his seat again, and they pretended to be working. He spoke loudly in their direction, "Don't know why it takes three people to wipe down the hostess stand." They laughed at him, but pretended to go back to work again.

He turned back to me. "I'm their boss. That wouldn't be right."

"Reece was Lina's boss, and that worked out for them."

"Okay, I'm their boss, and I'm not attracted to any of them."

I raised an eyebrow, looking over his shoulder. "Not even the one with her boobs hanging out?"

He spun around in his chair again before turning back to face me. "You said that to fuck with me, didn't you?"

I nodded at him, happy I could make him squirm a little. "When is this party?"

"Camilla said she booked the banquet hall on their anniversary—April 14th." He shifted in his seat, and I wondered if he was a little nervous.

I flipped through a mental calendar. "That's a little more than a month from now. A week or two before the wedding, depending on when they book it."

His smile filled his whole face as he leaned forward. "That's why I was thinking this plan would be perfect. We stay together until the party, and then go our separate ways. That way, if you wanted to have a date at the wedding—one that's not me, I mean—then we have our breakup and you're free to dance with whoever you want all night long."

He really thought this through. "Camilla mentioned that she'd been waiting to meet me for a while. Did you tell them I was dating you before I moved in?"

There was the nervous twitch again. "Not exactly. I told them I was seeing someone. I just got lucky when they walked in on you in the house the other day."

So his grandma hadn't remembered my name. Interesting. I didn't know why I felt a little disappointed, since I didn't want to be in an actual relationship with this man. "Is Camilla her only caretaker?" I asked before worrying if it was a bit of an overstep.

He shrugged a little, like he wasn't used to talking about his grandmother's condition. "My parents try to help, but from what I've heard from our cousins, Cami visits her at the assisted living facility more than anyone else. I'd try to visit, but I'm not on the list."

Damn, so helping him out, making this thing between us believable, would probably get him on that list. I really didn't want to help him, but I couldn't forget Nonna's mischievous smile and how much it mirrored his own. She was so important to him, and I wanted to help him spend time with her. But I also needed to look out for myself. "So, what do I get out of this plan?"

He put his elbows on the table and gave me his lady-killer smile. "A free place to live long enough to save up a ton of money?"

"Not juicy enough. I've got a real estate agent helping me. She'll find something soon." I left out the part that the realtor was my mom and she was struggling to find anything within the budget I gave her.

"But wouldn't you like to buy your own house?" Now he sounded just like my mother. "You could save enough for a down payment and take your time to find the perfect place. If you . . . ." He paused, looking over his shoulder to check for eavesdroppers before going on, "pretend to be my girlfriend for a few family outings, and then come to the anniversary party with me, you'll have a place to stay."

"For how long? Saving for a down payment in this economy is going to take much longer than a month."

"I'm not putting a deadline on how long you stay. The house is big enough for both of us. That's why I offered to paint the room. If you want to stay for six months, do it. A year, even. It's up to you." He tapped the table with the tips of his fingers. "You'd be doing me a huge favor. I want to make it worth it for you."

"And if I find the perfect place in two weeks?"

He cracked a small smile. "I need you to stay until after the anniversary party, at least. Once I have a chance to talk to my dad and make things right between us, the breakup can be as nasty as you want." His smile grew larger. "You can tell everyone how terrible I was to you, too."

I wondered how his dad would handle our impending breakup, but then thought about my friends. "Am I going to have to lie to everyone? You know I can't do that to Lina and Val." I already had one secret I was keeping from them, and it was burning a hole through me.

"Okay, we can tell them the truth, but I need this to

come off as real as possible for everyone else. Camilla is friends with Lizette, and I don't want her to find out because you met up with some dude at work."

"I would never bring a hookup to work."

He rolled his eyes. "You know what I mean, though. My parents are old friends with the Howell family, and the last thing I need is for my dad to see right through me. I couldn't take another rejection."

I sat at the table, contemplating my choices. I'd had no intention of helping him earlier, but knowing that I could save a bunch of money without having to touch my investments was enticing.

This was a bad idea. That kiss in front of his family had really messed me up, and having to pretend I was head over heels could get dangerous. Sure, that kiss had been completely delicious, but I hated that it was with *him*.

"Could you just stay with me until then? Please?" When I didn't respond, he whispered, "Don't make me beg."

I bit my bottom lip, thinking about him on his knees, begging. It reminded me of the last time he was on his knees in front of me, and I shivered. "What if I want you to beg?"

He let out a nervous laugh and splayed his hands on the table like he was about to stand. "Okay, fine, I guess I'll see if one of the girls over there will do it instead. It'd be easier anyway."

I put my hand over his. "Wait. I'll do it."

He leaned back in his seat, smiling. "You sure?"

The sly look on his face had me a little concerned, so

I took my hand back and placed it in my lap. "Under one condition."

"What's that?" He looked genuinely intrigued.

"We're not actually dating each other. I can still see other people and you can keep bringing random women home."

He rolled his eyes at me. "You can keep dating other people all you want, but be discreet about it. And don't bring any guys into my restaurants. I need my employees to believe this is real, too, since a lot of the staff are friends with my sister."

I blurted out, "And I'm not going to sleep with you." I felt like I was dropping into the deep end with this statement.

He scoffed and folded his arms across his chest. "Obviously. I'm not going to make that mistake again."

Rage boiled through my veins at the thought of the night we'd spent together. The night we never discussed. But under that rage was also a little shame. I hadn't even told my best friends about that night because I hated how much it had meant to me. How badly I had wanted it to turn into something more. "Oh, so you admit it happened, at least. That's refreshing."

Anger flashed in his eyes, but I somehow had the feeling he was thinking about my body under his. The feeling of his skin against mine.

The passion I thought we had between us, which turned out to be just some drunken lapse in judgment.

I thought about the phone that never rang the next day—or the day after that—and wanted to walk out of here, damning his family and this stupid agreement. But the thought of buying my own place, of not having to worry that another landlord could kick me out, kept me in my seat.

As if he read my mind, he said, "Listen, Blake. You don't have to worry about me trying to get into your pants ever again. I got it out of my system last summer, and I don't intend on doing it again." His hands balled into fists, his knuckles turning white. "It's the reason I thought you would be perfect for this plan. As soon as I'm back in my dad's good graces, we pretend to have a fight and you can go live your life without me, just like you always wanted."

I leaned forward, desperate to get the full details of this agreement so I could get the hell out of here. I pushed my half-eaten plate forward, my appetite gone, even for the most delicious food ever. "How's it going to work after we break up? I'm going to need more than a couple months to save for a down payment."

He shrugged. "The house is big enough for the both of us to live in without seeing each other. We're practically living like that right now anyway. I'll tell them you're moving out as soon as you can, but the market isn't exactly helping. Which is the truth." The corner of his lip went up in a smile. "Shit, being forced to live in a house with a woman who can't stand me might gain me some sympathy."

Living with him, pretending to like him was going to be difficult, but not impossible. "Fine, I'm in. As long as you're sure I don't have to be your date at Lina and Reece's wedding."

He rubbed his forehead. "Jesus, Blake. I don't care

who you bring to the wedding. I just need your help getting back into my parents' good graces."

I leaned back and chewed on my cheek. "How many family events are we talking about?" Hopefully, we looked like we were whispering sweet nothings to each other, not preparing to claw each other's eyes out.

He shrugged. "Not sure. Hopefully three, maybe four more hangouts with Camilla. Maybe lunch with Nonna or my cousins."

"Sounds good to me." I wiped my face with the cloth napkin, thinking that I had just signed a deal with the devil and knew I couldn't get out of it. "Is there anything else you think we need to talk about, or can I go?"

He let go of a breath he had been holding. "I think that's it." Then his eyes scanned over my blouse. "Thanks for wearing something nicer than what you had on this afternoon. I like that color on you."

I glanced down at my hot pink top before standing up and putting my hand on his shoulder. "I appreciate the compliment, Salmon."

His eyebrow popped up. "Salmon? Okay, that one's actually terrible."

I couldn't fight my smile. "I know. As soon as I said it, I realized it should have been saved for an email."

"How much time do you spend thinking up nicknames for me?"

"I'll never tell."

Our eyes met, and his gaze was warm. Not the cozy kind of warm . . . the destructive kind. Molten lava slowly devouring an entire neighborhood warm.

Goosebumps traveled down my arms, and I wondered

if I should lean down and kiss him goodbye. But then I remembered the sound of his voice as he whispered my name when he joined his body with mine not so long ago, and I froze.

It had felt so real in that moment. I couldn't believe how foolish I had been.

I ran my eyes down his jaw and touched my fingertips across the rose tattooed on his neck instead, my mouth dry. "Thank you for dinner. It was delicious."

He just nodded before saying, "I'll tell the staff you liked it."

I looked into his eyes again, ignoring the stitch in my chest that his emotions pulled out of me. "Guess I'll see you at home." I wasn't sure what else to say, but I was ready to get out of here. Away from the heat emanating from his body.

"Don't wait up for me. I probably won't be out of here until three or four."

I patted his shoulder again. "Wasn't planning on it, babe."

Chapter Seven

I sat down at my computer in my office for the first time since this morning and let out a sigh. Today had been absolute chaos. Between a Bridezilla whose wedding wasn't even until the end of the week, the restaurant still being shut down for the kitchen remodel, and a toddler who pooped in the swimming pool, I hadn't had a single minute to myself since ten this morning.

I was supposed to leave an hour ago, but I felt guilty leaving before our maintenance team was done sanitizing the pool, so I thought I would catch up on some emails before taking off for the night. It wasn't that I was avoiding my fake boyfriend . . . to the point where I hadn't seen him for more than ten seconds at a time in the last five days. It was because of my deep devotion to tourists and their vacation plans. Obviously.

I clicked open my email server on my desktop and started reading through facilities requests and complaints from unhappy customers. By the third email, I was practically cross-eyed.

There was a knock at my door and I called out, "Come on in." In walked the last person I wanted to see tonight. "Hooray, my boyfriend's here," I said in a flat tone.

He cringed at my lack of excitement, but sat down anyway. His leather jacket was open, showing off his black V-neck T-shirt and the tip of the tattoo across his chest. He put his helmet on his lap, and I forced my eyes back to my computer.

His voice had a slight wobble to it. "I'm glad you're still here. I need a favor."

I glanced quickly from my screen to him, catching him chewing on his bottom lip before I looked away again. "Why? What are you up to?"

He tapped his fingers against the top of his helmet. "It's my sister. She wants to go out for drinks tonight."

It had been a long day, and I really just wanted to curl up on the couch. "So go have drinks with her."

He shifted in his seat. "Well, she thinks you're going to be there, too."

I pushed away from my desk and leaned back in my chair, finally looking at him fully. "And why does she think that?"

He glanced down at the floor, and if I wasn't so fed up with him, it would look adorable. "Because she might have planned the whole thing after I told her you get off work at five." I ran my fingers through my hair, not sure how to respond. Communication was definitely not our strong suit. "Look, I don't want to lose an opportunity for her to see us together."

I glanced at the clock on the corner of my computer screen. "But it's already after six thirty."

"Which is why I was glad to find you still here when I left the restaurant." I looked down at my clothes. They were nice, but not exactly what I would wear out with friends. He must have noticed because he said, "I need to stop by the house and take a quick shower. You can change, too, if you want to. Then you can ride with me to the bar."

Regretting our stupid agreement already, I stared up at the ceiling. "I'm not riding on the back of your motorcycle."

"I figured you would say that. We'll take my car."

"Your car?" In the two weeks I had lived at his house, I hadn't seen him drive anything other than his bike, which he kept parked in the driveway. I hadn't been brave enough to snoop through the garage, but now I wanted to know what was in there.

He stood, reaching for the door. "I'll see you at the house in half an hour?"

I looked back at my computer screen, realizing that there wasn't anything in there that couldn't wait until tomorrow morning. "Fine. Let me close up here, and I'll see you at home."

Sal had told me to meet him here, but there was no sign of him anywhere. His motorcycle hadn't been in its usual spot, so I worried the house was empty. I came into the kitchen and called out, "Saltine, are you here?"

I really was running out of words that started with *Sal*.

After listening for a response and not hearing him, I went down his hallway, calling out for him again. Passing the laundry room, I noticed that his bedroom door was open.

I peeked inside his room, glancing over the four-poster bed, and focused on the en suite bathroom vanity on the far wall of the room. I froze as I found him standing there, completely naked. He was standing right outside his shower, wiping his face off with a towel, and my traitorous eyes scanned his perky backside.

It brought me back to the last time I had unabashedly stared at his ample rear-end. I had thought it was the alcohol coursing through my veins that night making me wonder if I could balance a wine glass atop his rounded muscles, but here I was, stone-cold sober, wondering the same thing all over again.

He continued drying himself off for what felt like half an hour before he looked over his shoulder, finally spotting me. "What the hell, Blake?"

I let out a yelp and threw my hands up. "Sorry! I'm sorry. I didn't mean to walk in on you."

He wrapped the towel around his waist and took a few steps toward me. My eyes instantly lingered on the water droplets tangling with his tattoos and chest hair, and my heart started racing. He took another step closer to me, like he knew what my attention was fixed on. "What are you doing in here?"

I closed my eyes and started walking backward. My ears felt like they were on fire. "Sorry, I was looking for you so I could ask what I should wear tonight, but I couldn't find you." I kept inching back until I felt my back hit the doorframe. My sweaty palms ran against the wall, guiding me into the hallway. "I didn't see your motorcycle outside, so I wasn't sure if you were even home."

"Stop acting like you've never seen a naked man before. Open your eyes."

I followed his command, but trained my gaze on the hallway before me instead of his exposed skin. "Sorry."

He took another step toward me. "Stop saying you're sorry."

I turned and looked at him, and started to say I was sorry again, but bit my tongue. I hoped the awkwardness oozing out of me came off as being embarrassed by walking in on him and not the hormones raging through my body begging me to throw myself at him.

It would only end badly, I told myself.

I looked at the ink across his chest. Remembering running my hands over the chef's knife that spanned from the top of one perfectly sculpted peck to the other was not helping me one bit. I needed to suppress these feelings deep, deep inside.

"Okay, so why did I find you in my room watching me get out of the shower?"

I shook my head. It was going to be very difficult to get the image of his legs flexing while he dried himself off out of my mind. "I wanted to know where we were going tonight so I don't make a fool out of myself in front of your sister again. Do I wear jeans, slacks, a skirt?"

He smiled, and I had to remind myself that he was

not my actual boyfriend. That I still hated him. "We're meeting Camilla and her friends at a bar down on State Street." He twisted to look at the clock on his nightstand, and my eyes lingered on the rose tattooed on his neck. It looked more realistic with actual water droplets sitting on his skin. "I'm sure they've been drinking already, so we should get going before they get hammered. Anything you want to wear will be fine."

Then he turned back to face me, and our eyes linked. Instead of agreeing and going to my side of the house to get dressed, I just stood there, staring at him like an idiot, unable to breathe. He didn't move, but the distance between us seemed to shrink by several inches.

A water droplet fell from his earlobe and landed on his shoulder, snapping me back to the present. It made me wonder something. "Why were you showering with the door open?"

He laughed. "Just a habit, I guess." He stepped out into the hallway, invading my space. "I've lived here a long time without a roommate. I must have forgotten to close it."

I stared at the tile floor. "Oh," was all I could think of to say.

When he didn't speak, I glanced up at him, wondering if I should bring up the night we had spent together. But now wasn't the time. Sure, I wanted to know why he thought it was a mistake. If it had been something I had said or done. Maybe I just wasn't his type.

But I also didn't want to break the spell of whatever was going on between us.

He flexed his pecs, and I hadn't realized I had been

staring at them. He gave me his sly smile. "Anything else, or should we both get dressed?"

I fought the urge to return his smile. Digging into our feelings would have to happen another time. "Nope. Give me a few minutes, and I'll be ready to go."

I met him by the front door. If I'd thought my palms were sweaty before, I realized that was nothing compared to how they felt right now. I didn't know why I was so nervous. Sure, getting his naked form out of my mind would not be easy, but there wasn't a chance we would ever be something more. Maybe I just really wanted to make a good impression on his sister.

He looked amazing tonight, in black jeans and a black T-shirt. I was concluding that his entire wardrobe was just V-necks and chef's jackets, which wasn't a bad thing.

He opened the door for us and guided me outside. We walked down the walkway to the garage, and he typed a code into the number pad next to the closest door. "Are you okay?" he asked, catching me off guard.

"Yeah, I'm fine." I had been feeling a little off mentally, but I figured it was because I had been working so much lately. Not that I was about to be going on a fake date with the guy I had been practically obsessing over for the last several months.

The garage door rolled up, revealing a white Audi R8 parked within. "Isn't that the same car Iron Man drives?"

He laughed, and I hated how much I enjoyed the sound. "That's actually why I bought it."

"Okay, that's adorable."

He flicked a switch on the wall, turning on the lights in the entire garage. I stepped in and looked around. The garage was huge and full of vehicles. In the bay next to his car was a small tractor and a ride-on lawn mower, which I assumed was for the groundskeeper. His bike was tucked in next to those, but in the next spots were a rusty old truck and two classic-looking cars. I walked around to the second classic, looking for a badge to identify what it was, when I noticed the little blue car next to it. "Is that Lina's car?"

He laughed and pointed past it. "Yeah, and Reece's." I glanced up at the black Porsche, the one Reece had traded his annoyingly green one for a couple of months before they skipped town.

Sal came to stand next to me. "They were concerned about where to store them while they traveled, so I told them to keep them here."

He pointed to the other vehicles. "These were my grandpa's. I run them all about once a month, but I haven't had the time to drive them like I would like to."

I looked up at him, surprised at how generous he could be sometimes.

He glanced down at his watch. "We should get going, yeah?"

I nodded at him, and he walked me over to his Audi. His movements weren't as graceful as they usually were—he seemed almost jittery. Maybe he was as nervous as I was. Without a word, he opened the passenger door and helped me get in.

A moment later, he slid into his seat, clicking the

buckle of his seatbelt. "I wanted to buy something ridiculous when I first started making money from the restaurant, and this was it."

"That's sweet." The car purred to life as he started it and pulled out of the garage. The sound of the engine made me totally understand the feeling of wanting to do something wild once in a while. "How long did it take for you to start making money?" As soon as I asked, I knew it had come off a little strong. "Sorry, that was rude. I was just asking from a business standpoint."

He patted my leg, which I hadn't noticed was bouncing up and down. "No, I didn't think it was rude. I know you think about business before anything else." I glanced at him sideways, and he added, "That wasn't meant to be rude, either."

He stopped the car, waiting for the security gate to close behind us before answering my question. "I got pretty lucky and started making money after the first year. You're going to make fun of me, but I had some trust funds set aside and was able to burn through them setting up the first two locations. Living at my grandparents' house has helped, too. Maintenance and utilities cost quite a bit, but not having a mortgage helped me open one every two years since I got started."

I leaned my head against the headrest while he took us down the winding road toward the highway, and I remembered the time I thought about taking his motorcycle down this street. It was just as fun in this car, but I wouldn't admit it out loud.

"I want to open a bed-and-breakfast. I've been planning it since college." Unsure of how the plan I had kept so close to my chest all these years just tumbled out of me, I sat there, a little shocked. I'd mentioned the idea a couple times to Lina and Val, but in more of a "one day when I win the lottery" idea, not something I was actually putting into motion in a few years. My own mother didn't know.

He took a tight turn, and I gripped the edge of my seat. "Why don't you?" He made it sound like it was just that easy.

Letting out a breath, I seriously thought about my answer. "I love my job at The Pacifica." He glanced at me from the corner of his eye like he didn't believe me. "I do, really. It's a lot of work most days, but I like the challenge." When he nodded like he understood what I meant, I went on. "Also, I was just offered a promotion, and I don't think I'll be able to turn it down." Saying it out loud had just given me more clarity than the last couple of weeks of dwelling on it. I had been dreading telling Lizette that while the money sounded nice, my heart wasn't invested in working for the corporation.

"Hmm" was all he said, as if he knew I was sitting here mulling over my entire life.

My phone buzzed in my purse, so I pulled it out. It was a text from Val in my group with her and Lina: *What are you girls up to tonight? I'm bored.*

Lina's text came in quickly: *We flew into Berlin last night, but I couldn't sleep. I just got out of bed, about to make breakfast, but I have nothing planned until this afternoon. Want to watch a movie over FaceTime?*

My fingers itched to tell them I would ditch my plans and meet them, but I had to tell the truth. Well, maybe not the whole truth. I had decided to wait to tell them about my arrangement with Sal until they were both here in person. That way, I would be in too deep for them to talk me out of it.

So I sent: *Sorry, ladies. I'm out on a date. But I can catch up with you guys later.*

Val sent a question mark and an eggplant emoji and then said: *On a scale of one eggplant to ten eggplants, how hot is he?*

I turned my screen away from Sal, just in case he saw the text, and looked him up and down. I thought about what I would have said before our mistake. Before I knew that he didn't really want me.

I sent ten eggplant emoji and a few fire ones, too. But then I typed: *Don't get too excited, though, this one's a catch and release.*

Lina sent: *What's wrong with him? It can't be any worse than the pregnancy fetish guy . . . .*

Before I could reply, Val sent: *Please tell me you'll sleep with him before sending him back to the ocean?*

I laughed, and Sal looked over at me. "What's so funny?"

"I told Lina and Val I was going out on a date. They're asking me about him. Well, you."

He gripped the steering wheel a little tighter. "What are you telling them?"

I paused, wondering how much to tell him now, too. "Well, they don't know it's you, so they're asking me how hot he is. Val says I should sleep with him." The tips of his ears turned red, so I laughed and texted them: *I don't think I'll end up in bed with this one. But he's pretty to look at and he's got a nice car. I don't think we have a lot in common.*

It was kind of the truth, even if I was omitting who I was actually talking about.

Lina sent: *Send us a picture!*

So I took a selfie, making sure not to catch Sal in the picture, and sent it to them. I had to admit, my hair looked flawless with a little bit of a wave to it, and the red lipstick I had put on right before we left the house had been a great idea. If he were anyone else, I would be shocked if he didn't try to sleep with me.

Val replied: *Not of you, dork.*

I sent: *Sorry girls, that's the best you're going to get tonight!*

They sent me a series of sad-face emoji before they started planning their evening together—or morning, in Lina's case—so I tucked my phone back in my purse, ignoring the fun they were going to have without me.

We pulled up to the bar, and for some reason, the universe was smiling down on us and we were able to find on-street parking right outside.

He parked and came around the front of the car, opening the door for me before I'd grabbed my purse and gotten out on my own. He held his hand out to me, and I stared at it for a few seconds. I knew we were playing pretend, but something about his outstretched hand felt serious.

I looked up into his eyes, and I wondered if he was thinking the same thing. "Just to be clear, we play the parts and go back to ourselves tomorrow."

His eyebrows scrunched together for a moment before he smiled. "Sure. Playing pretend one date at a time."

I looked down at his hand for a few more seconds before placing mine in it. His fingers slipped between mine, and my heart jolted. I gave myself a pep talk.

We're just playing parts so I can find a great place to live. That's it.

We walked into the bar together, and he spotted his sister sitting at a high table with two other girls. Camilla waved enthusiastically as we came closer, and Sal lifted his free hand in a little wave back.

This was too much. Bile rose in my throat as my heartbeat doubled it's pace. Pretending to be his girlfriend had seemed easy when it was just an idea, but as we walked up to real people who knew him and loved him, I didn't think I could do it. There had to be another way for me to save money. Maybe I could just move back to Bakersfield for the time being.

"Sorry we're so late," Sal called out when we were a few feet away. "Blake walked in on me getting out of the shower, and she lost her fucking mind."

The skin on my face started to burn. I gave him the meanest look I could muster, but he threw his head back, laughing. He really was ten-eggplant-emoji hot, especially when he laughed like that. On the outside, he looked so tough—the black clothes and tattoos making him seem unapproachable. But the easy way he laughed, the way his eyes lit up when he smiled, took my breath away. Okay, maybe faking this was going to be a little easier than I thought.

"That's not what happened, and you know it," I said, hoping his sister didn't believe we were late because I had thrown myself at him.

He shook his head, biting back his smile.

"You two are so cute together!" Camilla called out. She seemed a little tipsy, and judging by the giggles coming from her friends, they were, too.

Sal let go of my hand, pulling out a chair for me. As I sat down, he leaned in, his lips grazing my ear. "Sorry, you looked like you were spiraling into your own thoughts. I had to say something to get you out of there." Then he kissed my cheek. "Just relax." He took the spot next to mine, and I hung my purse on the hook under the table between us.

I was certain that in the history of the universe, there had never been a single person who was able to relax after being told to, and I was not going to be the first.

I wrung my hands together in my lap. I really was getting lost in my own thoughts. His hand rested on the back of my chair as he said, "Hey girls, this is Blake." Then his eyes met mine again. "My girlfriend." His eyes dipped briefly to my lips. In any other situation, I would have swooned.

Camilla giggled and interjected, "More like the love of his life."

The other girls let out sighs, and the one with long blonde hair gave me a little wave. "Hi, I'm Ericka. We never thought Camilla's brother would settle down." She winked at Sal before telling me, "Good job!"

"I'm Victoria," The short brunette said after taking the last sip of her drink. "It's true. Every time he comes out to happy hour, he's with another girl." Then her eyes doubled in size. "Oh, I didn't mean it like that."

I turned to face Sal and patted my hand on his cheek,

feeling his stubble against my palm. "Oh, I'm fully aware that he was not a virgin when I met him."

I looked back at Victoria, who still looked quite embarrassed, but Camilla spoke, breaking the ice. "Oh please, Salvatore hasn't brought a girl around for at least a year. We were worried he was going to join a monastery until he finally told us he was seeing you."

Thankfully, a server came by and took our drink orders. I got a vodka tonic and Sal ordered a Pepsi, which was unexpected. Of all the people I knew, Sal partied the hardest. At least from the stories Lina had told me. I nudged him with my shoulder. "Just a Pepsi?"

He gave me a sweet, small smile. "All I wanted was a Pepsi."

I couldn't help but laugh, wondering if he was referencing the song that came to mind or not.

We shared some appetizers and small talk. The girls were all lawyers and worked for the same firm as Camilla, who I had just learned also represented Sal and Camilla's family's business.

Feeling guilty about not asking Sal to tell me more about his sister on the drive here, I asked her a ton of questions about her job. She said they were corporate lawyers, but each of them had a different role at their firm.

She pointed to the brunette, who had drunk so much I was worried she would fall off her stool. "Victoria mostly works with contract negotiations." Then she looked at Ericka, who looked like she was taking her alcohol ten times better. "Ericka works mostly in business formation, and because I am our father's favorite child," she stuck her tongue out at Sal, "I focus mostly on mergers and acquisitions."

"A chip off the old block," he said warmly, but I wondered if it was a mask. He was eager enough to get back on his dad's good side that we were going along with this whole evening. Maybe being reminded that he wasn't the favorite hurt a little.

My attention turned back to the girls. I was glad I knew what they all did for a living—it made it easier to pretend I knew about them before tonight. Ericka asked me what I did, and I told her, "Oh, I manage The Pacifica. It's a resort right off of Cabrillo."

Her eyes lit up. "Oh, I know exactly where that is. It's on my short list of wedding venues."

Victoria chimed in, "She's been planning her wedding since she was seven. Still doesn't have the groom yet, though."

They reminded me of Lina and Val. I wondered which one was the wild one, which one was the reserved one, and which one was the independent one.

"So, what do you do as a manager?" asked Camilla.

Before I could answer, Sal jumped in. "Oh, she's not just a manager, she runs the whole damn resort. My girl is also up for a big promotion." He looked at me with that crooked smile.

I usually tried to avoid talking about what I did with strangers, because they always asked me for discounts or hookups, but Sal made me feel a little bit proud. "Yeah, I keep the place running smoothly most of the time."

He turned to me. "You're playing yourself down too

much. That place would fall apart without you. You literally do everything."

I let the warmth pool in my chest at his words. He could be so sweet when playing pretend.

The conversation turned to Sal and his restaurants. He shared how many reservations he had nightly, and how packed the rooms were, but it wasn't in a braggy way. It was in the same proud way he had talked about me doing my job.

A couple more drinks had been served when Sal put his hand on my leg. "Your purse is vibrating." He leaned in, dramatically whispering in my ear so everyone could hear. "Either it's your phone, or you and I need to make a trip to the bathroom together."

I smacked his hand away playfully and reached down, pulling my purse off the hook. "It's probably just Lina and Val in the group text." It continued vibrating, and I saw it was a call coming through.

Pulling the phone out, I was nervous when I saw my mother's name on the screen. I immediately answered it, covering my other ear with my free hand. "What's going on? Is everything okay?"

Sal looked concerned and turned his body toward me while I waited for my mom's reply.

"Oh, sorry, I was just looking at properties in Santa Barbara and—"

"What the hell? Why are you working so late?" I glanced up at the group, moving my phone away from my face for a second. "I'm going to step out and take this. It's my mom."

Sal pushed his chair back and stood, his brows knitting together. "Is something wrong?"

I waved my hand at him. "No, she's fine. I'll be right back."

I caught him sitting back down from the corner of my eye as I made my way through the crowd and out the front door. I stood on the sidewalk in the freezing cold, regretting not wearing a sweater. "Okay, I'm outside. So why are you up half-past ten looking at properties?"

"Where are you?" She seemed way too interested in my social life for my liking.

"At a bar. Answer my question." I rubbed my arms, trying to get some warmth into them.

"Was that a guy you were with?" Okay, she really was way too interested. I had to shut it down quickly.

"No. Answer my question."

"Ugh, you are no fun!"

"I am fun. Just not when you scare me half to death, calling me late at night."

"I'm always up this late. But anyway, a house came on the market today, and I know you don't have the cash you wanted, but I think it would be really great for you to check out."

"I'm not sure that I'm ready to buy yet." I wasn't ready to let go of my imaginary bed-and-breakfast, but I couldn't say it.

"I know, but I think you should go see it. Just to see if it's even your taste. You don't have to commit to anything, but I have to be honest, houses in your price range in your area are going to be few and far between."

"Fine, I'll go look at it, but I think I need a little time

before I actually put in any bids." I thought about what I could pull from the stock market, what I could pull from savings to make this happen without it hurting my future. This was happening so quickly.

"I'm emailing you the listing right now. I have a friend who lives nearby and can let you in whenever you have time this week. I'll send you her contact info in this email, too."

I heard her fingers typing frantically in the background, and I knew I had to say yes. "Fine, if it will make you feel better, I'll do it. I have to go, though. I'm out with a friend."

"I hope you and your *friend* have a really nice night." The way she said friend made me feel a little slimy. I didn't want her thinking about my dating life.

"Can I call you back in the morning, Mom?"

"Make it the afternoon. I'm going to try to sleep in tomorrow."

I told her I loved her and hung up before I went back inside. I weaved back through the crowd toward our table, spotting Camilla's friends dancing with strangers, along with a bunch of other people in the middle of the room. Sal turned to me as I sat down, a concerned look on his face. "Is your mom okay?"

"Yeah, sorry, she was excited about a property she found in the neighborhood I'm interested in. I told her I wasn't ready to buy, but she is insisting that I go look at it."

As soon as the words left my lips, I regretted them. Camilla leaned forward. "You're looking at houses? Didn't you just get settled?"

I tapped my fingers on the table, trying to figure out how to spin this, but he covered my hand with his, cooling my nerves. "You know I've been planning on moving out of Nonna's house for years. It's just too much house for me."

"I worry you won't feel that way when the two of you get married."

A knee-jerk reaction caused me to say, "I don't know about all that." Then I looked at Sal, at the weird expression on his face, and tried to fake a smile. I needed to step away from the table before I screwed up again, so I said the only thing I could think of. "Should we dance?"

The sparkle in his eye got even brighter as he stood up, still holding my hand. Then he glanced at his sister. "We'll be back in a bit."

As soon as we made it to the dance floor, the song changed from something fun and poppy to a 90s slow jam. I couldn't help but laugh about having to dance to a song about making love all night long.

He put his hands on my hips and pulled me tightly against him. "Is this okay? I can go get us some drinks at the bar if you're uncomfortable."

I laid my head against his chest. "No, this is fine." We swayed back and forth, and it reminded me of dancing with him the night of the going away party.

I really wanted to ask him why he hadn't called me all those months ago, but now was not the time. If the answer he gave me embarrassed me, it would be a mess trying to hide my tears in front of his sister and her friends.

Shit, maybe I did care about his opinion more than I thought.

"I hope I didn't ruin our plan when I said I was looking for houses. I should've thought before I spoke."

One of his hands ran up my back, and he rubbed the nape of my neck slowly. "No, it's fine. I've been complaining about living at Nonna's house for years. I've even offered to let Camilla take over the property, but she doesn't want it, either."

"You really don't want to live there?"

"Don't get me wrong, it's really nice. But there are way too many rooms, and it's not exactly my style."

I leaned back, looking into his eyes. "What is your style?"

"I'd like to live in a house overlooking the ocean. Something small and easy to maintain, but with a modern design."

I imagined the house he described, the perfect one coming to mind. "Like the beach house Lina and Reece rented?"

"Exactly like that house." His cheeks went pink, but I couldn't tell why.

In an effort to hide the butterflies flipping around in my belly, I laid my head against his chest again. "That house would be perfection."

The song changed to something upbeat, and we ended up in a group with Camilla, Ericka, Veronica, and the guys they had found to dance with. I couldn't remember a time I had this much fun without my best friends by my side. Sal was a phenomenal dancer, and so was his sister.

An hour or so later, we sat at our table, resting our feet and cooling off. A confetti popper burst behind me, causing me to jump in my seat. I spun around, finding a bachelorette party full of woo-girls next to us covered in glitter.

Suddenly, I missed my tribe something fierce. I felt like Cinderella, afraid the clock was about to strike midnight, erasing the magic that had been this evening. I leaned against Sal, knowing that he didn't want me the way I wanted him, and said, "Are you okay to drive, or should we call an Uber?"

He finished the last sip of his drink before setting the highball glass down on the table. Wrapping his arm around me, he squeezed me a little before saying, "Other than the sugar high those sodas have given me, I'm completely sober."

I thought back to the drinks the girls and I had ordered, and I realized that he really had just been drinking Pepsi all night. In fact, I hadn't seen him drink at all since moving in with him.

I stood up, and the room spun around me. "Well, I'm glad one of us knows how to get home."

He put his hands on my hips, helping me stand upright as we walked out with his sister and her friends. While we waited on the sidewalk for their ride, he pulled me tight and tucked my head under his chin, his warmth coursing through my whole body.

Camilla smiled wistfully at us and nudged Ericka. "One day I'll have what they have."

I remembered to play up my part, and I reached up and rubbed my hands across Sal's arms.

Soon, the girls were gone, and we were in his car, headed down the dark, winding roads. I felt a little sad that tonight's game was over. A brief spark in my chest wished that this could be real. That we could go back in time to that night and I could find out what I did wrong. What I did that made him change his mind about me.

"I wish I could fix it." I said without thinking.

He looked sideways at me. "Fix what?"

The thought that I was about to tell him what I felt for him and that he would reject me again was too much to bear. He had been pretending at the bar, and I needed to get that in my head. "Never mind. It's nothing."

"You're really cute when you've had too much to drink, you know," he said as he pulled up to the security gate and punched in his code.

"Your sister isn't here, Sal. You don't have to keep up the jig."

He pulled into the garage and parked the car. "Did you just call me Sal?"

I looked at him, shocked. "No." Calling him by his name meant I was letting him crack the shell I had built between us, that I was letting him in. I promised myself I wouldn't do that.

He laughed and pointed at me teasingly. "Yeah, you did."

I adored the sound of his laugh. It made the air feel like those confetti poppers from earlier. But then I remembered that everything between us was fake and the car went from feeling intimate to cramped.

I opened the door and got out. "You need to get your

hearing checked, Salsa," I said as I stumbled to the front door of the house.

He slung his arm over my shoulder, steadying me while he unlocked the door. We made it to the living room before he turned me around, gripping my waist in those large hands.

I didn't know where to rest my eyes. His were mostly green tonight, and they seemed to see right through me. I looked down past his lips, to the tattooed swirls peeking out from the neck of his shirt.

I closed my eyes for a second, not able to handle the heat gathering in my lower belly, but that made it worse. His aftershave—sandalwood and something else . . . eucalyptus, maybe . . . took over my senses. It was as if I had my nose pressed against his neck, his scent enveloping me.

I forced my gaze to meet his again, and something I couldn't define fluttered through his eyes before he bit his bottom lip, like he was considering his next words carefully.

I narrowed my eyes at him. "What is it?"

"Tonight was great."

I needed to focus on our purpose. Not the want for him I felt in every bone of my body. "Yeah, your sister seemed to really buy it. I think you'll get an invite to the party in no time."

He tugged me closer, the warmth of his legs pressed against mine, capturing me in a fog. "No, I meant hanging out. It was fun." He reached up and ran his fingers through my hair. I closed my eyes and leaned into his hand. "You have a little something . . . ."

I felt a tug before opening my eyes. He held a piece of confetti between his fingers.

I mumbled, "We should get some of those poppers for Lina's party," but at the same time he said, "Can I ask you something?"

A giant yawn came out of me, one of those loud ones you can't control, and he looked over his shoulder at the clock hanging on the wall. "Oh wow, I need to get you to bed."

The closeness of his body and the connotations of him putting me to bed caused a shiver to run through me. I thought about finding him coming out of the shower earlier and wondered what it would be like to take one with him. Blood pumped faster through my veins as I leaned closer against him. Thinking of his fingers covered in soapsuds, running up and down my arms. Across my breasts. Moving down lower.

Maybe he did want me like I wanted him. There was only one way to find out. I closed my eyes, pushed up on my toes—

And stumbled forward into the space he had vacated as he let go of me and walked away. "Do you want a water or a couple ibuprofen?" He launched himself into the kitchen, opening the cabinet and grabbing a glass. His voice was higher pitched than usual. I must have embarrassed him with my ridiculous display of misplaced affection.

"No, um, I'm fine." I mumbled, feeling more rejected than before.

He turned on the faucet, filled his glass, and then chugged the entire thing. Finally knowing how much I repulsed him, I squeaked out, "I'm gonna go to sleep. I'll see you later."

He put down the glass, wiped his chin and replied, "Sure thing. Thanks again for coming out with me tonight. Camilla loved you."

I walked to my room without bothering to reply, peeled off my clothes, and snuggled into the orange bed. I felt completely dejected. Right before passing out, I grabbed my phone and typed into the group text with Lina and Val: *Yup, I was right. The date was a dud. Maybe I'm just destined to be alone forever?*

Chapter Eight

Another week passed, and thankfully Sal and I only bumped into each other a few times, nothing long enough to count as an actual interaction. I saw the woman who came to tend to the horses every morning more than I saw my fake-boyfriend roommate.

Things had calmed down a little at the resort, most of the construction having moved to the suites on the top floor, but the restaurant was still shut down—which was a giant headache.

On the bright side, Lina was in town for a few days, so I was meeting her and Val for lunch. I walked into the restaurant and found the two of them already seated, looking over menus.

I slid into the booth next to Lina and gave her a hug. "How is our world traveler?"

Her smile lit up the room. It was great to see her so happy. "I'm wonderful, but I'm getting really antsy about the wedding." She banged her hands on the table, like a drumroll. "And as of an hour ago, we have a date picked, and a venue booked!"

I grabbed her in a side hug. "I'm so happy for you!" Sure, I had secretly wished she and Reece would choose The Pacifica, since it was the most beautiful resort on the West Coast, but I understood it wasn't always a happy place for them.

"Well, when's the big day?" Valerie asked.

"April 21st. The hotel we found is on a little patch of beach a few miles up the coast. They'd been fully booked for a year, so we put ourselves on the cancelation list. As soon as I landed this morning, I saw they had left a message that a couple had canceled. The hotel was willing to book us if we left a deposit, so I called Reece and asked him if he was down for it. He agreed and now we're settled." She clapped her hands. "It's really happening."

Seeing the excitement in my best friend's eyes filled my cup with joy. Val and I tried to pry information out of her about what we could do to help, but Lina swore she and Reece were keeping it small and easy to handle.

Halfway through our meals, however, the topic turned to the bachelorette-stag party I was supposed to be planning with Sal.

"We haven't talked about anything, actually. We have the guest list, and that's it."

Valerie rolled her eyes. "You haven't talked to the person you are currently living with?"

I bit back the gut-reaction to defend myself, frustrated that Val was pushing me on this. But I knew she was just playing around, like she always did. "Well, until today we didn't have a date, so we couldn't really book anything. Besides, I've been so busy at work that I pass out as soon as I get home. I haven't even seen him for days." I had wanted to wait as long as I could to tell them about fake-dating the best man, but I knew I was out of time. "Also. We kind of have something going on."

Lina bumped me with her shoulder. "Ooh, sounds spicy."

Any playfulness in my tone disappeared. "No, there is absolutely none of that between us." He made it very clear that this was strictly business.

I thought about how I had tried to kiss him and felt the shame from that night all over again. I couldn't believe I had done that.

Valerie pointed her fork—which had a piece of romaine lettuce hanging from it—at me. "You're going to have to give us more details or our thoughts are going to be smutty as hell."

I sighed. "I agreed to be his fake girlfriend while I'm staying with him so that his dad will invite him to some anniversary party."

They burst into uncontrollable laughter. Which should have made me laugh, but it felt like they were laughing at me instead of with me. It just made me angry.

I balled up the napkin in my hands. "I knew I shouldn't have said anything to either of you."

Lina wiped moisture from her eye with her fingertip, her face serious. She knew they had hurt my feelings. "Sorry Blake. It's just that you spend most of your energy trying to convince us you hate him. The last thing any of us would have expected is for the two of you to pretend to date each other."

Val grinned like a snake, and I knew she was about to cross a line. "You two are totally going to fall for each other and start fucking like rabbits. I can see it now."

I waved my hands at her. "Not on your life. I'm not going to be that stupid again."

Based on the looks on their faces, I realized I had let my secret out, and I had zero chance that they had misheard me.

Fuck.

Valerie clapped her hands. "Oh my God, finally."

Lina's eyes shot to Valerie and then to me. There was shock plastered on her face, but a little guilt there, too.

"What do you know?" Something told me I was about to be very upset with my friends.

Lina's squeaky "Nothing" was a classic tell. She was a terrible liar.

My eyes narrowed on her, my voice as calm as I could make it. "Lina. Tell me what you know."

She held up her hands as her words spilled out quickly. "Reece said it was a secret and I couldn't tell anyone that I knew. That it wasn't his story to tell. He only told me because we promised not to keep secrets from each other." Her brow furrowed. "And I thought it was best if you told me yourself. So I've been waiting."

Val bit into her fist, her eyes as big as saucers. Which meant she had probably known, too. I shifted toward her. "You knew I slept with Sal, too? And you didn't say anything?" The grimace on her face told me everything. "What the hell, you guys?"

Valerie waved her hands frantically. "I swear I didn't think Lina knew. Joey told me to keep it between us, too."

I slammed my hand on the table, drawing attention from the people sitting at the table next to us. I didn't care if everyone heard this conversation at this point. "How did both of your boyfriends find out about this?" Then I paused, knowing the answer to my question. "He told them, didn't he?" I could kill him.

I had no idea what to say. Complete mortification filled my every bone. I was not one to share my bedroom exploits, even with the two of them, and because of what happened after I slept with Sal, I was hoping to take that night to the grave.

But that asshole went and blabbed about it to all of his friends.

Lina looked at me with those big brown puppy-dog eyes. "Please don't get mad. Sal called Reece for advice a few days after it happened."

"He went to Reece for advice? Why?" I was downright enraged at this point, the skin on my face heating.

Lina continued, "Well, when things went down the way they did, he was confused. That's why Reece asked me not to say anything."

I turned toward Val. "And you?"

Val put her hands in her lap demurely, like she was trying to be serious for the first time in her life. "Sal asked Joey what he would do in the same situation, and Joey asked me because he had no idea what to tell him. He's never had a one-night stand before."

I pushed my plate away from me. I would rather deal

with the family that had let their small child flush a washcloth down the toilet this morning than have this conversation. "So, Sal called it a one-night stand?"

At least I knew where his heart was now. No wonder he was so disgusted when I tried to kiss him.

Val's hands flew up in surrender, and she looked concerned. "No, it wasn't like that at all. He seemed genuinely upset about all of it."

Sure. Upset that he had slept with me. I started to tell them just that, but something Lina had said echoed in my ears. "Wait. What do you mean when things went down the way they did?"

Lina's forehead scrunched up when she said, "He said you were gone the next morning without leaving a note."

Val chimed in, her voice soft. "He told Joey you ghosted him."

Then Lina added, "We kind of felt bad for him. He sounded totally defeated."

I gasped, and I was sure it came out louder than it should have, but I couldn't believe the bullshit I'd just heard. "What the actual fuck! I didn't fucking ghost him!"

Lina's eyes shot to the group of older ladies at the table across from us as they looked over, offended. I wanted to flip them off, but I held it in. Her tone was soft as she admitted, "I'm sorry. I should have told you as soon as I heard." She looked at Val. "We both should have."

Valerie nodded. "I guess I was just waiting for you to say something, and when you didn't, I assumed you didn't want to talk about it. You know I've had my share of regrettable hookups, so I totally thought you wanted to just leave the past in the past. I'm so sorry."

Lina added, "If you want to talk about it, we want to hear what really happened. But if you don't, we'll forget it ever happened."

I let out a breath, staring down at the table. "It was the night of your going away party. We had way too much to drink, and even though I was still kind of pissed at him for his stupid birthday party last year, I couldn't stay away from him." Thinking about how horrible those women had been to Lina made me even angrier. I picked up my napkin and crumpled it into a ball. "Sal and I ended up on the dance floor together and—I hate to admit—the man can dance."

I closed my eyes for a second, thinking about his body pressed against mine. The way we found the same rhythm in that dark, sweaty bar. It was a lot like the way we had danced last week, and my heart clinched a little tighter. "Anyway, we were tipsy . . . which mixed with the dancing . . . ." I shook my head, trying to forget the feel of his breath on my skin. "I lost my head, and one thing led to another. We ended up in an Uber headed to my place." The feel of his callused hands pulling the straps of my blouse off my shoulder, replacing them with his mouth, played in my mind. It had felt scandalous letting him undress me in the back of someone else's car, but at the time, I didn't care.

"I peeled him off of me long enough to pull his phone out of his pocket and put my number in his contacts. I took a bunch of stupid pictures of us together to stop myself from sleeping with him right there in the car." I was glad they were on his phone and not mine, so I hadn't been able to obsess over them for several months, debating whether or not to delete them.

I paused, deciding to skip over what we had done once we got inside my house. That was no one's business but my own. "Long story short, the next morning, I woke up in my bed with him curled up around me. My phone was blowing up with calls and texts from Paige because of an emergency with the computers at the front desk that I had to take care of, so I got dressed in the dark, scribbled a note on a napkin on the kitchen counter for him to call me later, and ran out the door." I didn't want to think about the sweet conversation we'd had before we fell asleep the night before. When we had whispered our hopes and dreams while sharing a pillow. When I thought we were starting something together.

Val leaned forward the way she always did, right before she solved the world's problems. "So, were you just really busy handling the emergency and didn't call him back?"

"That's the thing. He didn't call."

"And you didn't try to call him?" Lina's question had been the most frustrating one yet.

"I don't have his number."

Val folded her arms across her chest. "That's a really stupid excuse. You could have asked any of us for it. Or hell, walked right into one of his restaurants and confronted him face to face."

I stared at the wood grain of the table, feeling the scrutiny and shame I had been overcome with the days following our night together. "So I could look like a crazy woman? No thanks. He could have called my office or come by the resort if he really wanted me."

"So you really haven't talked to him about it?" Lina's voice was quiet, full of concern.

I shook my head. "I literally hadn't spoken to him until we got together after shopping for Lina's dress, which was awkward as fuck, by the way. He didn't bring it up, and neither did I, so I figured we were just going to pretend it didn't happen. Until he said that it had been a mistake the other night."

Lina turned in her seat, facing me. She put her hand on my thigh. "We'll figure this out."

"I don't want to figure it out. I want to forget it happened, find my perfect house, and move on with my life."

Then Val, with her knack for perfect timing, asked, "Was the sex really sloppy or something? Was his dick crooked? You can be honest with us."

I closed my eyes, thinking about how we had slammed into walls, licking and biting like feral beasts all the way to my bedroom. How his fingers dug into my hair, pulling it just the way I liked before he plunged his hand down the front of my jeans.

I let out a slow breath and looked at the girls again, trying to fight the tears forming in my eyes. "That's the part that really sucks. It was really good. The best I'd ever had." Turning my gaze up to the ceiling, I wanted to be anywhere but here. I felt the sharp pain in my chest, the one that had been there since a few days after our night together. "I thought we had a connection. It wasn't just about the sex. He was sweet and funny." He still was, if I were being honest with myself. I had wanted something more from that night. An actual relationship with him. "The worst part is that I really liked him." It cut like a knife knowing that not only did he play me, but he lied about it to his friends.

Then Valerie asked, "So why not talk to him about it now?"

Lina added, "He must have felt something, too. Otherwise, he wouldn't have asked Reece for advice."

I put up my hands. "No. We both agreed that it won't happen again. It's just not in the cards for us."

Val jumped in again. "Right. So two people who clearly had feelings for each other slept together, but it didn't work out. And now they're living together and pretending to date each other. Makes sense."

Lina's mouth pressed into a frown. "Why didn't you think you could share this with us earlier?"

I rolled my eyes. "Because he doesn't have feelings for me. I don't know what he was doing when he told Reece and Joey that whatever happened between us was my fault, but believe me, my feelings were completely one-sided."

Val leaned in. "How do you know that for sure?"

I covered my face with my hands, tying to hide my embarrassment. "Because I tried to kiss him a week ago, and he literally jumped to the other side of the room."

I peeked through my fingers just in time to see Lina's hand cover her mouth. "You didn't."

I nodded, confirming one of the worst moments of my life. I tucked my hands into my lap, forcing myself to be brave, and let them in a little. "We had been out on a fake date with his sister and her friends. We got home, and I swore there was something pulling us toward each other. That whole invisible string thing. But I was wrong about him. Again."

Val gave me a sweet smile. "Blake, we want you to talk to us about stuff. We know you like to bottle things up, but we were literally put on this earth to take care of each other."

Lina tilted her head and added, "We just want you to be happy. If you're going through something, we want to know."

"I know. I just love both of you so much, and I didn't want to make a big deal about it. He's obviously very good friends with both of your boyfriends. If we got together and it didn't work out, it would change the whole dynamic of our group, anyway. It's not worth the risk." I ignored their skeptical looks and continued. "I had a one-night stand with a really hot guy. It's happened before, and it will happen again. I just so happen to live with this one. My mom will find a place for me soon, and I get to use this time at Sal's to save some more money." I just needed a few months until I had enough in the bank for a down payment.

Eager to change the subject, I brought up the other issue stressing me out. "Also, Lizette offered me a job at corporate, and I don't want it. I'm afraid that I won't look like a team player if I turn it down, though."

Valerie said, "Jesus, Blake. When did that happen?"

I flipped through the dates in my head. "Umm, like a month ago?"

She seemed a little upset, which was rare for Val. "A whole month? And you didn't say anything?"

"With the wedding and the new store, I didn't want to be a burden on you guys."

"Nothing matters if you're miserable. Nothing. Fuck the store. Fuck the wedding." Valerie looked over at Lina. "Respectfully, I mean."

Lina laughed but added, "She's right. Lord knows we've spent hundreds of hours this year complaining about our problems. We want to hear yours, too."

I smiled and promised I would let them in more often.

Lina folded her hands on the table. "So, why don't you want the job at corporate? Reece and Lizette are playing nice again after he called her when you lost your house. I heard it's gotten a lot better at the main office now that his dad's retired." She knew better than anyone else what it was like at The Pacifica—what it was like at The Howell Group, really. And she had a bigger reason to hate corporate than anyone, since they were the reason she left the resort.

"Fuck it." I threw my hands up. "I might as well tell you everything." Their brows furrowed in stereo. "I've been playing the stock market for a while, and I've been doing really well. I've also been investing in some high-yield savings, and while it's tied up right now, I've got a pretty good chunk of money to play with. I was going to use it for something else in a couple of years, but I think it's going to have to go toward a down payment on a house."

Val caught on to the part I was worried about telling them. "Something else?"

It was time to start being completely open with the people who cared about me the most. "I want to open a bed-and-breakfast."

"That's awesome." Val sounded nothing but supportive.

Then Lina added, "I bet if you tell Lizette she would help you get it up and running."

I flopped back in my chair, relieved that they didn't think it was a terrible idea. "If I wasn't also navigating the real estate market, I might think about it. But all that money is about to be gone."

"The cool thing about money is that you can always make more of it later." Val's smile was bright, and I regretted not telling either of them earlier. I made a promise to myself to actually let them in more, not just to tell them I would to make them feel better.

"Speaking of making more money. How's the new store coming along?" I asked her, ready to move away from my problems.

Valerie put her face down on the table dramatically. "Can we talk about anything else? I have a month and a half before it opens, and everything is going really well."

I laughed. "So you're freaking out because it's going well?"

She sat up, her mouth twisted into a grimace. "Exactly. If things are going well, what the hell is going to knock me on my ass soon? It's against the laws of the universe for everything to work out flawlessly." She picked up her fork and speared the last piece of lettuce in her bowl. "I'm having nightmares about fires and floods and earthquakes."

Lina finished chewing a bite of food and said, "I think it just means that you've kept this project organized and you know what you're doing this time around."

Val shrugged her shoulder. "Joey said the same thing. But I don't know. The universe is always up to something." She wiped her mouth on her napkin and set her focus on me again. "So, if Sal is most definitely not going to be your plus-one to the wedding, who is?"

After Sal rejected me again the other night, I had doubled down on the online dating app. I had spent the last week swiping, messaging, and had even sent a few pictures that were dirtier than I would ever admit to my friends.

I pulled out my phone and opened the dating app I had been glued to every spare minute this week. "Let me show you a couple of my current options." I scanned through the guys I had connected with and showed the girls a few of my conversations.

"Are you sure you should be casually dating with a fake boyfriend at home?" Lina asked. I thought she was joking, but after a beat I realized she had asked it honestly.

"When we agreed to our . . . arrangement, I made it very clear that I wanted to bring someone that was not him to your wedding. Which is even more important to me now that I know he didn't want to kiss me the other night." I pulled up a picture of the guy I liked the most on the app. "This guy is a landscape architect. His name is Dustin. His eyes would look great with my bridesmaid dress, don't you think?" Most of his pictures were of him hiking the hills surrounding Santa Barbara, but my favorite was the shirtless one at the beach, walking his golden retriever puppy.

Valerie leaned in on the last picture. "Ooh, I could take a bite out of him."

"I know, right? He asked me to meet up with him tonight, but with Lina being in town, I told him I'd get back to him in a few days."

"Actually," Lina started, "I'm having dinner with my mom tonight, so if you want to go out with him, you should."

"Hmm, maybe I will." I went back through the app and showed them the next guy I was interested in before they could ask any more questions about Dustin.

"Ooh, he's adorable." Val said as she pointed to the tall, dark-haired guy.

"Adrian is a bartender and likes to go jogging. I told him he could take me out next Wednesday, since I have the next day off. In case it goes really well." He seemed a little too good to be true, but I was willing to find out what his flaws were. "Worst case, it will be a free meal."

Lina asked, "Which one do you like better?"

"I haven't met either of them yet, so I'm not sure. I still have some time to figure that out, though." Glancing down at Adrian's picture, I already felt a spark between us. He had a brilliant smile. "I'll keep you both updated."

The conversation turned back to Lina's wedding plans, and before I knew it, I had to go back to work. My shoulders felt lighter knowing that my best friends knew my worst secret and my biggest dream, but I also hoped they believed me when I said nothing would ever happen between Sal and me again.

After an afternoon of cranky guests and even crankier employees, I locked my office door and slung my bag over my shoulder, trying to ignore the amount of work that needed to get done before we could reopen the kitchen for all the summer weddings that were going to be here before we knew it. Instead, I focused on how much fun I was going to have with Dustin tonight.

Maybe if I tried to kiss *him*, he wouldn't act like I had the plague.

As if I had conjured him with my thoughts, my phone rang with his number on the screen. "Hello?" I asked, hoping he wasn't calling to cancel on me.

"Hey, Blake. Look, I'm having an issue and was wondering if we could change things around a little for tonight?"

I closed my eyes, trying to ignore the frustration I was feeling. "Sure, what's up?"

"Well, my car has been in the shop all week. It was supposed to be done today, but they needed to order a part that won't be here until tomorrow."

"So, do you want to reschedule?" I didn't want to miss this date. I had been looking forward to a palate cleanser since my fake date with Sal that ended so poorly. Hoping this was just a slight problem, I started walking down the long hallway toward the lobby.

"No, not at all. I still really want to see you." The smile in his voice reassured me a little. "I was just hoping you could come pick me up?"

Luckily I had cleaned out the trash from my car

yesterday, so I wasn't too afraid to have a hot guy ride with me. "Sure. Text me the address, and I'll meet you there. Is now still a good time?"

"Yeah, sounds great." I said goodbye to him and made my way out of the resort. It was the first time in weeks I could get out the door without being stopped multiple times to put out other people's fires, so I needed to get out before someone caught me.

Fifteen minutes later, I pulled into an apartment complex and found a spot closest to Dustin's address. I looked around, noticing the neat landscaping and freshly painted walls. This was a good sign that he probably wasn't a sleazeball.

I sent him a quick text: *I'm here, just parked outside.*

He sent a reply: *Sweet, I'll be down in a few.*

But it wasn't a few. It was more like a several.

If I would have known he was going to take so long, I would have gone home and changed. Or at least tried to freshen up in the bathroom before leaving the resort.

Over ten minutes later, he came down the staircase and into view. He flashed me that sparkling smile, and all the time I had been waiting disappeared.

He came around the passenger side and got in. "It's nice to meet you in real life," he said as he reached over for what I thought was going to be a hug, but as my arms went around him, his lips pressed against the corner of my mouth in the most awkward way.

I tried to play it off as funny, but I couldn't help but be a little annoyed. Who kisses before you even really meet? Lina and Val were going to have a field day with this moment.

I pulled away and turned the car back on. "Is everything okay? You seem like a lot is going on."

"No, life is great. I just got back from walking Rufus and then had a bit of laundry to fold."

So he was folding laundry while I sat in the parking lot waiting for him?

I noticed he hadn't put on his seat belt, which was a pet peeve of mine. "Your seat belt is right there." I pointed, trying not to sound passive aggressive.

"Oh, we're just going down the street. I think I'll be fine."

I wrapped my fingers around the steering wheel tightly. "Nah, I think it would be best if you just put it on. Statistically, we're more likely to be in an accident close to home."

I swore he rolled his eyes before reaching for the belt, but he took a few seconds before clicking it into place.

How had this guy been so perfect on the Internet but was such a big mess in person?

"So, what kind of music are you into?" I asked as I put the car into reverse and began driving to the restaurant.

"I listen to a little bit of everything. How about you?"

I smiled. Maybe the first few minutes with a new person were destined to be awkward. "Same. I'm really into whatever's on the radio, but I have a special weakness for showtunes."

"Showtunes? What's that?"

Did this man live under a rock? "You know, musicals? Fiddler on the Roof, Dear Evan Hansen, Hamilton?"

He shrugged, pulling a piece of dog hair off his jeans.

"Hmm, never really thought about that kind of music, I guess."

I tapped my fingers on the steering wheel. We had talked about TV and movies on the dating app. I knew we had that in common, but I didn't know what else to talk about.

Luckily, we pulled into the parking lot of the Italian place—his choice. I wasn't in the mood for Italian food, since it had been tarnished by a man who didn't want me for the rest of my life, but it was easier to just go than to have to explain why I didn't want to see another ravioli again.

This place was nice, though. It was a massive chain restaurant that probably couldn't even be classified as real Italian food anymore, but their breadsticks were good.

We got out of the car, and he reached for my hand. I was not one for public displays, but I thought it was sweet that he was trying to be romantic, so I slipped my hand into his. "This is my favorite restaurant. I come here all the time."

I smiled as we walked in the door. "I haven't been here in years."

We put our names in with the hostess and sat on a bench to wait for our table. I looked around and wondered if Sal's Place was ever going to turn into a franchise like this. Without thinking, I said, "My roommate owns a few Italian restaurants, so I don't come to this one very often."

Dustin's face lit up with excitement. "Oh yeah? What does she run?"

"He." This was about to get weird. "My roommate is

a guy." I started to tell Dustin about Sal, but I didn't want to spend the evening talking about the guy I was trying to get over. "His food really is great." Much better than what we were about to eat, which shouldn't have made me feel as disappointed as I did.

"You should have told him we were going out tonight. Maybe we could have gotten a discount or something."

That was the last thing I would have wanted to do. For many reasons. "I'm only staying with him temporarily. It's a long story, but I needed some housing and he stepped in and let me stay with him, so I'm kind of all out of favors right now."

He gave me a wary look, but went on, "That was really nice of him. Is he into you or something?"

"Blake? Your table is ready."

Thank goodness for the hostess. I did not want to think about how to spin my latest failure into light conversation.

So instead, I jumped up like my butt was on fire. "Right here. Thanks so much!" Dustin stood up, too, and we followed the hostess to our table.

The meal was relatively painless. There wasn't a lot that we had in common. Apparently, Dustin used his conversation skills on the app and saved little for the actual date.

Which was a bummer, because he really was nice to look at. His blond hair was soft and had a slight curl to it, and his blue eyes were even more vivid in person.

At least the food was good, despite not being the most delicious food I'd ever eaten. When the server dropped off the bill and a handful of candies, Dustin patted his lap a few times. "Oh, shit."

"What is it?" I wondered what was wrong.

"My wallet. I forgot it at home. I'm so sorry."

I reached into my purse and pulled my wallet out. "No worries, I just got paid, anyway, so it works out."

He put his hands on the table. "I'll get the check next time, I promise."

I didn't know how to tell him I had already decided there would not be a next time, so I just smiled at him. "You ready?"

He took my hand again and walked me out to the car. The entire time, I really just wanted to peel my hand off of his and wipe it on my slacks. It didn't fit right, like it was too small, or maybe his fingers were too short.

We got into the car, and after I had to gently suggest more than once that he put his seat belt on, I knew for certain I would not be going out with him again.

Halfway to his house, he broke the silence between us by pointing out the window. "Hey, do you think we could stop by the grocery store? I'd like to pick up a few things for lunch tomorrow."

I thought for a split second about opening his door and kicking him out of my car, but I had forced him to wear a seatbelt, so he wouldn't go flying out like I was currently imagining. "Um, you don't have your wallet, remember?"

"Oh, yeah." He laughed a little. "Sorry, I forgot about that." Then, after a short pause, he added, "Could you spot me a twenty?"

I took a deep breath in through my nose and let it out

through my mouth to stop from yelling at him. "You know what, I've got a really early day tomorrow, and it's getting late. I think I'm just going to have to drop you off."

He smiled, oblivious to the anger fuming from me. "Oh, that's cool, too. I just figured because we were close to the store and all."

I nodded and continued driving. I couldn't get him out of the car quickly enough.

Once I parked, he had the audacity to try to kiss me again. I held my hand up, which turned into an awkward handshake, but I didn't even care. "Thanks for tonight, Dustin. But I think we're just going to have to stay friends."

He gave me a cute smile, making me wish it had turned out better. "No worries. Friends are cool, too."

As soon as he was far enough up his sidewalk that I knew he wouldn't turn around and ask me to run another errand for him, I pulled out my phone and sent a text to the girls' group: *This date was the worst. Even worse than the baby-hungry dude last year.*

I tucked my phone back into my purse and started the lonely drive home.

My phone rang as I pulled into the driveway, and I answered it. Valerie's voice filled the inside of my car. "You can't just text a bombshell like that without following up on why it was terrible! I need details!"

"Sorry, I was driving. Maybe it wasn't as bad as the 'I wanna put a baby in you' guy, but it really was up there." I parked the car in the gravel driveway and turned off the engine.

Val said something, but I was fumbling with switching from Bluetooth to the phone as I got out of the car and missed it. "What?"

"I said, what could possibly be more disturbing than telling someone you want to get them pregnant before they've even finished dinner?"

I tucked the phone between my ear and my shoulder as I dug through my purse for my house keys. "Well, first he called me to come pick him up because his car was in the shop."

"Well, cars break down. That's not a deal-breaker."

I slipped through the door and put my purse on the table in the entryway. "He tried to kiss me before the date even started. And then he wouldn't put his damn seat belt on." I leaned against the kitchen island counter, looking out the big picture windows.

"Do you think you're picking out negatives because of some other reason? Some hunky tattooed reason, maybe?"

"Absolutely not. This guy couldn't hold a conversation and didn't even bring his wallet, which isn't even the worst part!" I closed my eyes, feeling angry about the date all over again. "He asked me to loan him twenty bucks for groceries while I drove him home."

A voice coming from behind me, which was definitely not Val, said, "Wow, you sure know how to pick them."

I leapt up and spun around, finding Sal standing in front of the stove, turning on a burner. I had been so concerned about telling Valerie the details of my date that I hadn't noticed him on the other side of the room. "I didn't know you were here," I said to Sal. Then I said into the phone, "I'm going to have to call you back."

His eyes had a twinkle in them as he smiled. He gestured to my phone while putting a kettle on the fire. "Please, don't stop this riveting conversation because of me."

I gave my attention back to Val, who I was pretty sure was trying to hide uncontrollable giggles. "I'll call you in the morning."

"Tell your boyfriend I said hi. I hope he's not too jealous of your terrible date."

"I hate you, Valerie." I said to her sweetly.

"I love you too!" The sound of her laughter cut off as she hung up the call.

I put my phone in my back pocket. "You're not usually home this early."

He turned his back to me, opening a cabinet, and I felt like he was trying to keep his full attention away from me. "Tuesday nights are usually pretty light, and since I haven't taken a day off in a few weeks, I figured I'd stay home tonight."

He pulled out two mugs and laid them on the island. "Would you like some tea?" he asked, like standing together at the kitchen island talking about our day was a daily routine.

Without thinking, I smiled a little. "Thanks." Maybe he wasn't so bad after all. Sure, the thought of kissing me disgusted him, but as Dustin had said, *friends are cool, too.*

He rifled through another cabinet and pulled out a wooden container. He opened it, pulled out a paper tea package, and slid the box toward me. I thumbed through the different types until I found a chamomile one that looked yummy.

"Honey?"

My heart sparkled at the nickname before I looked up at him and saw him shaking a little bear in his hands. "Um, yeah, thanks," I mumbled. He laid it on the counter and moved to the fridge.

As he opened the door and pulled out the milk, I couldn't help but admire how deftly he moved around in the kitchen, like he was made for it. I watched him as he opened the dishwasher I had loaded earlier and emptied it, putting every dish in its place without a word.

The kettle whistled, so he turned off the heat and poured the water into our mugs. He squeezed honey into mine before holding his hand out for my tea packet. I handed it over and watched him put it in my mug before pouring milk into his own. He gestured with the jug, asking if I wanted some, but I just shook my head.

The silence between us felt sacred, like we both had so much to say but were choosing to just be together in this moment.

Or he was just trying to be nice since I was living in his house.

He pulled a spoon from the drawer and placed it in my mug before sliding it over to me. I whispered, "Thank you," before sitting on a stool, stirring the honey through the darkening water.

He sat his elbows on the counter and leaned forward. The room suddenly felt smaller, like he was taking up more space. "So, you wanna talk about it?"

My heart leapt into my throat. I had practiced what I

would say to him a hundred times before, but now that I had his undivided attention, I didn't know what to say first.

Do I bring up how he slept with me and ignored me the next day? Or how my friends said he lied to them about it?

Or should I start with how I awkwardly tried to kiss him the other night?

Oh God, was I his Dustin? Asking for a place to stay and thinking there was something more going on between us than there was.

He tapped his spoon against his mug twice, bringing my attention back to him. My eyes met his as he said, "About your date, I mean. Do you want to talk about how bad it was?" Then he pointed his spoon toward the tv in the next room, "Or do you want to find something bad to watch instead?"

My bravery popped like a balloon. He didn't want to talk about us, he just wanted to be nice. The tea was an olive branch, and it was up to me to decide how to receive it.

I picked up my mug, deciding to be a nice roommate, and said, "Sure, let's see what we can find on Netflix."

Twenty minutes into an episode of a dating show where strangers were locked in a house and told to pair up, I had tears streaming down my face from laughing so hard. Sal had insisted that we watch the UK version, since the accents were easier for him to make fun of.

"Oh, for fook's sake," he said, repeating something a contestant had said earlier, and I burst out laughing again.

The couples were going on dates with people that weren't their partners, and although they were trying to be serious, everything they said turned out to be hilarious.

When the contestants filed out of the van and back into the house, I pointed at the screen. "I feel like if a gust of wind came up, it would knock that whole house down like a deck of cards."

"Right? It looks like they only used two-by-fours and like three pieces of plywood to build the whole thing."

The couples came together again in the backyard, where a bikini-clad blonde with too much lip-filler was manning the barbecue grill. She opened it, all proud of herself, revealing that she had been making dinner for everyone. "Oh, I love a good baked potato."

He laughed. "That looks appetizing to you?"

I shifted in my seat, turning toward him a little. "Okay, maybe not those baked potatoes. But add some butter and a ton of sour cream and it's basically my favorite food."

He nodded, a gleam in his eye. "Good to know."

I sat my empty mug on the coffee table and tucked my legs under me. Sal reached behind himself, grabbing a chenille blanket and tossed it at me.

I thanked him and he replied with a "No problem."

The contestants were making their way to the backyard to confront their other halves when Sal asked, "So, speaking of poorly built houses, how's your house hunt going? Have you gone to see that house your mom called you about?"

"I'm actually going tomorrow morning before work."

And before I could stop myself, I continued, "You could come with me, if you want."

When he didn't say anything, I added, "You know, to practice being a couple or whatever, so next time we see your sister we're less awkward."

He nodded slowly, just as a girl in a string bikini slapped a guy with a permanent sunburn on the screen. "Yeah, I could make that work. For practice purposes."

"Is nine too early? I know you're usually still sleeping then, but I could ask the real estate agent to meet us later?"

"No, that sounds great." He stood, stretching his arms over his head. "I should probably head to bed, though."

I pointed to the TV. "Don't you want to see how this episode ends?"

A blush rose up his cheeks. "I've already seen this whole season. I won't spoil it for you, though." He reached down to pick up our empty mugs and their spoons. "I'll see you in the morning."

Chapter Nine

I left the orange bedroom the next morning, dressed for work, but ready to see this house. My mom had already sent like fifty texts asking me to send her pictures of what I liked and what I didn't so she could find the perfect house for me over the next few months. I thought back to the house Lina had rented. To that perfect kitchen and magnificent view. I sent her a link to a Pinterest board I had been putting together to help her out on my way down the hall.

The smell of bacon wafted from the kitchen, and I found Sal manning the stove, dancing to a pop song blasting from his Bluetooth speaker on the counter.

He spun around, smiling, and my breath got stuck in my throat. He was so fucking beautiful.

I had to remind myself that I didn't like him because he didn't like me. The last thing I wanted to be was some heartsick woman pining for a guy who wasn't interested.

He pointed to a stool with his spatula. "Have a seat. Breakfast is almost ready."

"I was just going to have a cup of coffee and a granola bar."

He went back to the stove, slowly stirring scrambled eggs in a pan. "Nonsense. You've got too many things to think about today to go into it with an empty stomach."

"You sound like my mother."

He looked at me over his shoulder, cringing. "Worse. I sound like my father."

Again, moving like the kitchen was built for him, he grabbed plates, cups, and cutlery, and before I knew it, I had a full breakfast sitting in front of me.

He slid onto the stool next to mine and poured himself a glass of orange juice before offering it to me. "Thank you." I felt the same comfortable way I had last night when he offered to make me tea. Like he was taking care of me. I poured some orange juice into my cup before spearing a fluffy egg with my fork. I took a bite and instantly knew eggs would never be the same again. "How is it that whatever you cook tastes better than everything I've ever eaten before?"

He laughed and dug into his breakfast. "Nonna taught me how to scramble eggs when I was about six years old. So you can blame her for that."

"Good job, Nonna." I took a few more bites before I noticed he had stopped eating. His plate still had food on it, but he had set his fork down and was staring at me. I swallowed the food in my mouth and asked, "What is it?"

I might have imagined his face turning pink when he said, "You make little noises when you're eating." It was my turn to blush. His voice sounded deeper as he said, "Sorry, I shouldn't have said that."

I shook my head and filled my fork with eggs, ultra-aware of the way I was eating. "I hadn't realized I was making noise."

He picked up a slice of bacon and took a bite. After a few chews, he said, "I like them. They're adorable. They kind of remind me of—" He paused, shaking his head. "Never mind." Then he took another bite of bacon.

I nudged him with my shoulder, curious to know what he had almost said. "Tell me." I prodded, as I took another bite.

He shoveled what was left on his plate into his mouth and stood. As soon as I'd decided he wasn't going to answer me, he put his plate in the sink and lifted a sultry gaze to me. "It reminded me of other sounds you've made before."

One look. One sentence. That's all it took to turn my core to fire.

I bit my bottom lip, remembering what he had done to cause those noises I knew he was referring to. How his body had felt so pleasantly heavy over mine. The filthy words he whispered as he glided in and out of me.

How he had cupped my face in his hands and stared into my eyes, saying, *"Yes, Blake. Come for me. Just like that,"* right as I lost myself to him.

My heart thumped several times in my chest, but I couldn't look away from him. Those hazel eyes that had devoured me that night had caught me in a trap.

Something clanked in the sink, making me jump. As I looked down to the tile floor, Sal turned around, grabbed the pan off the stove and began rinsing it. I finished what was left of my breakfast, being extra mindful to not make a peep, and came around to the sink to rinse my plate off, too.

Aware of the thick silence between us, I opened the dishwasher and started loading it. Sal's body was so close —it felt like he was pressing it against me. I wondered if he felt the same way as he took a few steps away. He checked his watch before saying, "We should probably get going or we'll be late."

Once I slipped the last dish into the dishwasher, I stood up straight, trying to speak, but my voice was gone. I coughed, clearing my dry throat. "Yeah. Do you want to ride with me or . . . ?"

His voice was barely a whisper as he said, "No, I'll follow you on my bike. So both of us can go to work after."

I stood, wiping my sweaty hands on my bright green slacks. "Sounds like a plan." And I headed toward the front door.

We walked through the open front door of a gorgeous house right at the edge of a cliff. The sound of waves crashing reverberated through the entryway. "There is no way in hell I can afford something like this." My voice echoed off the white tile floors.

"We're just here to get a feel for what you like." His voice was soft behind me, like he was standing closer than I thought he had been.

A blonde woman with a hot pink pencil skirt came around the corner. She looked about my mom's age, but her style looked more like my own. I immediately wanted to ask her where she got her floral blazer. "Hi," she sang brightly.

I reached out, shaking her hand. "Hi there, I'm Blake."

"Nice to finally meet you. I'm Theresa." She looked from me to the giant standing behind me. The way her eyes raked over his body caused my jaw to clench. It definitely was not jealousy or possessiveness making me feel this way.

"And I'm Sal," his voice rumbled as he reached out, taking her hand.

I felt the tension in the room rise a little, so I jumped in with, "It's short for Salmonella."

Her eyes met mine again. "Excuse me?" But Sal had burst into laughter, putting his large hands on my shoulders.

"Okay, that might be my favorite nickname you've come up with so far."

I turned to him, unable to hide my smile. "I have to admit, I'm kind of proud of it myself."

Theresa looked between us, her eyes scrutinizing. "So are the two of you . . . ?" She drifted off at the end of her sentence.

I thought about telling her we were dating, but this woman knew my mother.

"Just friends." Sal and I said at the same time.

She nodded, like she didn't believe either of us.

"Well, come on in and let me show you around."

She walked us through the living room, pointing out the big picture windows. It was really beautiful, with modern yet comfortable-looking furniture. Sal went straight to the kitchen and let out a groan.

"What is it?" I saw nothing wrong with the white quartz countertops and stainless-steel appliances.

He spread his arms across the room, which went from one end of his fingertips to the other. "It's not big enough."

"This house is huge compared to the one I just moved out of. Besides, anything larger is going to be way out of my price range, not to mention more house than I need." I was prepared to settle if it meant not draining my finances.

"I agree. The house itself is too big for what you want. But this kitchen is dismal at best." His eyes scanned the cabinets and the countertops.

"I don't cook, remember? As long as the fridge can hold takeout, I'm fine."

Theresa started to say something, but Sal pointed at the stove. "How are you going to entertain in here? You can't even roast a turkey in that thing."

He had a point. The oven wasn't even half the size of the one in Sal's house. "You're confusing me for you. I've never cooked a turkey in my life, and I don't plan on it anytime soon."

He leaned his hip against the counter. "Yes, but could you see your future husband trying to make dinner for your children in here? Where would they sit?"

My brain went into overdrive. "I don't want either of those things. You know that."

Something passed between us. A silent understanding, like he finally believed how I felt about marriage and children and knew I wasn't going to waver. He leaned forward, propping his elbows on the counter and nodded. "Okay, so what if your partner wants to cook dinner for Reece and Maggie and their future kids when they're visiting?"

I thought about correcting him about my best friend's name, but the thought of Reece and Lina and a bunch of kids running around filled me with sparking joy. My ears became warm as I played out the scenario in my head. I knew I was wrong, but I had hoped that when he said partner, he was talking about himself.

I said the only thing I could muster. "You have a good point."

Oblivious to the weird communication going on between Sal and me, Theresa typed something into her phone. "This is good information, Blake. We know you want a kitchen for entertaining and a smaller square footage. I'll add that to the notes I'm sending to your mom."

The rest of the house tour was like walking through a fog. All I could think about was coming home to someone who made dinner and roasted turkeys on holidays. Someone who wanted to be with me, even with my boundaries. And I couldn't get anyone who wasn't Sal to come to mind.

I noticed bedrooms but couldn't remember anything special about them. When we made it to the primary bedroom, I was disappointed that there weren't two sinks in the en suite, but I knew if I said something about it, he would bring up an imaginary partner again.

We finally found ourselves in the driveway. I thanked

Theresa and assured her that my mom would call her soon to brainstorm. She extended her hand to Sal, holding a business card. With a wink, she said, "It's nice that you're such a helpful friend to Blake."

He reached for the card. "No problem. Someone's got to look out for her, you know."

She hadn't been listening to what he said, judging by the way she was looking at him. Like she wanted to eat him alive. "Call me for anything, okay?" He started to pull his hand away, but she held on to the card. Her voice dropped. "Anything."

He gave her the smile I'd seen him give women on the dance floor, but this was the first time I'd noticed it wasn't genuine. "Sure thing, Theresa."

We went out to the car, and I put my hand on the door handle. My phone vibrated in my pocket before I thanked him for coming, and without thinking, I pulled it out and checked it.

It was a notification for a geocache in the area. I clicked it and saw that it was just a few yards away. Thinking I would come back on my day off and look for it, I took a screenshot to remind myself.

"Is that the geocaching app?" Sal asked over my shoulder.

I cringed, not wanting him to tease me about my nerdy hobby. "What do you know about geocaching?"

He slid his phone from his pocket and showed me he had the same app on his home screen. "I've only been doing it for about a decade."

Trying to hide my shock was difficult. I wasn't a gatekeeper by any means, but the thought of this guy who was all hard edges and dirty jokes climbing a tree or crossing a creek to find hidden treasure was not one I'd ever come up with on my own. "I figured you were a Muggle."

He laughed, "There's a lot you don't know about me yet, Blake." Then he paused thoughtfully. "Is this what you were doing the night I found you in the parking lot?"

I felt my skin blanching. "Maybe."

He let out a laugh. "It's why I was there, too. Did you find it?"

"No, some jerk scared the shit out of me and then wouldn't go away, so I couldn't keep looking." I glared at him, but it felt more playful than anything else.

"For what it's worth, I kept looking after you stomped off, and I couldn't find it." He chewed his bottom lip, and it sent tingles through my spine. "Maybe we could go back soon and look for it together?"

We had spent a few months getting to know each other before Lina and Reece moved away—before we slept together—but knowing this about him melted my icy heart.

"Yeah, I would like that. Should we find this one while we're here?" I clicked through the app, pulling up the information for the nearby hidden package.

He pulled it up on his phone, too, before answering me. "Sure. Lead the way."

I started walking down the street and found an area between two houses that was covered with overgrown grass and weeds. "Looks like it's somewhere over here."

"What size is it?"

"It says it's a regular one, but half of the time I don't

trust those ones." Sometimes the app was a bit frustrating, without much detail other than difficulty, terrain type, and cache size.

He stepped through the grass, moving bushes around. "So how often do you go geocaching?"

"I try to find new ones on my days off, but I've been so busy lately I haven't been able to look for any."

"There are a few great ones in our neighborhood." He paused, his body freezing. "My neighborhood." He paused again, digging around another bush. "You know what I meant."

I looked through a bush near his. "My brother Jake and my college roommate are the only people I know who do this."

"Maggie and Val don't go with you?"

I laughed. "I've taken them a few times, but they usually start talking like pirates, which is more distracting than helpful. It's more of an adventure I like to do solo, anyway." I started to ask him more about his geocaching adventures when I saw a shiny green box. "Think I found it."

I wiggled my arm through the bush and pulled out the plastic container. It was the size of a small Kleenex box, and I couldn't wait to see what was inside.

Sal sidled up against me, and it took all my effort not to lean into him. I popped the lid off the container and he said, "Ooh, this is a good one!"

It was filled with a bunch of little things: rocks, a couple of Lego bricks, a small 3D printed pine cone and even a Hotwheels car. I pulled out the well-worn paper log and handed the container to Sal. "Want me to put both our names on it?" I asked as he sifted through the treasures in the box.

He looked up at me and smiled, like I had asked him if he wanted to dance. "Yeah, I would like that."

I reached for the golf pencil in the container and found the first blank line on the log. This cache had been visited at least a hundred times, which always made me feel like there were more people out in the world like me than I had thought.

I wrote: Blake & Sal, and today's date and rolled the log back up.

"I'll be right back," he said as he handed the container to me. He jogged down to his motorcycle and grabbed his backpack, pulling something out of the front zipper.

When he made it back to me, he held his hand out, showing me a small compass in the palm of his hand. "I always leave these."

I picked up the compass. It was no larger than a quarter, and I recognized it immediately. I had seen it in at least a dozen caches around town. My eyes traveled from his hand, up his arm, and finally rested on his eyes.

I could feel my heart softening, knowing that he had many layers that were peeling back. Luckily, I didn't have to say a word as he took the container from me and dropped the compass inside before sealing it back up.

I pretended to be busy logging our find in the app on my phone, but really I was trying to calm my beating heart. Months ago, I had slipped into deep feelings for him, and in this moment, I started feeling them again.

He put the cache back where we had found it and stood across from me. "Should we get going?"

I found it hard to reply. I mumbled a "Yeah" and started walking toward my car. Once inside, I buckled myself in and rolled my window down. He was still standing outside my car, so I told him, "I appreciate your help this morning."

He held up Theresa's business card. "Hell yeah, where else would I get the phone number for someone my mother's age who wants to fuck me?"

I barked out a laugh, covering my mouth with my hand. "It wasn't like that."

He perked up an eyebrow and gave me a devilish grin. He copied the tone Theresa had given him when he repeated, "Anything."

I knew he was trying to be funny, but all I could think about was wanting him all over again, and I needed an excuse to get out of there. "Well, guess I better head to the office."

He looked down at his watch. "Yeah, I need to get going, too." He tried to hand me Theresa's card through the window. "Here, you take this."

"I already have her number."

He rolled his eyes. "I don't care what you do with it, but I don't want it." I laughed at him and took it, stuffing it into my cup holder. When he wiped his hands on his jeans, I laughed again, this time a bit louder.

I started the car but didn't want to let him go just yet. He tapped the window frame. "Well, I guess I'll see you later."

I nodded. "Don't worry, I won't wait up tonight. I know you'll be out late."

He hesitated before saying, "Thanks, Blake."

I watched him walk away and get on his bike through my rearview mirror. It reminded me of the first time I'd ever seen him. I had picked Lina up from that nightclub when she called me sobbing. From that heartbreaking party that almost split her and Reece up for good.

I had seen a glimpse of Sal through my rearview mirror on his birthday and instantly felt a connection. Just one look pulled him into my heart.

No matter how angry I was at him for being at fault for even a little bit of my best friend's sadness, I couldn't get him out of my head. I had wanted him from that first moment, and I'd be lying if I said I didn't want him still.

It really fucking sucked that he didn't feel the same way.

Maybe the girls were right. I was blaming him for something he had no control over and should forgive him for it. Before I could dwell any further over the feelings churning inside me, I put the car into drive and took off for the resort.

I clicked send on yet another email asking the contractor for an updated timeline on our restaurant, which was currently in about a million pieces. I hadn't heard back from my last two emails or the voice mail I'd left three days ago and had been unable to catch him when he was on-site. My next step was somehow finding his home address so I could sit in his driveway until he gave me a date I could start telling wedding parties and family reunions we could cater again.

He had originally promised us it would take three months, tops, but we were pushing into month four and there were still no booths in sight.

Paige's voice sounded in my ear. "Blake, Lizette is here and would like to meet with you. Should I tell her you're available?"

I hit the button on my radio handset. "Thanks for asking, Paige. You can send her in."

Two minutes later, Lizette came in the door, closing it behind herself, and plopped into one of the chairs facing my desk. "To what do I owe your visit?" I asked.

She kicked off her red-bottomed heels and dug her toes into my rug. It still threw me off when she removed her business facade and acted like an actual human being in front of me. "I'm having a late lunch with a friend at a restaurant down the street, so I figured I would stop by and pretend to talk numbers with you, so the board thinks I'm more than just a figurehead."

I smiled at her. "So, taking over the family business isn't all that it was chalked up to be?"

She closed her eyes, laying her head back. "I think I'm starting to understand why my dad was such a jerk all the time. Every time I think I've got a decision made, I have to present it to the board, and half the time it gets shot down." She opened her eyes again, looking at the edge of my desk. "I really wanted to turn the company around, start doing more good, but every time I get ahead, they reel me back in."

"That's got to be so frustrating." I thought about telling her what a pain in the ass it had been running this property, but she was still my boss, and I didn't want to sound like I couldn't handle it.

She leaned forward. "Speaking of corporate bullshit . . . . Have you thought about the job offer?"

I gripped the edge of my desk, knowing she was going to hate what I had to say. "Actually, I think I'm going to turn it down. I like it here, and I don't think I'm ready for more." It wasn't the complete truth. Really, I had my heart set on my bed-and-breakfast and wasn't ready to give it up yet.

She tapped her firecracker-red fingernails against her cheek and let out a brief hum. After a second she said, "So what you're saying is that you're not totally set on saying no."

I laughed. This woman was the most persuasive person I'd ever met. "How about right now it's a no, but I reserve the right once renovations are finished to change my mind?"

Her eyebrow arched, like she had caught me in her trap. "I love that idea." Her phone went off in her purse. "Hold on, let me get this."

I turned toward my computer, clicking through this month's expense report as she spoke to whomever she was having lunch with. I approved a budgetary request while she told the other person to just meet us here so they could walk, since parking at the restaurant nearby was impossible.

She hung up the phone and tucked it back into her purse. "Sorry about that. My friend and I try to have lunch once a month to catch up, but I told her about the divorce last night and she's freaking out, trying to make sure I'm actually okay."

"And are you? Okay, I mean?"

She held up a hand. "Not you, too!"

"You know we're all just concerned about you. It's a big deal."

"Honestly, it's more of a formality. He's still my best friend. We just weren't . . . . How did my therapist put it? Romantically compatible." Her eyes met the ceiling. "Hell, we hadn't had sex in over a year. You would have thought I would have noticed something was up."

"Damn, that's a long time." But when I thought about it, the last time I'd been intimate with someone was almost around the same time she had. I was pretty sure Sal spent his free time sticking his dick in anything that breathed, though. With a face like his, how could he not?

"Just promise me you'll get an ironclad prenup when you get married. Zeke and I were able to split pretty easily because of that beautiful little document."

I rapped my fingers on my desk. "Oh, you don't have to worry about that. The unmarried life is the only one for me."

"Good for you. Don't let anyone make you compromise. That's what got me in my mess in the first place." She wasn't the only person who had urged me not to compromise lately. I guess I had been doing that a lot . . . letting others have their way so I didn't rock the boat.

There was a knock at the door and Lizette scurried to put her shoes back on. Once she was ready, I called out, "Come on in."

And because nothing in my life could ever be simple, Lizette's friend, who chose right now to walk into my office, was none other than my fake boyfriend's sister, Camilla.

My heart leapt out of my chest and I was suddenly glad I hadn't complained about the single life to Lizette like I had just been about to.

"Oh, thank goodness you're here." Lizette stood and pulled Camilla into a tight embrace.

As soon as they let go, my fake boyfriend's sister turned to me, waving her hands in excitement. "Oh my gosh, Blake! Izzy didn't tell me she was hiding out in your office!" She looked around. "Your resort is gorgeous!"

I stood and walked around the desk, wrapping her in a hug. "Thanks so much for stopping by." I hoped my voice sounded confident and she didn't feel my heart bursting out of my chest.

Lizette looked between us. "I should have known the two of you knew each other. This town is so small."

Camilla sat down in a chair, pointing for Lizette to sit back down. My palms went slick with the thought that they were making themselves comfortable.

"Blake is shacking up with my brother."

Lizette's eyes shot to mine questioningly, and I took a moment to walk back around my desk, using it as a shield from the two of them. "That I am."

"Reece told me you had found a place, but he didn't mention it was with his best friend. Why didn't you tell me you were staying with Sal?"

Camilla bit her bottom lip and giggled a little. "Oh,

she's not just staying with him. Those two have been knocking boots for a while."

Heat crept up my neck, and I shrugged a shoulder. "Guilty."

Lizette slapped my desk. "What the hell, Blake? Here I was complaining about the death of my marriage for the hundredth time, and you were hiding this from me!"

Camilla clasped her hands together. "That's it. You're coming to lunch with us. I want to hear all the stuff you can't say around my brother."

At that moment, the concierge's voice in my earpiece interrupted our fun little chat. "Blake, there's a deliveryman here for you. He says you have to sign for the package."

I held up my finger and then pointed to my headset, letting the women in my office know that someone was taking to me. "Yeah, that sounds great. Thank you, Alex."

Then I turned back to Lizette and Camilla, thankful for the excuse that had just dropped into my lap. "Sorry, ladies. I came in a couple hours late this morning because of an appointment and there's just too much going on for me to take a lunch. I'll have to catch you next time."

Lizette stood, taking a step toward the door. "Well, you're missing out, but as your boss, I understand." She gave me a wink, which made me thankful how far our friendship had come the last year. Lord knows how many nightmares I'd had about her taking over the resort last summer.

Camilla stood, starting to say goodbye to me as Lizette opened the door and let out a squeal. She was not the type to ever show emotion outside of my office, so I panicked.

I recognized the deliveryman's muscular arms and knew I was extra fucked. He had a styrofoam cup from my favorite smoothie shop in each hand, which I definitely did not order. My work life and my pretend personal life were about to come crashing together.

Sal and Lizette spoke a million miles an hour, the excitement of bumping into each other apparent. It was a little unnerving seeing my serious boss so animated.

She pointed to his hands. "What are you doing here? Did Cami invite you?"

He turned a little bashful and his eyes met mine. "Actually, I was bringing a token of apology to my . . . ." He paused, as if asking me for permission to go on with our ruse in my personal space. I quirked my lip in a smile, knowing if we wanted to be believable, this would be the place to do it. "Um, girlfriend."

Lizette smiled at me. "Oh wow, I didn't realize you two were *together*, together. I figured you were just hanging out." She nudged Sal with her shoulder, a gesture that was alien coming from her but showed that she had more layers than even I knew about. "Good job."

He handed me a smoothie, and I thanked him, which made me wonder why he had said it was a token of apology. My stomach flipped. Was this about sleeping together? Had he finally come here to talk about it?

Camilla pointed at his legs. "What's with the basketball shorts? Shouldn't you be at work?"

He took a long drink from his straw, obviously avoiding her question. "I just came from the gym."

She put her hand on her hip, giving him a skeptical look. "I thought the reason you go to the gym at 2 every morning is because it's too people-y during the day?"

He reached around my waist, putting a tentative hand on my hip. It felt like those hover-hand pictures you see from Comic-Con, so I leaned into him, letting him know he could touch me here.

He answered her, "Yeah, usually I like to go after I close up the restaurant, but Blake and I had been house-hunting this morning, and I needed to blow off some steam."

I turned, looking at him, wondering what kind of steam he had built up when my headset blared with Alex's voice again. "Paige, did you see him?"

Paige's voice jumped in half a beat later. "Yes. I'm standing in Bob's office right now. He has his arm wrapped around her."

Bob was our head of security, and he had an array of screens across one wall showing the view from every camera on the property. Which meant Paige was watching our entire interaction live. At least she didn't have sound. I pushed down the button on the radio clipped to my pants and spoke. "You're on the wrong channel again. Time to switch to two, so I don't feel like firing both of you before you leave for lunch."

Alex's voice was higher pitched as she said, "Oh crap, sorry. We didn't mean it, Blake." As soon as I thought she was done, she spoke again. "Is he your boyfriend?"

Thankfully, everyone standing outside of my office was busy having their own conversation and had no idea that my employees were gossiping about us on the radio.

"Let's keep it professional while corporate is in the building, ladies."

I came back into the conversation, listening as Sal told Lizette how his newest location was going. "It really is a dream come true."

"That's amazing. I'm proud of you." Her genuine smile worried me a little. If she was this comfortable with him, how was she going to treat me when we had our big pretend breakup?

His hand tightened on my waist. "Speaking of dreams, has Blake told you about her bed-and-breakfast plans?"

My stomach dropped. I had told him that in confidence.

I thought back to spilling my secret to him in his car. Had I actually mentioned that it was a secret?

Fuck. Maybe I hadn't been clear that he was the only person in the world that knew I was serious about it. And now my boss knew I was planning on becoming the competition.

Lizette's eyes lit up, though, which was a little reassuring. "She hasn't said a single word about it." Then she looked at me. "Is this why you don't want to take the promotion? Are you going to leave me?"

I chewed on the inside of my cheek for a second. "I'm not sure if the bed-and-breakfast is ever going to happen. It was just an idea I was toying around with, not like an actual plan or anything."

Camilla punched Sal's shoulder playfully. "Is this why you're finally moving out of Nonna's house? Are you going to turn it into a hotel?"

Holy crap, this was moving way too quickly for me. He turned his head, catching my panicked eyes. "We hadn't really talked about it, but I won't lie and say I hadn't thought about it."

Lizette squealed again, the way that made me wonder if her brain had been swapped with someone else's this morning. "Please let The Howell Group be an investor! This could be so much fun. Something fresh to bring life into the brand."

"Don't the two of you have lunch reservations or something?" My heart raced, and I was desperate to get them away from me.

Lizette checked her watch. "Yeah, we've got to get going. But let's reconnect about this later, okay?"

I gave her a noncommittal nod before Camilla asked, "What are you two doing for St. Patrick's Day? We should all go out!"

I was suddenly thankful for how much work I had to catch up on this week. "Sorry, I'm so busy here this week. The renovations are a lot right now."

Sal added, "Yeah, I'm working, too."

"What about Saturday?" I had a feeling we would not get out of hanging out with them so easily.

Sal answered before I could think of an excuse. "Sorry, we're overbooked with St. Joseph's day this weekend. Maybe some other time, though?"

I made a mental note to look up what St. Joseph's day was later on, since I'd never heard of it, but Camilla asked, "What about lunch on Monday? That way Nonna can come too?"

Gah, I couldn't deny spending time with Nonna.

"Sure, I should be able to clear some time in my schedule for that." I looked at Sal for confirmation.

"Monday works for me, too," he answered. Camilla said she would let us know when and where once she made sure it was a good day for Nonna, then she gave us both tight hugs and she and Lizette made their way down the hallway toward the lobby.

As soon as they were out of earshot, I pointed down the hall. "What the hell?"

He looked down the corridor, like the answer to my question could be found there. "What?"

"Any other secrets of mine you want to tell my boss?" I was so embarrassed, which made me angry at him for blurting out my business.

He cringed. "Shit. I didn't know it was a secret. I'm sorry, Blake." I stood there, staring daggers at him. "I know you really want your own hotel, and I want to help make it happen. I thought you would have told her about it."

I caught the camera in the corner of my eye and wondered how many people were watching us on the screens in Bob's office. I finally took a sip from the smoothie Sal had handed me ages ago.

Of course, it was pomegranate lime, my favorite flavor. I wondered if he had asked my friends what I liked. "You want to come walk with me outside? My staff is already blowing up the radio with gossip, which will only get worse if we duck into my office." Even more so if we looked like we were arguing.

He nodded, and I led the way down the hall, through the lobby. When we crossed past the concierge desk, he gave Alex a little wave, which I knew would just feed into the scandal of my dating life.

I pushed the button on my radio. "I'm going to take a fifteen-minute break. Don't let the place burn down while I'm gone."

Paige replied, no doubt watching Sal and I walk across the grassy lawn from the camera screens. "You got it, boss."

I took the earpiece out and wrapped it across the back of my neck, so I could still hear it but not be distracted by it.

We waited for the crosswalk light to change in awkward silence and found a park bench to sit at on the beach. Not quite ready to dive into the conversation we needed to have, I took another sip of my drink. "How did you know this was my favorite flavor?"

He shrugged in a way that made his rough exterior look young, boyish. "Just a lucky guess." He took a sip of his. "And it's my favorite flavor, too."

I sat mine in my lap and gestured to it. "You said it was a token of apology. Assuming you weren't planning on coming in here and telling Lizette my most sacred secret, what were you sorry for?"

His eyes met the waves crashing against the sand. "Well, I was putting on my helmet when I realized I had steamrolled the entire visit to the house this morning. It was rude of me, and I should have let you answer Theresa's questions without my commentary. Then I went to the gym to get it out of my head, but I knew I needed to come talk to you. To clear the air."

My stomach sank. I didn't realize that I had been

subconsciously wishing he was here to apologize for telling our friends I had *ghosted* him, but knowing it wasn't why he came was a bit of a disappointment. "Oh." I tinkered with my straw, twisting it around in circles. "I hadn't noticed, to be honest."

"I was supposed to be there to support you, letting you find out what you wanted, and I took that away from you. Which I guess I've done again just now." He looked up, meeting my eyes with his. "I'm sorry."

His words felt genuine. I felt them in my bones.

"Actually, I was thankful you brought up your opinions. I wouldn't have noticed the kitchen was too small or what I was going to do in it if you hadn't spoken up." I paused, worried about the truth that was about to spill out of me. "And it's probably a good thing that you told Lizette about the bed-and-breakfast. I've been terrified that she would fire me over it. But now it feels almost tangible."

The air between us felt charged. This seemed like more than just an apology.

He shifted in his seat, turning to face me more clearly. "There is something else I wanted to ask you."

I gripped the styrofoam of my smoothie a little tighter. "Uh huh?"

His eyes drifted off to the group of children building a sandcastle just down the beach. He started to speak, and Paige's voice blared out the earpiece hanging around my neck. "Blake, I know you're on a break right now, but there's a dog loose on the third floor. Bob left for lunch, and I can't get it to come to me. I didn't think there were dog-friendly rooms on the third floor?"

Her panicked voice covered whatever Sal had said. I spoke into the radio, "10-4, I'll be there in a minute." And then I looked back at Sal. "I'm so sorry about that. What were you saying?"

He shook his head, smiling. "Any more luck on the wedding date search?"

I felt like someone had just pulled the needle off a record player. This was not what I had expected him to ask. "Um." I tripped over my words. "I guess it's going okay." He knew how badly my date went last night. Did he want to hear all the details?

He patted my leg before standing up. "Good. I'm glad. I just know that you're making a lot of compromises to go along with my charade, and I don't want your personal life to suffer." Here was that word again. Compromises. Maybe I had been making too many of them lately. He took another drink and turned to face the water. "I didn't know my sister was going to be here today, or I wouldn't have come by."

"No, it's okay. I'll talk with Paige about keeping my private life more private." He followed me as I stood and walked down the sidewalk toward the resort. "I'm sure I'll have a date for the wedding lined up any day now. Nothing I can't handle." My heart felt tight as the lie left my lips. The more time we spent together, the more I wanted him to be my wedding date. But he didn't want what I wanted, so it wasn't worth thinking about.

We walked until we came to the main door of the resort. He reached up and grazed my elbow with his fingertips. "Thanks again for all this. I'm sorry I'm dragging you into my problems, but I'm glad you're my partner."

I nodded, feeling my emotional fortress on the rise again. "Hey, I have a weird question."

He took a step closer, the smell of eucalyptus and motorcycle exhaust invading my senses. "You can ask me anything."

"The night I moved in with you . . . who were you on the phone with?" His forehead bunched in confusion, and I realized that he probably didn't remember. And that me remembering made me look like I had been obsessing over it. Even though I hadn't been. "You told them Reece's friend was staying at your place, so they couldn't come over."

His eyes lit up, and he laughed a little. "Oh, Marianna? She's really awesome."

"The same Marianna from your work?" My predictions were right. There was definitely something going on between them.

He nodded. "Yeah, we usually have game night once a week. She's—"

Paige's voice screeched from my earpiece, "Oh my God, Blake, I am freaking out. Please get up here!"

"You should go. I'm needed upstairs, apparently." He held the large wooden door open for me.

"I'll see you later." I held what was left of my smoothie up. "Thanks again for the treat. You didn't have to."

"I know, but I wanted to." I waved goodbye and ducked through the door, stuffing my earpiece back in.

"Paige, I'm on my way." I ran all the way up the

stairs, so I didn't have to wait for the elevator, and threw my empty cup in a trash can on the way. I rushed onto the third floor and was relieved when I found them. My assistant was crouched into a corner, trembling, while a tiny brown Pomeranian paced back and forth across the hall.

I bent down, making kissing noises at the dog. "Come here, sweetheart." I sang at it.

It ran to me, leaping into my arms. As I stood, I looked down at Paige. She shook her head wildly. "No way. How the hell did you do that? I tried telling it to come to me and it just stood there growling."

I pet the dog on the top of its head. "The trick is not letting it know that you're scared." I reached for its collar, finding a name tag. "Okay, Penny, let's call your parents."

Paige stood up, dusting her pants off. "Well, statistically, you're more likely to be injured by a small dog than a large one."

"I'm sure you're right, but Penny's just a little lost baby. Aren't you, Penny?" I rubbed her behind the ears and pushed the elevator button with my elbow.

Maybe I was a little like Penny—lost and scared and lashing out at people who were just trying to help me. I'd had it set in my mind my whole life that relying on people, needing people, was a burden to them. When my parents were struggling financially, when Jake and I were small, the worst thing we could do was add to that pressure.

But maybe some people needed to be needed. Maybe letting my friends in, leaning on them more often, was what was best for me in this stage of my life. Letting them hear about my problems, giving away some of my stress, was good for them, too. The thought shifted my perspective on a lot of things. I wasn't a burden. I was a human with fears and aspirations. Dreams that might have a chance of coming true if I wasn't worried about holding on to them so tightly.

Paige tried to pet Penny as we stood in the elevator, pulling me from my revelations, but the dog gave her a little growl. I scratched behind her ears, and she calmed down again. "Sorry. I don't know why she's being weird with you." We got to the bottom floor, and the door slid open. As we stepped out, we were greeted by a frantic couple. I handed over the dog and nicely reminded them to keep their dog on a leash while on our property.

By the time I made it back to my office, I hoped that rescuing a dog was the most difficult thing that would happen this week.

I sat silently, but my brain drifted off to Sal's question about my date to the wedding. Was he concerned because he had already found one? I wished I hadn't been interrupted when he was telling me about Marianna.

The thought made me a little nervous. Maybe their game nights had turned into something more in the last few weeks and he was going to bring her to the wedding. Maybe he hadn't wanted to kiss me because he had been kissing her.

I was sure she was nice, but I hated her a little bit now.

Chapter Ten

I hurried into the restaurant, embarrassed that it was twenty minutes past the time we'd agreed to meet. This was not how I wanted Sal's family to get to know me. I scanned the busy steakhouse, finding our party already seated at a table in the corner.

I smoothed my skirt, trying to calm my nerves as I approached the empty chair behind Sal. He was deep in conversation with Camilla, sitting across the table from him. Their grandmother sat next to her, and two women I didn't know sat at either end of the table. "I'm here now, sorry."

Sal stood, wrapping his arms around me in a welcoming hug. He was really great at making this believable. "Hey, honey."

I pushed up on my toes to kiss him hello, for the sake of our audience, but as if he suddenly remembered the last time I tried to kiss him, he turned his cheek to me. After pressing my lips to his smooth skin, I turned to the rest of the table. "I'm so sorry I'm late. The contractor finally showed up to update me on the kitchen renovations, and I couldn't get out of the office."

Sal pulled out the chair for me, motioning for me to sit down. After he sat, he put his hand on my knee, calming me. "I just got here, too, actually," he admitted.

Camilla smiled from across the table. "Lizette called me an hour ago and said she wasn't going to make it. We were just wondering if you two were going to stand us up, too. "

"Sorry, you're stuck with me." I laughed a little as I said it, before realizing that in a little while we'd have to stage our breakup, and I might never see her again. I ignored the pain the thought caused and focused my energy on their grandmother and the other ladies at the table. "Good afternoon, Nonna." She smiled at me and said hello before I nodded to each of the women I hadn't met before. "It's nice to meet you both . . . ."

"This is Blake." Sal finished my sentence. Then he gestured to the curly-haired brunette on the end next to him. "This is my cousin Giovanna." Then he pointed to the woman on my right, "and this is her sister Bianca." Giovanna looked like the younger sister, maybe twenty-five, but Bianca looked to be about my age. "Their mom is our dad's sister."

I gave each of them an awkward little wave. "It's nice to meet you both."

"So," Camilla started, "how busy was the restaurant this weekend?"

Sal leaned back in his seat. "Our busiest yet."

Nonna leaned forward a little. "Did you call your father, Salvatore?"

I caught the slight grimace on his face before he smiled at her. "I did, actually. He didn't answer, but that's beside the point." His hand left my leg and moved to the nape of my neck, rubbing slow circles with his thumb. I wondered how much of it was to calm him as well as me. "What did the rest of you do for St. Joseph's Day?"

Because I was too chicken to ask him last week when they brought up the holiday I'd never heard of, I had instead relied on my Googling skills and found out that St. Joseph's was like Italian Fathers' Day. No wonder Nonna was concerned if he reached out to his dad.

The cousins talked about having dinner with their families, Camilla admitting that she hadn't seen their father either, and the server came over with a tray of food. Sal leaned toward me. "I ordered you a baked potato, since you said you liked them the other night, but I can ask for a menu if you want something else." He pointed to the plate that was being placed in front of me. "Butter and extra sour cream? I think that's the way you said you preferred them."

I blinked a couple of times, shocked that he remembered. Here was one though, made just the way I liked it, in front of me. The smile I gave him was absolutely genuine. "Thanks, Sal. That's what I was going to order anyway."

He nudged me with his shoulder, speaking quietly enough that only I could hear him. "What, no nickname today? You don't want to call me Saliva in front of my family?"

I mixed up my potato with my fork and scooped up

my first bite. "I'm running out of good ones, Saloon." I took a bite, loving how good this meal was.

His loud laugh caused everyone else at the table to glance our way. "You're too adorable," he said, and for a second it felt real. Like we could actually be together.

The rest of the table had started talking about the party Camilla was planning for her parents while we ate. A few minutes later, I remembered the other task Sal and I were supposed to be taking care of. "Oh, the venue is booked for the wedding, so we can start planning the party."

Giovanna looked at Sal, her eyes bursting with excitement. "Did I just hear the two of you say you're planning a wedding? Oh, my gosh!" She dropped her fork and clasped her hands together.

I held up my hands, needing to put an end to this quickly. "Oh, no way. We are not getting married." I scooped another bite onto my fork. "Ever."

I looked up at the rest of them just as I realized the mistake I had made. We were supposed to look like we were going to become the perfect nuclear family, not a couple of people who wanted to live within their own boundaries.

Sal just shrugged, lifting a forkful of steak to his mouth. "She's right." He ate his food, carefully chewing as the rest of the table waited for him to elaborate. "Blake and I aren't planning on having kids, either. So there's no need to get married." He said it like it was something we had discussed extensively, not that we were making this up as we went along.

Nonna raised an eyebrow at him. "What do you think your father is going to say to that?"

He turned to me, and when his eyes met mine, it didn't feel pretend. "He'll just have to realize that the two of us are a family, kids or not."

It took every effort to finish my lunch. To not launch myself at him, kissing him senseless. I was in deep trouble, catching these feelings for him.

The rest of the meal went by quickly, and as Sal paid the bill, refusing to let any of us pitch in, Camilla asked, "Drinks tomorrow night?"

I didn't have anything going on, but Sal answered, "Sorry, I have . . ." he turned away from me, looking a little bashful. "I have plans. How about Thursday?"

I knew that look. He was most definitely hiding something. Someone. The heaviness in my stomach made me realize he was probably going out on a date with that Marianna girl. I bet he was planning on bringing her to the wedding and I'd be stuck going solo.

As soon as we had all said our goodbyes, Sal having pressed a chaste kiss to my cheek, I rushed to the privacy of my own car.

I needed to get over him. Whatever I was imagining was going on between us was not real, and the faster I replaced these feelings with someone else, the better. Pulling out my phone, I opened the app I had been neglecting while thinking this fake relationship could become something more. I scrolled through a few accounts until I found Adrian, the bartender I had told the girls about when Lina had been in town last, and clicked his profile.

He was perfect. Had a great job, seemed responsible based on the short messages we'd sent back and forth, and was not a muscular restaurateur who seemed to invade my every sense whenever he was around.

I sent a message: *Hey. Wanna go out for drinks this week?*

Two days after asking him out, I walked into a dark restaurant just outside of town, finding Adrian sitting at a table in the back. He was cuter than he looked in his pictures, which was a surprise, since usually the guys I met online weren't as good as their portfolios.

His black hair was cropped short, and his T-shirt was so tight I could see the outline of his chest. As he smiled, I felt butterflies in my stomach. He hadn't asked why I wanted to meet somewhere far from the crowded nightlife of downtown, and I was thankful I didn't have to give my reasons.

I looked him up and down as I made my way to him, hiding the disappointment I felt when I didn't see a single tattoo showing on his skin. His eyes were just plain brown, too. No trace of green in his irises.

Not that there was anything wrong with brown eyes. I had brown eyes. But hazel had become my favorite lately.

"Thanks for meeting me so late," I said to him as I walked up to the table. It was already past seven, so we had agreed to just hang out for appetizers before seeing where the night took us.

He stood and gave me a hug, already being a gentleman. "No problem. You look so beautiful."

I tugged at my blouse absentmindedly. "Thank you. I'm sorry I didn't have a chance to freshen up after leaving work."

I had brushed my teeth in the bathroom before leaving the resort, but I didn't want to run into my fake-boyfriend roommate before he left for work, so changing wasn't an option.

Adrian pulled my chair out for me, and I took a seat, thanking him again. We looked over our menus and ordered some spinach artichoke dip. "The bread they bring out with the dip is seriously so good." He said, pointing to it on the menu.

The conversation went well, and we really hit it off. We listened to similar music and liked the same movies. He didn't really enjoy reading books, but he liked true crime podcasts, and when I told him those were basically audiobooks, he laughed with me.

The only thing we didn't have in common was that he was really into fitness, but he promised he would never make me wake up early in the morning to run a 5k with him.

After an hour and a half, we found ourselves in the parking lot, standing next to my car. When his hand reached for my hip and he pulled me against him, I knew I was done for. His lips pressed against mine, and I became aware of how long it had been since I had been with someone else. Losing the ability to think logically, I said, "So, I'm off tomorrow. Want to go somewhere we can get more comfortable?"

I felt his grin against my lips as he kissed me again, his

fingers slipping under the hem of my shirt. "I thought you'd never ask. My roommate is home, though. Can we go to your place?"

I pulled back and saw the lust I felt mirrored in his face. "I'm renting a room in kind of a weird neighborhood. Follow me?"

He nodded and stepped back, pulling out his car keys. "I'll see you there."

I made the drive to the house in record time and punched in the stupid code. I should have called the security company and programmed my own number, but I was still telling myself that I would be out of here soon.

I parked my car in my usual spot, and Adrian parked next to me. Thankfully, there wasn't a motorcycle in sight, nor was there a light on in any of the windows.

Adrian met me at the door of my car. "Wow, I expected you to be living in some slum by the way you made it sound earlier." He scanned the large acreage around us. "Whose house is this?"

I got out of my car, grabbing his belt loop and pulling him toward me, feeling a little reckless. "A friend of mine owns it. I'm not staying here long." Sure, it wasn't exactly the truth, but I really wanted to sleep with him. My core ached just thinking about it. I felt that telling him the man who owned the house was my pretend boyfriend would shut that down real quick. I wasn't about to cock block myself.

His lips met mine, and we stumbled to the front door together. It took me three tries, but I got the front door unlocked, and we slipped inside. "My room is just through here and down the hall." I mumbled into his neck as I dragged him through the entryway.

His fingers reached for the button of my slacks, and I reached down to stop him. "Wait until we get to my room." I whispered.

"I want to bend you over and take you right here," He said into my ear. I lost all restraint and reached for the button of his jeans.

A grunt from the other side of the room stopped us in our tracks.

I looked up from Adrian and found Sal, the worst human with the worst timing, sitting comfortably on the couch, his feet propped up on the coffee table. The house was completely dark except for a single table lamp lit next to him.

Sal had on a skin-tight black V-neck tee-shirt, and I would have made fun of him for obviously flexing his arm muscles on purpose if I wasn't so frustrated that he was home right now. I had so many questions for him in that moment, but instead I asked, "Are you wearing glasses?"

He pressed the book he was reading against his chest and looked beyond annoyed we had interrupted him. "A lot of people who wear contacts sometimes have to switch them out for glasses, Blake." His tone was so condescending that I wished I had a glass of water to throw at him.

There was no way in hell I was ever going to admit how fucking sexy he looked sitting there with those dark frames on his face. Those tattoos peeking out from his shirt. Those fucking hazel eyes.

I hated him so much.

I looked back at the man I was planning on taking back to my room and doing unmentionable things with. The one I had hoped would stay the night. The one that would call me the next day. "Sorry, I didn't realize my roommate was going to be home tonight."

Adrian kissed my neck before stepping away from me. I could tell he was sizing up the brawny man sitting so casually on the couch.

"Hey, I'm Adrian. It's nice to meet you." He reached out his hand for Sal to shake, but Sal just eyed it over the top of his glasses frame. A few seconds passed, and Adrian tucked his hand into his pocket.

I stepped a little closer to Sal. "You told me you weren't going to have an issue about this."

Adrian looked between the two of us, a skeptical look on his face. "Am I getting in the middle of something?"

Sal turned to him, the fabric of his T-shirt stretching across his chest. "I'll put on my headphones when you take her to her room. I know how loud she can get."

My blood boiled over, and I clenched my hands into fists. "How dare you?"

His eyes finally met mine, and I couldn't help but feel a spark when I noticed his glasses weren't black. They were dark green and made his eyes look even brighter than usual. "It's true, though." Then he looked back at Adrian. "At least it was when she and I slept together." He placed his book facedown on the coffee table and stood. He patted Adrian on the shoulder as he walked past him, headed for his bedroom. "Good luck, buddy. She likes to get wild."

I covered my face with my hand, trying to hide my embarrassment. "I'm so sorry about him. He's the worst."

Adrian took a large step away from me. "Is this some kind of weird fight you're having with your boyfriend?"

I tossed my purse onto the coffee table and reached for his hand. "Oh God, no. Sal is not my boyfriend. I'm just staying here while I'm in between places."

He looked down the hallway Sal had disappeared down. "But the two of you are sleeping together?"

I let out a deep breath. "It happened once, months ago. Before I even moved here. It was a huge mistake, I promise." I pulled him toward me, trying to lead him down the opposite hall to my room. "Can we just forget this happened and go back to our original plan?"

He looked at his watch on his free wrist, and that's when I knew nothing would be going any further tonight. "You know what? I have an early day at work tomorrow. I should probably head out."

I tried to blink back the tears forming in my eyes. Without fail, as soon as I found a guy that wasn't psycho, someone stepped in and ruined it.

"Yeah, of course." I walked to the front door, opening it for him.

"I'll call you soon, yeah?" He gave me a kiss on the cheek, and I had the feeling this was the last time I'd ever see him.

As soon as I saw his headlights disappear down the drive, I spun on my heel and stomped down the hallway. Banging on Sal's bedroom door, I was ready for a fight.

"You better get your ass out here and explain yourself."

After a long minute, he swung the door open, causing me to stumble forward. He had followed through on his promise, with a set of headphones covering his ears, but he had lost his shirt in the process.

I found myself face to face with the tattoos scattered across his chest that I had been trying to forget about for months. But tonight, instead of wanting to run my fingers across them, I wanted to shove him away from me. How had he taken everything that was building up between us and acted like a jackass tonight? "Why the fuck would you say shit like that to my date?"

He pulled one side of his headphones away from his ear, heavy metal blasting out of the speaker. "Sorry, I didn't hear you. Did you need something?"

So this time I yelled louder. "Why the fuck did you act like that, Sal? You're not my fucking boyfriend."

He stepped closer, and I wondered if it was because he knew it would make me lose my train of thought. The smell of eucalyptus and sandalwood filled my senses with him only an inch away. "Why are you in my doorway and not riding the douchebag you dragged home?"

"You fucking scared him away with your alphahole behavior."

A smile cracked on his lips, and he didn't say anything as he slipped off his headphones and tossed them onto his bed behind him.

"What? Spit it out." I felt like I was practically screeching at him.

"Maybe I'm just an alphahole, as you put it. Besides, you should thank me."

I threw my hands in the air. "You're fucking deranged!"

"No, I just know what kind of guy he was. I could tell by the way he looked around the house when you walked him in. He was more interested in the money he thought you had than in you, and that's not okay with me."

"Oh, you are so full of yourself. He was all over me when we came in the door." I should have let him take my pants off when he'd wanted to.

Sal leaned against the doorframe—the irritating way that tall men could lean against a wall and make it look like they held it up themselves. "Trust me. He wasn't good for you. I did you a favor by sending him home."

"I can't fucking believe you said those things about me. That you talked about . . . *us* like that." My voice cracked, but I wouldn't cry. Not in front of him, at least.

He exhaled deeply, raking his fingers through his hair, and his whole demeanor shifted. His shoulders slumped like I had figured out his bullshit. "Fuck, Blake, I'm sorry." He looked back up at me, regret filling his gaze. "I didn't mean it. Any of it. My jealousy just took over, and it was out of my mouth before I thought twice."

I wanted him to deny it. I wanted him to give me something else worth fighting about. If I stayed angry, I wouldn't fixate on him admitting that he was jealous.

I jammed my pointer finger against his brick wall of a chest. "You don't get a say in my life. You have no right to an opinion about who I date, and you don't get to talk about me like I'm some object for your pleasure. I'm a fucking human being."

"I know. I acted like an idiot. I didn't like seeing his

hands all over you, and I regret what I said." His honesty was unexpected, and it took a little of the wind out of my sails.

"What you did tonight was not okay." Knowing there was nothing else I could say, needing some time to process the heavy truth he had just given me, I turned around and started for my room.

"I got a phone call from Reece this morning." I stopped in my tracks. Was Reece concerned that Sal and I hadn't started planning the party?

I turned my head over my shoulder, looking at him. "We need to plan the bachelorette party, I know. I'll get right on that as soon as I don't want to stab both of your eyes out."

He pushed his glasses up and rubbed the bridge of his nose, looking exhausted. "It's not about the party. We can throw that together later."

I took a step toward him, worried. Now that I thought about it, I hadn't heard from Lina for a couple of days. "Is everything okay? No one's hurt?"

He waved his hand, clearing the thought, and put his glasses back into place. "It's just—" He pushed away from the doorway and came to stand directly in front of me. "Blake." My heart skipped a beat at the way he said my name with concern in his eyes. He reached out, touching my elbow before dropping his hand.

Okay, now I really started to worry. Every terrible scenario about my best friend flipped through my mind. Had there been an accident? Were either of them hurt? They spent a lot of time in new cities . . . . Had they been robbed? Was there an issue with a tour stop? Were they going to have to cancel the wedding? My heart threatened to jump out of my throat.

"I did call."

My eyes met his, confused. "What? You said Reece called you?"

He folded his arms across his chest, but not in defense. It looked more like defeat, like he was trying to make himself smaller. "I called you. The next morning. I called you, and when a guy answered and said I had the wrong number, I realized you had played me."

I ran my fingers through my hair, and suddenly all I could smell was Adrian all over me. His musky cologne filled every pore of my body. I wanted to believe Sal, but I was haunted by the ghost of the man who had his arms around me ten minutes ago. The man that could have been something if it weren't for the one in front of me.

The man who didn't need to be something if the man in front of me was telling the truth. Had he really been jealous tonight? Had he really called me last summer? My heart raced, and I felt panic creeping in. "I don't. I can't." I couldn't think with him so close.

"Why won't you ask anyone for help?" His question came out of nowhere. "And why do you push away the people who want to take care of you?"

His inquisition sent me over the edge. "I'm not the one on trial right now, Sal."

"Oh, so that's what this is? My trial."

"Tell me why you were jealous." I knew I was deflecting, and I wasn't going to be able to much longer. He could see right through me.

Sal swallowed, his Adam's apple bobbing. "You know

what? Forget it." He took a couple of steps toward his bedroom. "We can talk about this later. Or never again, if that's what you'd like."

I wanted to talk about it. This conversation had been consuming me for the better part of this year. But I needed to process it first. What would his phone call mean? Why would he be jealous if the thought of kissing me sent him running? Why had he really scared off the only good date I'd had since—well, since him?

Did I really want whatever was going on between us? Would it be worth it?

I needed to know exactly what Reece had said to him. I needed to talk to my best friend. Whatever they'd discussed had the power to change our relationship forever.

"I, um. I have to go."

"Goodnight, Blake." His voice was barely a whisper.

I spun around on my heels and raced down the hallway.

Halfway to my room, I stopped in the living room to grab my purse, and I spotted his book laying open on the coffee table. The one he had been reading when Adrian and I came in the door.

It was a swoony romance novel with a man and a woman riding a horse across the beach together. The spine had been cracked a hundred times.

This man was something else.

The way Sal had acted this evening was not cool. Even if he had more information in that moment than I did. Even if the sight of Adrian's hands on my hips bothered him.

It was not a healthy way to express his emotions.

I picked up his book and slammed it shut, causing his saved spot to disappear into oblivion. It was petty, but I couldn't stop myself.

I rushed into my room and peeled my clothes off, double-checking that the door was closed behind me. I had to get the smell of Adrian off me.

And I needed to get the visions of Sal inside of me, out of me.

I dug through my purse, pulling out my phone, and sent a text to Lina: *I'm having a bit of a boy emergency and need to talk. Can I call you in like twenty minutes?*

I threw the phone on my bed and stuffed my clothes into the overflowing hamper.

I stepped into the bathroom and started the shower before going back to the bed, checking my phone. I'd hoped whatever time zone Lina was in would be one where she was awake. It was well after midnight here, and I knew she was somewhere in Europe.

Lina's text popped up: *Sure, we're just finishing breakfast.*

I replied: *Perfect. Gotta take a shower first and then I'll give you a ring.*

I set the phone down on the counter and got into the shower. It wasn't even warm yet, but I didn't care. I let the water wash over me, trying to organize my thoughts from most important to least.

Did Sal want me the way I wanted him? Or was he

mad I was moving on from him and had found someone that could potentially make me happy?

What did this mean for him and Marianna?

As I rinsed the shampoo out of my hair, I had to ask myself: Did I actually want to be with him?

After all this time, after all the snarky comments and all the bullshit we hadn't discussed. I'd lived here a month, which sometimes felt like the blink of an eye. Other times it felt like forever. It paled in comparison to all the months before, when I thought he hadn't called. Hadn't given a shit about me.

I ran conditioner-soaked fingers through the length of my hair, wondering if Sal and me was even a relationship worth pursuing.

My soapy loofah skimmed across my torso, and my thoughts shifted to Adrian's hands on my skin. He had been crazy hot, and my skin tingled at the thought of him. If things had gone the way I had planned, he was supposed to be joining me in this shower right about now.

But was Sal right? I thought back to the conversation at the bar. He had asked several questions about how much money I made and what my goals were for the future. But I figured that was just small talk you have with someone when you're trying to decide if you want to sleep with them or not.

As I continued to wash myself, the hands I had been thinking of turned to larger, more callused ones. The night we had spent together returned in perfect clarity. I closed my eyes and thought about his lips tracing down my body. How Sal had gripped my hip tightly with one hand and sent me to heaven with the other.

I opened my eyes and turned the water to cold. Now was not the time to think about how he had made me come harder than anyone else ever had. How, even worse, it seemed like we would have made something beautiful together.

I quickly rinsed my hair and effectively cooled my body down. I didn't want my need for sexual touch, for emotional connection, to drive my choices.

As soon as I was dressed in pajamas, my hair wrapped up in a towel, I grabbed my phone and called Lina. Sal had asked me why I didn't ask for help, why I pushed my friends away. Well, this was me not doing those things.

I hated how well he knew me. Better than I knew myself.

She answered on the first ring. "That was twenty-five minutes, and now I'm officially worried about you."

I laughed. "I'm a mess, Lina."

"Well, I could have guessed that, since it's the middle of the night in Santa Barbara." She paused for a moment. "Tell me what's going on."

The story of the last week spilled out of me. I told her how I had run into Camilla and Lizette at work, and how Sal was there. And how Sal had asked me if I had found a date for the wedding. Then I told her about reaching out to Adrian after figuring out that Sal probably had a date, based on how he acted at lunch with his family.

I told her about my date with Adrian. How we got along well and how attracted to him I was. Finally, I took a calming breath and told her how Sal had caught us coming in the door like a couple of hormonal teenagers and blocked the only cock that had come near me in longer than I cared to admit.

"He told Adrian good luck. That I like to get *wild*, Lina."

She let out a gasp, and I was relieved that she was just as shocked as I was. "Wow, okay, that's a lot to unpack."

I pulled the towel out of my hair and brushed through it with my free hand. "It gets worse. Which is why I called you."

"Hold on." She told someone she would be right back, and the loud room she was in became quieter, like she had found a more private area. "Okay, I'm sitting down. Hit me with it."

"He said that Reece called him."

"Oh." Her line got even quieter, and I had the feeling she had covered the microphone with her hand, but I heard whispering. It sounded like Reece asking if everything was okay.

"Any idea of what that could have been about?" I asked, knowing by her unease that she knew all about the phone call I was asking about.

"Well." Her pause was pregnant, like there were a million words packed into those four letters.

"Magdalina Herrera, tell me what you know."

The line was silent for several more seconds. "I really think this is a conversation you should have with Sal."

"Nope. Let me talk to him."

Her voice went up a pitch, like it always did when she lied. "I don't know who you're talking about, Blake."

"You know exactly what I mean. I heard him in the

background, so you might as well let him explain himself."

There were rushed whispers, which began to sound exasperated, before Lina finally responded. "Okay, you've got both of us on speaker."

"What the fuck, you guys! Stop meddling in my life and tell me what's going on." I didn't care who heard me. I wanted them to know how frustrated I was.

"Hello to you, too, Blake." Reece's deep voice came through the phone. When I didn't reply, he went on, "Look, Sal is my best friend. He's the only person who stuck by me through everything."

"I'm well aware of that, but I need to know what you said to him this morning."

He let out a sigh. "I called him to talk about bakeries in town, and I asked him if he knew anyone locally who we could hire for the wedding cake." He quickly added.

"Uh huh." Okay, I hated weddings, but I did love cake. That was probably the best part of any wedding I'd ever been to.

"And after he gave me a few names, I asked him if the two of you wanted to go taste them for us. But he said that you probably didn't have time because you were busy trying to find a date for our wedding."

"Okay, so that's slightly true, but I don't see why that's any of his business."

Lina's voice was louder than before. "He was frustrated because he has feelings for you, and you're too damn blind to see that he wants you to be his date to the wedding. He wants you to be his person, you dummy!"

Reece mumbled, "Well, that's certainly one way to tell her."

Lina replied to him, "What? She needs to know how he feels."

"And he needs to be the one who tells her."

I jumped into the conversation. "You guys, this makes no sense. He didn't even want me to kiss him the other night, remember? And besides, I think he's seeing someone."

"Who?" Their voices rang together.

"Marianna. She's a waitress at his restaurant."

Reece let out a laugh. "Did he actually tell you that?"

So he did know about her. Great. "Well, no, but he mentioned her."

"Marianna is his cousin. They play Dungeons and Dragons with a group of friends all the time."

I really did feel like a dummy. I was jumping to the worst conclusions, like I always did when I was scared about something. "Oh. I didn't know that."

"Which is why I think you should talk to him about all of this, not us." Reece sounded sweet, like he really had my best interests at heart.

Lina chimed in, "Maybe not tonight, though. You're too wound up."

I started to argue, but she was right. "Okay, I'll sleep on it."

"And Blake?" Reece's voice rumbled through the phone. "We love you. And we love him. Whether you decide to be together, to stay friends, or to hate each other for stupid reasons for the rest of your lives. That's not going to change."

"I love you guys, too." I was glad my friends were there to support me. If I had talked to them sooner, I could've avoided a lot of this heartache. No more pushing people away.

I hung up the phone and lay back in the creamsicle bed. This was a lot to take in, even though I still didn't have a lot of information.

The possibilities spiraled through my mind. I thought about what it would be like if I let Sal in. If I let go of the anger I had been holding on to and let him tell me his side of the story.

Chapter Eleven

I crawled out of bed the next morning, having slept a collective twenty minutes the entire night. I hoped I was home alone, but I had a feeling I wasn't.

I dragged myself into the bathroom and had a look at myself in the mirror. Poking the bags under my eyes, I knew it would be obvious to anyone who saw me that I hadn't slept last night.

At first I had tossed and turned, wondering if I should just go knock down Sal's door and confront him against Lina's advice. But I knew that if I let my emotions lead this conversation, it would just end badly.

So I tried all the techniques I had learned over the years anytime I'd been struck with insomnia. I counted sheep. I imagined myself riding a bicycle through town. I had even squeezed my eyes tightly and pretended I was a mermaid swimming through the ocean, making friends with all the sea animals.

That last one had always worked on my worst sleepless nights, but last night it gave me no relief.

By four a.m., I had given up and decided I needed to physically exhaust myself. It was too dark to go for a walk, so I reached into my bedside table and pulled out the rabbit-shaped device I knew would take the edge off.

No matter who I tried to imagine lying on top of me —first Adrian, then Henry Cavill, and then finally the tattooed mafia leader from the last smutty book I had read—they all turned into a man with a dark mohawk and a rose inked onto the side of his neck. It took all of my energy to clear him from my mind.

Half an hour later, I had tossed the vibrator onto the foot of my bed and given up. My body only wanted one thing, and I wasn't sure I was willing to give in.

But now it was seven. The sun was shining its bright-ass rays through my window, and I was tired, horny, and honestly pretty hungry.

Splashing water on my face, I brought myself back to the present. He probably wasn't even here.

I took care of my restroom needs, brushed my hair and my teeth, and hoped I could slip out, grab some cereal from the kitchen, and hide in my room for the rest of the day.

I opened the door, and the smell of breakfast cooking hit me like a ton of bricks. Not only was he home, but he was twenty feet away.

I tiptoed into the kitchen and found him, his back facing me, leaning over the stove. There were piles of bacon, sausage, and potatoes on the island, enough to feed ten people.

I panicked, worried that he had people coming over. Maybe his Dungeons and Dragons friends. I didn't know much about the game, but I knew it took a bunch of people and it lasted for hours. I'd always wanted to try it but didn't know anyone who could show me how.

I didn't want to be in the house if his friends were over, so I backed up a few feet, thinking I could get dressed and slip out the front door without being noticed.

I bumped into the couch, and he spun around, spatula in hand. "Oh, you're up." He had those damn glasses on, which reminded me of the only few moments I had felt any pleasure in my bed last night . . . when I had been thinking of how they brought out the green in his eyes.

I held my hand up. "Don't worry, I see you're having people over. I'll be out of the way in just a few minutes."

His brow furrowed together. "What people?"

I pointed to the heaps of food between us. "There's enough food here to feed an army."

A small smile splashed across his face, and he reached up, rubbing the back of his neck. "Oh, that's just for me." His eyes met mine for a few beats of my heart. "Or us, if you wanted to stay."

"There's no way the two of us could eat this much."

He shrugged. "I cook a lot when I'm stressed."

I walked to the island, leaning my hands on the edge. "Your entire career is based on cooking." I wondered if food had something to do with his love language. It made sense, him being a chef.

He flashed me a small smile, which sent a shock through me. I bit my bottom lip, hoping the pain would stop the butterflies floating around inside. If I had been thinking of that smile last night, it would have sent me over the edge.

"Maybe I'm just stressed all the time?" He turned back to the stove, cracking eggs into a skillet. "Look, I'm sorry for coming between you and that guy last night. I should have spoken to you privately instead of making an ass out of myself in front of him. The things I said . . . ."

"Are you apologizing to me or the eggs?"

He turned, leaning a hip against the counter so he could keep an eye on the stove while talking to me. "I let my emotions get the best of me. It won't happen again."

I laid my elbows on the edge of the island. "You said you had no problem with me bringing guys home."

"And I didn't. I don't, I mean." He sighed, and his shoulders dropped like they had last night. "I'm going to do better."

"You're the one who asked me if I had found a date for the wedding."

"I know. I thought it's what you wanted and was trying to make you happy."

I stood there, silently watching him as he fried eggs for us and put them on plates. It had felt a lot like the other morning, but the air was different. We weren't here to play pretend, and whatever conversation we were having was going to ruin me.

He slid a plate in front of me and handed me a fork as I took a seat on the stool, thinking he would sit next to me like he had done last week.

Instead, he stood on the opposite side of the island, not touching his plate.

I really wanted to tell him about my phone call with

Lina and Reece, but I was afraid to, so I said, "I like your glasses."

He took them off and twirled them slowly in his hands. "I tore my last set of contacts the other day, so I have to wear these until my new ones come in the mail."

"You should wear them more often. They look good on you." I was still mad at him, but I could feel my anger fading. Thinking about the last conversation we had, I tried to find a place to start. "I'm sorry I closed your book, making you lose your spot. I was mad at you and shouldn't have lashed out."

He winked at me, and I almost turned to putty. It wasn't fair having a conversation with a man this good looking. "I wasn't actually reading it."

So he had been waiting up for me. I had to fight the smile spreading across my face. "Was it just not interesting enough?"

He leaned forward, making the feet between us feel like inches. "I've read that one enough times to recite it in my sleep. You know damn well that I was sitting on that couch waiting for you to come home." A cloud passed through his eyes before he went on. "I just didn't think you'd have a friend with you."

"And why were you waiting to talk to me?"

He seemed to hold his breath for a few seconds. "Like I said, I got an interesting call from Reece. He had called about wedding cakes, but somehow we ended up talking about you."

"I talked to him after you went to bed, and he said the same thing to me."

He raised his eyebrow. "So, he told you what he told me?"

I shook my head. "I think Lina tried to, but Reece said I had to get it out of you instead." I tapped my fingers on the counter nervously. "So you really called me after we had . . . ." It was hard to say. It made it feel too real. "After we spent the night together. And you thought I gave you a wrong number?"

He dug in his pocket for his phone, tapped the screen a few times and scrolled for several moments. Without a word, he laid it down on the table, facing me. He pointed to where his call log said "Blake Thomas" three times, showing that he had called me multiple times on June 6. The day after Lina and Reece's going away party.

I pushed my untouched plate to the side and looked down at the phone. "I never got these."

"I know."

I clicked the little "I" next to the number for more information, and my contact page came up. A picture we had taken in the Uber showed at the top. A picture I had used when I put my information in his phone. Then I looked down and saw what the issue had been. "This isn't my number."

"Yeah, I kind of figured that when an angry-sounding dude picked up the third time I tried to reach you and said you had obviously given me the wrong number to get rid of me."

"Why didn't you say something? You could have reached out, come to my work, or asked Lina or Val to call me."

He ran his hand through his hair, which was messier

than usual. That hair that had felt so smooth in my fingers so long ago. "I thought about it. But I was ashamed that you'd given me a wrong number on purpose, like what we'd had together meant nothing. And then a week passed. A month. Six months. When I finally had the courage to talk to you about it, so much time had gone by that I figured you'd moved on."

I whispered more to the phone than to Sal. "I didn't want to get rid of you. I hadn't moved on." Then I realized the mistake and looked up at him. "The first two digits after the area code. They're switched. I must have typed them in wrong in that damn car."

I frantically tapped the screen, going through the motions to fix the error. This had been my fault. I was the reason he didn't call me. "But the next morning, I left a note on the kitchen counter for you."

"There was no note. Your roommate was making breakfast, which was a little awkward, but the counter was clear."

I should have known Chelsea would have thrown it away. She was always tossing out my mail or receipts I had left on the counter like I didn't even live there.

"I wish you would have seen the note. I practically begged for you to call." All of this was from one stupid typo. I couldn't believe it.

He took a few steps back, leaning against the counter next to the stove. "We were drunk, Blake. It should have never happened."

My breath caught in my throat as I looked into his eyes. "You really believe that?" My voice sounded alien. Like someone else's whisper.

He answered with a small shrug. "Don't get me wrong, it was a lot of fun, but neither of us had the ability to make rational decisions that night. Drunk people can't give consent. So, yeah, it was a mistake."

"Wow." I stood up, backing away from the kitchen island. This was the opposite of what I thought he would say.

"That came out wrong." He walked around the island, finally standing in front of me.

I waved my hands in the air. "I get it. We can be just friends." My eyes filled with tears, my vision going blurry.

"Dammit, Blake, I don't want to be friends with you."

I gasped for air. "I'm just going to go back to my room." I turned to walk down the hallway, but his hands wrapped around my arms, stopping me.

His breath met my lips as he admitted, his voice low. "I want you to be mine."

"But what about—" Before I could ask, his mouth covered mine and his arms wrapped around me.

I melted into him as I tilted my head slightly, letting him kiss me more deeply.

After a few minutes, he pulled back slightly, his hands roving down to my bottom. "I've fucking missed you so much." He gripped me, lifting me up, and kissed me again.

I wrapped my legs around his waist, feeling the same electrical charge I had the first time he kissed me like his life depended on it. "I want you so badly, Sal. I want us." It came out surprisingly easily. Like I had held it in for so long that it came tumbling out.

His lips trailed from my mouth to my neck, to my

shoulder, and he started walking us down the hallway. He kicked my bedroom door all the way open, and I was glad I hadn't shut it all the way. I didn't want his hands to ever leave my skin.

When he laid me across the bed, pressing his body on top of mine, I knew I wasn't going to last much longer. All of my fantasies from the last several months were right in front of me.

He propped himself on his hands and stared into my eyes. Into my soul. "You're mine, Blake. Got it?"

I nodded, my voice a breath of a whisper. "I'm yours."

He leaned back, straddling me and gripped the hem of my pajama shirt, so I sat up an inch, letting him pull it off of me. His eyes went to my breasts, his hands cupping them on instinct. As he leaned down and took one into his mouth, a moan escaped me.

He licked the skin between my breasts and looked up at me. "Those fucking noises you make. They're what have been getting me through all these months."

The hard length of him pressed against me through his sweatpants as his grip on me tightened. He licked the tight peak of my other nipple. "You are mine, and I am yours." He bit down on the tip of my sensitive skin, and I moaned again, this time grinding my slick core against him.

He came back over me again, his breath skimming over my lips. "Tell me I'm yours, Blake."

"You're mine, Sal." My voice was quiet but sure.

He grazed my lips with his before pulling back again. "Tell me we're doing this, for real." He shook his head slightly. "No dating other people, no more hiding how we feel."

I felt myself hesitate. I wanted him, but there was more we needed to talk about before diving in.

He sat up, his hips pinning me to the bed. "I can't go any further with you unless we're serious."

I didn't want to talk any longer. I wanted him. Every part of him. I balled his shirt into my fists, pulling him back down. "I am yours and you are mine. We've been playing this game for too long to deny it."

He kissed me again, growling. "You're mine."

"I'm yours." I pulled his shirt over his head, tossing it to the floor. "Now fuck me before I change my mind."

He plunged a hand down the front of my pajama shorts, his fingers rubbing against my panties. "Oh, I'm going to fuck you until you forget your own name."

I reached down, grasping him through the front of his pants, and he sucked in a breath. Without a word, he pulled back, gripping both of my wrists in his hands, moving them over my head, pushing them into the mattress. "If you touch my cock again, I'm going to come. And I know we both want more than that."

I tried to pull an arm free, but he had an iron grip on me. "You don't want me to test that theory?"

He squeezed his eyes closed. "Blake, it's been a really long time for me, and I'm barely holding it together as it is."

I rolled my hips under him, trying to feel his cock any way I could. "How long?"

He opened his eyes, giving me that stare again that

threatened to consume me. "Since the last time I had you."

Oh.

That was not what I expected him to say.

"Um, same here." I admitted quietly.

He held my hands where they were, but kissed me again, this time sweetly. Softly. "You're all I've been able to think about, Blake. No one else measures up." He shifted my wrists, moving to hold them with one hand, and his eyes moved quickly to a spot above me. "Well, what's this?"

He picked something up, and I heard my vibrator come to life as he pressed the button. I had forgotten to put it away last night.

Another wave of wetness drenched my thighs as he held it up between us. I was no stranger to sex toys, but I had only ever used them solo. He pressed the tip of the toy to my nipple with a sly smile. Watching him look down at my body with those dark eyes as my rabbit shook, my arms still pinned over my head, sent me over the edge. Shocks of pleasure ran down to the tips of my toes, my thighs wrapping around him tightly.

"You're so fucking pretty when you come." He turned the vibrator off and tossed it on the bed. "We'll have to play with that later. The only thing I want inside you right now is me." He leaned down and kissed my neck, biting me gently.

I couldn't breathe, my body turning to liquid fire. His voice rumbled through my skin as he asked, "Did you make yourself come last night?" His free hand slipped into my shorts again, and I couldn't answer. "Tell me the truth, Blake."

"No, I couldn't." It came out as barely a whisper.

His fingers pressed hard against me through my panties. One of them raked up, finding my clit. "Were you thinking about me?"

I nodded, "A little bit."

"Do you usually think about me when you fuck yourself?" Another finger slid over to my skin next to the thin fabric between us, and I started to come undone again. When I didn't answer, his motions stopped, the pressure lifting. "Blake?" I closed my eyes, unsure if I wanted him to know the truth. After a few heartbeats, his finger on my apex pressed down harder. "Do you think about me when you come?"

A shiver ran through me, and I looked him in the eye. "Every time."

He grinned, that devious smile I adored, and moved his hand under my panties, plunging a finger inside of me. "Good. Because I can't come unless I'm thinking about this pussy."

Any resolve I had disappeared as a moan escaped me and my muscles clenched around him. He moved faster, shoving in another finger, and I shook under him. With my arms still stretched over my head, I should have felt helpless, but I felt more in control of this than anything I'd done before.

"Condoms. In the top drawer." I practically yelled out as I came again.

He let go of my arms, cupping my cheek in his hand.

"I love when you tell me what you want," he growled before kissing me again.

I pulled him tighter against me, my fingernails digging into his back. "I want you to fuck me, Sal. Now."

He pulled away from me and shifted sideways, reaching for the bedside table. I used his distraction to reach for his pants, pushing them down as far as I could.

He held the metallic packet in his hands, but I reached for it. "Let me put it on you?"

"You can do whatever you want, Blake. Anything." He really was mine. I wasn't sure if he was mine for this moment or mine for good, but right now I didn't give a damn.

I shifted to sit up under him as he perched up on his knees. I ran a finger up his length and loved the shiver that ran down his entire body.

As soon as I rolled the condom down, something snapped inside of him and he grabbed at my hips, yanking my shorts and panties off, throwing them behind him. He kicked off his sweatpants, which I realized were the only thing he still had on, and climbed on top of me.

I thought he was leaning down to kiss me, but instead he stopped, looking into my eyes. "You're okay with this?" I watched him lick his lips. "Once we do this, there's no going back."

"No going back, Sal. I've wanted this for too long." My voice sounded husky, but I knew I meant every word.

Being with Sal was even better than I had remembered it. He knew just what I liked, gripping my hips and pulling my hair with the most delicious tension.

He paused a few times to slow himself down, but

when he did, he told me how beautiful I was, and each time made me feel more connected to him than before.

When neither of us could hold back any longer, he slammed into me to the hilt and called out my name. My toes curled as he pressed his forehead against mine and came apart over me.

We laid there for several minutes, just holding each other. Being together.

He took a deep breath and rolled onto his side, taking me with him. Reaching up to tuck a strand of hair behind my ear, he asked, "Are we still okay?"

I laughed. "After that experience, you're concerned that I'm not perfectly content?"

He pressed a sweet kiss to my lips. "You know what I mean. You still want to do this with me?"

"Oh, I would do this with you every day." He rolled his eyes, and I realized he wanted a serious answer from me. I ran my fingertips down his arm. "Yes, I think we should give it a go."

He pulled away from me and stood up, and I felt cold all over. "Where are you going?"

He smiled and gestured to his lower half. "I've got to clean myself up. I'll be right back." He leaned down and kissed my forehead before going to the bathroom.

A couple of minutes later, he emerged with a warm washcloth in his hand. He motioned for me to move my legs and he pressed the warm washcloth against my core. "I can do that myself, you know."

He winked. "But I like having an excuse to touch you again."

I pulled the cloth away from him and stood, trying to

clean myself up without looking awkward as hell. I excused myself to the bathroom this time to finish taking care of myself, but when I came back to the bedroom, he was gone.

I threw on a T-shirt and shorts and found him in the kitchen, packing most of the food from earlier into plastic containers.

He had put his pants back on but had left the shirt off. It was probably wherever I had tossed it. I plucked at the waistband of his sweatpants. "Do you always wear pajamas without underwear?"

He laughed, kissing me on the cheek. The easy way he moved around me made me feel like we had been together for months, not minutes. "Blake, I haven't worn underwear in like twenty years." He picked up a piece of bacon and took a bite, like we were talking about the weather.

I felt my skin flush again, not knowing why the thought of him going commando every time we'd ever spent time together made me so hot. "Like, ever?"

He shrugged, offering me a piece of bacon, which I gladly took. "I wear boxers at the gym, but other than that, I don't like them."

I ate my bacon, wondering what the last hour was going to mean for the next few weeks, and after that, even. As if he was reading my mind, he asked, "So, what Camilla had said about the bed-and-breakfast . . . ."

I tried to remember the conversation. "Honestly, I was so anxious about Lizette's response when you dropped the bomb on her. I couldn't recall what your sister said about it."

He picked up the frying pan. "Do you want me to make you some fresh eggs? The other ones sat out too long."

I pushed up to sit on the kitchen island, grabbing another piece of bacon from the plastic container he had put them all in. "Only if you're going to make some for yourself. But first, tell me what you were thinking about the bed-and-breakfast." The one that I didn't think was ever going to exist until a few days ago.

He pulled the butter and eggs out of the fridge and went through the motions of preparing to fry them. "Camilla mentioned turning this house into your B&B."

I looked around. "In a perfect world, it would be great. But there's no way I could afford it. Especially since I don't have a place to live right now."

He cracked an egg into the pan. "First, you have a place to live. Second, if I'm an investor, you don't have to buy the property. And Lizette said her company wants a part of it, too."

I covered my face with my hands. "You know, this is turning into a giant snowball I'm not ready for. Before I told you, it was just a little dream I'd kept to myself, and now we're talking about properties and investors when I haven't even decided if I want to leave The Pacifica." It became a little difficult to breathe, with this responsibility suddenly in my lap.

Without hesitation, Sal moved the pan off the fire and spun around, fixing all of his attention on me. He pulled my hands away from my face gently before holding them in my lap, but my vision was blurring again. "Blake, it was just a suggestion, and I'm sorry for throwing it at you."

He didn't prompt me verbally, but I caught him breathing deeply and holding it, and on instinct I followed him.

"Sorry, it's just a lot on top of everything else that's going on." I closed my eyes, wishing I could disappear.

"I won't bring it up again. I just wanted you to know that I'll support you with whatever you choose to do." His voice was calm and reassuring. When he could tell my heart rate had returned to normal, he turned back around and finished making new eggs for both of us.

After he put the eggs on plates and put them next to each other on the island, he asked if I wanted him to warm up the bacon and sausage, but I told him no. I was hungry, but I wanted to talk with him more than I wanted to eat.

He sat down and dug into his food. I waited for a few seconds and then decided on the most important question I had for him. "How do you do that? Going from rough and possessive in the bedroom to cool and collected in the kitchen?"

He laughed, and I felt a little sad for all the laughs I had decided I hated in the past. "It's what you like. Why wouldn't I give that to you?"

I turned toward him on my stool. "How do you know it's what I like?"

"You told me." He paused, searching my eyes, with humor in his. I started to ask when, but my own voice rang in my ears from the time before. "When a woman tells you to wrap her ponytail around your wrist and hold on, you don't exactly forget it."

I felt my cheeks heat, but he picked up a bite with a fork with one hand and put the other on my upper thigh.

At his touch, more memories of that night became clear. I really had told him exactly what I liked, and he followed through with all of it.

"So, what do you have planned for the day?" he asked, pulling me out of the memories.

"Nothing glamorous, just a bit of laundry. How about you?"

He looked up at the clock on the wall. "I've got to meet a supplier in Malibu in a few hours. And then I think between all three locations, I'll be pretty busy until midnight."

"That makes for a long day."

"Come have dinner with me? I'll be downtown after about six. We can plan the stag party and talk about . . . ." He paused, making a gesture between us.

I bumped my shoulder against his. "Yeah, I would like that."

We finished our breakfast and cleaned up the kitchen, and the air went thick. He stood in the archway of the hall that would take him to the opposite side of the house. I stood at the kitchen sink.

My eyes scanned his toned torso as he pointed behind him with his thumb. "Well, I'm gonna go take a shower so I can get to work."

I felt the awkwardness of saying goodbye fill my veins. Instead of saying anything sexy or reassuring about starting a new relationship, I blurted, "Okay, well, I'll see you later."

He paused for a second before rolling his eyes and walking down his hallway.

I made the walk to my bedroom, wondering how I

could have made the conversation last a little longer. How I should have jumped on him before he said goodbye.

As I walked through the doorway, my phone rang. Wondering if it was Lina checking on me, I picked it up. It was a number that wasn't saved in my phone, but I answered it in case it was the contractor telling me the kitchen was magically repaired.

"Hello?"

"Are you going to come make out with me in the shower or not?" I could hear the laughter in his voice, but it made heat flow through me.

"Why didn't you ask earlier?" I spun around and started jogging toward his room.

"I had to make sure you gave me the right number this time."

I laughed and hung up on him.

I didn't make it two steps into his room before he wrapped his arms around me, kissing me like it was the first time all over again.

It was like all the animosity between us melted away, whether real or made up in my head, and I was enveloped by my person. He knew my wants, my needs, and my deepest desires, and I felt like I was on my way to knowing his, too.

Chapter Twelve

It took us another hour or so before Sal actually got dressed and went to meet his supplier. I was worried I had made him late, but he assured me he had planned extra time into his morning because he had hoped we would spend most of it together.

I felt the spark of a fun new relationship as I waved goodbye to him from the front door. How he was going to have the energy to run a successful restaurant chain after thoroughly exploring my body, I had no clue. I was ready for a nap, maybe another meal.

I snuggled up on the couch, grabbing the book that was still on the coffee table from the night before. I was hooked in the first chapter, following the woman who had been left without an estate after her father's death. She had been taken in by a kind neighbor whom she later found was a wealthy viscount who made her dreams come true.

I pressed the book to my chest after making it to the part where they kiss for the first time. My heart fluttered at the possibility of their new relationship, too. I understood why Sal had read it many times. Hell, I wanted to devour the rest of it right here.

But my eye caught the clock, and I realized it was after lunchtime. I stood up, grabbing a random receipt from my purse and using it to mark my place. After I put the book on my nightstand in my room and came back to the kitchen to figure out lunch, my phone buzzed.

I picked it up from the counter, realizing that I had never let Lina know how things had panned out. It was a text from Valerie: *Hey, do you still have the day off? Want to bring me lunch so we can catch up? I'm trapped at the new store, and I'm starving!*

I replied: *Tell me what you want, and I'll pick it up.*

Then I sent a text to Lina: *Long story, don't want to share over text and I don't know what time it is for you, but things turned out really well. I think he's my real boyfriend now? Let me know when it's a good time to call.*

I ducked into my bedroom, got dressed, then checked my phone. Val had sent me a screenshot of an order from a bistro near her record store and had written: *I took the liberty of ordering the soup and sandwich combo you always get, since it was in my saved orders.*

I replied: *Thx, I'm on my way.*

Half an hour later, I walked through the back door of her store, which had been propped open. She was sitting on the sales floor, music blasting while she sorted albums from a storage crate. I held up the paper bag containing our lunches. "Ready to eat?"

She jumped and let out a yelp, obviously not realizing I had come in the door. "Sorry, I was in the zone. I've only got a few more days to get everything ready for the soft opening, and then with the wedding coming up . . . ." She grabbed her curly hair, which was bushier than usual. "Oh shit, I still haven't made reservations for the rehearsal dinner . . . it's only a few weeks from now, and I feel like I'm losing it."

I reached a hand out to help her stand, and she took it. "If it makes you feel better, Sal and I haven't planned the bachelorette party, either."

"We both suck." Luckily, it sounded like my admission had made her feel better.

"We really do. Let's take a break and then see what we can do," I told her. Val was not acting like her bubbly self, but I understood the craziness. It surprised me I'd made it this far into my day off without getting a call from work.

"I think it feels like the big mess right before everything is done. But I'm still freaking out." We walked to the break room in the back, which was more decorated than I would have expected for a new location. Band posters hung on the walls, and cantina lights were strung across the ceiling. It felt more like a greenroom at a concert hall than the back room of a record store.

I unpacked our lunches, worried that Val looked more disheveled than I'd ever seen her. "It looks really great in here. On brand with the other location, but with a personality of its own."

She sat at the table, raising her shoulders finally. "Joey was here until two this morning hanging posters. Thank God for that man."

I looked around the room before sitting down across

from her. "Remind me to hire him for our next round of renovations at the resort. This looks amazing."

"Thank you. And thanks for lunch," she said around a bite of a roast beef sandwich.

"You're the one who paid for it. All I did was pick it up."

"It was the least I could do for someone who's going to spend the rest of her day off helping me sort and put away about ten crates of records."

I laughed. "Oh, there's the real story."

She looked sheepish, a look that was very not Valerie. "I mean, if you would like to?"

Even though I was exhausted from last night, I patted the back of her hand for a brief second. "There is nowhere else I'd rather be."

We finished our lunch, and she quickly put me to work. As I unpacked boxes of records and put them in alphabetical order, I asked her where her employees were. She admitted she was worried she was burning them out already. She had told them to take today and tomorrow off so they would be ready for the soft opening on Monday. The grand opening next weekend would be here before we knew it. "So you're planning on just burning yourself out?" I couldn't help but ask.

"Be careful, Blakey, you're starting to sound like me."

I laughed. "Well, when our group doesn't have a voice of reason, someone has to step up."

"I promise I'll take a vacation as soon as we're up and running. Joey is playing in Sacramento in May to prep for the next tour, and I'm going to go with him."

We talked more about her plans, and as soon as I had

made it to the bottom of the third box, her phone rang. "Ooh, it's Lina!"

She answered, putting it on speakerphone. "Hello from inside the new store! Blake's here too!"

"Thank goodness!" Her voice sounded exasperated. "I called Blake's phone three times before calling yours. We're having an emergency."

I dropped what I was doing and rushed over to Val's side. "What's going on?"

"The wedding venue canceled on us." She sounded like she had been crying. Like she was about to start again any second now. "We were told that it was a possibility since our spot was filling in a cancelation, but we thought it would be fine." She took a wavering breath. "Sure as hell, the bride and groom got back together, and now their wedding is un-canceled and ours is back at the courthouse."

"Didn't you sign a contract? Isn't that illegal . . . or at least immoral?" Valerie asked.

"They came in with a ton of money that we couldn't match." I could tell she was trying to hold it together, but her words spewed out quickly. "Now we're going to lose the DJ deposit. And oh my God, the money I've already sent the florist—"

"Lina, we'll figure this out." Val started, her voice soothing.

I rushed to the break room, where I found my phone sitting on the table. There were several missed calls and a text from Sal. It took everything in me to ignore my texts while I opened my work calendar and headed back to where Val stood, leaning against a shelf of half-filled record crates. Val was reassuring Lina that the courthouse was perfect for what they wanted, and we could find somewhere for the small reception.

I scanned through the events calendar at The Pacifica. "Okay, here's the deal, we don't have any openings for the weekend you originally planned, but I do have both the beach and the large ballroom upstairs open on Sunday the 16th. I know you weren't planning on The Pacifica, and you'll have to see if your other vendors can deliver five days early, but at least it's not the courthouse."

"Let me talk to Reece and see what he thinks, and I'll call you right back." She must have been frantic because she didn't even say goodbye before the line went dead.

Val and I went back to sorting records, but our speed definitely declined as we discussed other options. I had been heart set on them getting married at The Pacifica, but it was their day, and I wanted them to start this new journey where they would be comfortable.

Fifteen minutes later, Val's phone rang again, and I picked it up as quickly as I could. Lina started talking before we could ask her a single question. "Okay, Reece is in. The florist is okay with moving the date. Surprisingly, the DJ was okay with it, too. Sunday isn't the busiest night for a wedding, so we got lucky there. We'll have to find a new officiant, but worst case we can have someone get ordained on the internet the day before."

Val leaned toward the phone. "And your flights?"

"Reece is on the phone with the airline right now. He found one that comes in pretty late Friday night. We're going to have to cancel some bookings here, which sucks, but it is what it is at this point. We probably shouldn't have scheduled gigs this close to the wedding anyway." I started logging the new wedding date into the master calendar for work when her voice became panicked again. "Oh God, the bachelorette party and rehearsal dinner! You guys have worked so hard, and now we're going to have to cancel those, too."

Valerie's eyes met mine, and we silently decided right then and there to never tell our best friend we hadn't actually planned anything yet. Valerie used her calmest voice when she assured Lina, "Oh honey, don't worry about those. We'll be able to make it work." She looked at me and mouthed, *"What should we do?"*

Thoughts fired through my head rapidly. "Sal and I have his parent's anniversary that Friday night. We can do the rehearsal that Saturday, as long as it's before the guests for the wedding we have booked that night start setting up. Let's do the party right after the rehearsal? Make it a rehearsal-stag-bachelorette extravaganza?"

"Would that be okay for you guys? With Val's new store and the resort, you're both so busy right now." Lina's voice sounded a little calmer, like she knew we could figure out this puzzle, even if she was freaking out.

"I put you on the calendar, but I'll call Kathy and make sure she gets the ball rolling for setup and teardown."

"No, I'll call her, since she's still working part time for me. I've got to tell her which sessions I need to cancel to make this work, anyway." In our panic, I had forgotten that our events coordinator at the resort also handled Lina's schedule, since they had become friends while Lina was our photographer.

My mind started going through the steps that needed to be taken to pull off a wedding in a little over three weeks. And then I remembered one big kink in the plan. "Crap. We have sort of a small situation at the resort." My mind spiraled, trying to figure out how to solve the problem I'd been dealing with for longer than it should have been.

Lina's worry crept into her voice again. "Wait, what's the situation?" She whispered into the phone, "Is it Ezra? I thought he got relocated to the East Coast?"

I laughed, having forgotten that her ex-whatever had also worked at The Pacifica. No wonder she and Reece had reservations about getting married where their relationship had begun.

"No, we sent that dude to the resort with the most snow in the entire Howell Group. Hopefully he's miserable." I paused, having thought of a solution. "Our kitchen is in pieces, and the only thing the contractor is good at is extending his deadlines, so we've been stuck having our clients bring in their own caterers."

Val looked at me, having thought of the same fix. "What if we call Sal?" Then she leaned into the phone, like she was telling Lina a secret. "Blake's boyyyyfriend can probably cater your reception."

I opened the text from Sal, which was asking how my day was going. I tried to hide my little swoon at his thoughtfulness, keeping my head in the current problem. "Let me ask." I hit the call button, and he picked up on the second ring.

I heard loud clanging noises in the kitchen before he spoke. "Hey babe, how are you?"

It was hard to not squeal internally when he called me babe, but I was a woman on a mission. "We have a problem."

"Oh shit, what did I do this time?" He was trying to be humorous, which was adorable, but I had to stay on track.

"It's kind of a long story, but the wedding venue canceled on Lina and Reece. The only night we can book them at The Pacifica is the Sunday after your parents' party. We've got the space for the ceremony and the reception, but we don't have a working kitchen, and I doubt it will be ready in three weeks."

"And you need me to cater?" He had read my mind.

"Yes."

"Sounds good. Tell them to text me the details when they have them, and I'll start planning the menu."

"Thanks . . . babe."

I heard the smile in his voice. "You're welcome, babe."

Valerie rolled her eyes. "Oh my gosh, Lina, she's doing that gross googly-eyed thing."

"I'll see you tonight?" I asked, eager to get off the phone in front of my nosy friend.

"Can't wait," he said before I hung up.

"Okay," I said to Lina, still on Val's phone. "Sal said he would handle the catering. Problem solved. Just send him a text, and he can set it all up."

"Wow, you guys are amazing. I'm going to text Kathy and see what I need to do. I'll start looking for an officiant as soon as we get off this call." She blew out a loud breath. "I'm so glad I have you all."

Valerie added, "We love you guys so much. Oh, and Joey and I are going to taste the cakes tomorrow. I'll see if the bakery can do a rush order. Worst case, we find somewhere we can get a ton of cupcakes and build a tower or something."

"What would I do without you?" Lina was back to her joyful self.

"You'd probably still be in a not-relationship with that Ezra douchebag," Valerie told her, and I caught her laughter through the speaker.

I told Lina goodbye and went back to sorting records. The two of them discussed the logistics of the cake tasting and what else needed to get done before the big day, like picking up the dress and the suit Reece had custom ordered for the ceremony.

After a few minutes, we told Lina we loved her and couldn't wait to see her, and Val hung up the phone.

Val and I made it through at least a thousand records before we found ourselves lying on the floor, fingers sore and backs exhausted. We had tried to talk a few times, but it always threw off our organization, so we cranked the sound system up and got the work done.

During the last stack of vinyl, we had rolled through explosive giggles for no reason, which was how we ended up on the floor, staring up at the ceiling together.

"Thanks for using your day off to save my ass." She looked over at me, and I could swear there were tears in her eyes. My heart clenched. She rarely got so emotional.

"Honestly, it was nice to just zone out and get something done for once. Every project I've started lately still isn't done. Thanks for giving me a rewarding task."

She laughed at my positivity, even though I meant it. It had been a nice way to spend the afternoon with my best friend.

After a few minutes of stretching my lower back, my phone rang. I had completely forgotten about my other missed calls when Lina called, and I hoped none of them had been important.

I crawled across the floor to where I had set my phone and answered it.

"Hey baby, I have some great news!"

I covered the microphone with my hand and whispered, "It's my mom. I'll be right back."

Valerie yelled as loud as she could, "Hi Eleanor!"

"What are you ladies up to? Tell Valerie I said hi!"

I called out to Val, "Mom says hi!" before telling her we were getting the new record store ready for its opening next week.

After catching up, hearing about how Jake's baby was growing strong, and all about the lady at the grocery store who cut her off at the checkout earlier this week, she said, "Oh, I almost forgot about the reason I called! I think I found a few houses for you to check out!"

I rubbed my forehead. My mom always held off on the good news until the end of a call. "You know, you could have started with that."

She laughed. "I don't hear from you as often as I used to. I need to get my chats in somehow!"

My heart warmed. She really was the best. "Sorry. I'll call more."

"No, you won't." She let out a cackle of a laugh and

then went on without skipping a beat. "Anyway, I just sent you an email. Open it up."

I put the phone on speaker and opened my email. There were three links to listings above the picture of her smiling brightly in her email signature. No wonder she was the best agent in Bakersfield for so many years in a row.

I clicked the first link and scrolled through the information. It looked like it was the right size but it needed some renovations. The price was nice, but I was already living without a kitchen at work. Did I want to wait several months while the one at home was remodeled, too? "Put the first one on the maybe-if-we-can't-find-anything-else list."

"Okay, I'll write that down. What about the next one?"

I went to the next link. "This one is way out of my price range." Not only would this eat through all of my investments, but I'd have a huge mortgage tying me down for the rest of my life.

"I think the owners will negotiate. It's been on the market for six months, and they're eager to sell." She sounded hopeful, so I clicked through a few more pictures.

It was beautiful. A crisp white kitchen with all new appliances. But when I got to the backyard, it left me wanting more. "Is that concrete?"

My mother sighed. "Yes, the backyard is tiny and, for some reason, it's been completely paved over. But, in time, you can get that fixed. It's not like you wanted to have dogs or kids playing back there." She did have a point, and a little part of me felt like she finally understood what my needs were.

"True. This one's a little more maybe than the first one." I closed it out and clicked the link for the last house in her email. It wasn't an official listing, just a document filled with pictures of the property. "Oh my gosh, Mom, I've been in this house before!"

Valerie rushed over to me, having been listening the whole time. "Let me see!" She looked over my shoulder. "Whoa, that's the house that Lina and Reece have been renting when they're in town."

My mom sounded proud. "This is the one I was most excited about." Again, she left the best thing for last. "The owner called Theresa's office and said they were thinking about listing it but were still on the fence. Since I told her to call me if anything in that area came up, she called me so we could see if you wanted to look at it before it officially hits the market."

"What are they asking for?" It was basically the perfect house for me—two bedrooms and located right on the beach. Fully updated and modern, but with plenty of space for entertaining in the open living area.

"That's the thing. The owner said they're open to any offers, and they're willing to finance the sale themselves. I ran some numbers, and I think we can make it work if we get them to take a bid that's below-market." I got a little excited. My mom was the best in the business, and I trusted her to get a great deal. "We're going to have to use most of your savings, and it will definitely eat into your investments if you don't want an astronomical mortgage." I think she knew I cringed at that because she added,

"Honestly, I don't think you'll find anything better than this for a long time."

My savings. My bed-and-breakfast money. Curse Chelsea and Connor and how they fucked me into this situation. May they eternally burn in Landlord Hell for evicting me before I was ready to be thrust into the world like this. But I really loved the beach bungalow, and the house before it on the list wasn't bad, either. "Do you think buying right now is a good decision?"

"Blake, my darling daughter, I would not have recommended this if I didn't think it was a good idea financially. The locations of these properties are perfect, the amenities are just what you wanted, interest rates are low, and I think we can get either of them for well below market value."

My nerves began to swell, but I looked over at Val, and her calm demeanor gave me some peace. I would have to put off my dream for a little longer.

But was that even true anymore? Lizette said The Howell Group would invest, and Sal practically offered me his house. I would have to compromise and share the B&B. It wasn't the original plan, but plans change.

"Are you still there?" My mother's voice jolted me out of my head.

"Yeah, sorry, I was just thinking."

"Well, I hate to wear my pushy real estate agent hat, but if you're interested in any of these houses, we need to let Theresa know so she can show you the properties."

A thrill ran through me. "Let's look at the second and third one." Then an idea hit me. "Wait. Can we put in a bid for the third house, since I know I love it, and I'll go visit the other house in case it doesn't go through?" In case it really was too good to be true.

"I think that's a great idea." I was glad my mom was here for this. It was a little overwhelming how fast everything was moving, but I knew I could trust her to steer me in the right direction. I paced in front of the phone as we talked numbers. Val chimed in a few times, which I was grateful for, since she owned a house and two record stores. By the time we were done, I was excited about this new adventure.

Sure, the owner of the bungalow could turn down my offer. But my mom had sent a text to Theresa while we talked about budgets, and she said I could go see the other house whenever I had free time next week. This was really happening.

It wasn't until we hung up that I realized how late it had gotten. I looked up at Valerie. "Oh shit, I have to go. I told Sal I would meet him for dinner."

"Your boyyyyyfriend." She giggled. Somehow, it felt like she had known this was going to happen all long. She put her hand on her hip. "I love how content you look now that it's all falling together." I rolled my eyes, not willing to take the compliment. "No, Blake, I'm really glad that you're finally happy again. It's been a while."

It had been a while, and I wouldn't admit out loud that I was apprehensive the bottom would fall out of something before too long. Hopefully I was wrong.

Sal had texted me to meet him at his location in Carpinteria, which was only fifteen minutes from Val's new store. Lina said it was her favorite, but I didn't think it had anything to do with the food.

I spotted Sal's motorcycle parked out front as I pulled into the lot. I probably should have gone home and changed, but I was already running late as it was. My dusty jeans and T-shirt would have to do for this place that looked like you had to wear a blazer and a tie just to get in.

As I walked through the large wooden door, a *maître d'* with a bright smile on his face immediately greeted me. I let him know I was here to see Sal and stood back in the lobby, wondering where they would seat me in this packed house.

I had only been here once before, but I had forgotten how fancy it was. Gold chandeliers hung from the ceiling and plush red booths lined the walls, bringing me into what felt like an Italian restaurant on a movie set.

Sal came out of the kitchen, and the muscles in my cheeks pinched as I tried to hide my grin. He looked so at ease in his element as he walked through the restaurant. Everyone else was in a hustle to get work done, and he just strode across the floor, waving and smiling at patrons. This really was his happy place.

He was in front of me before I knew it, wrapping his arms around me, kissing me like I was the only other person in the building. I melted into him, grabbing the lapels of his black chef's coat, pulling him closer to me. "You hungry?" he asked, his voice deep.

"For your food? Always."

He walked me to a table near the back, closer to the kitchen. "I can't hang out for too long, but I figure we can talk while we eat."

I smiled at him as he held the chair out for me, only sitting down once I was settled. "I totally understand." Then I admitted, "You look so hot when you're at work."

He nodded at me. "I could say the same thing about you. Why do you think I visit you at the resort so much?" His eyes scanned me up and down, and I didn't think he was focusing on my clothes. "There's something about a confident woman I can't resist."

"I don't feel very confident lately. Every time something gets fixed, another situation falls apart." I hadn't even told him about the issues with the bachelorette party and the rehearsal dinner yet.

He leaned back in his chair, stretching his arm across the back of the one next to him. "That happens here, too. It took me a long time to stop letting it get to me."

"Hopefully that will rub off on me, too."

"It will. You're doing great." My stomach did a little flip just as a waitress brought us dishes we hadn't ordered. She placed my favorite ravioli in front of me and a plate of chicken parmesan in front of Sal. "Sorry, I put the order in as soon as they told me you were here. You liked it so much last time, I figured you wouldn't mind."

I took my napkin, shook it open, and placed it in my lap. "No, this is great. Thank you." It was nice that he knew what I liked, regardless of where we were. After a few bites, I remembered why I had really come tonight. "So, about the bachelorette party. We need to talk."

He tapped the table with his free hand. "I have a confession to make."

I had no idea where this was going. "Uh-oh."

"I've pretty much planned the whole thing. Maggie said that you mentioned axe throwing, so I booked reservations for a party bus to take us there first and then to a restaurant near your resort that has a bocce ball court in the garden. And then when you said they had to move the wedding up, I called and moved all the bookings to Saturday night. I told them we might need to change the date again, since I didn't know what Val planned for the rehearsal dinner, but everyone was pretty flexible."

Sure, I was relieved, since I hadn't wanted to plan the event in the first place, but I felt a little weird that he had left me in the dark. "When did you find the time to do all that?" The restaurant industry didn't exactly afford for a lot of downtime, and I could only imagine how overwhelming it was to run three locations.

He shrugged, taking another bite of his dinner. "It's not a big deal. But I wanted to run it all by you before finalizing everything, since we had agreed to plan it together in the beginning."

"Thank you, so much." I stared at my hands, wondering why he hadn't wanted to share the mental load of the party with me. Or even discuss it with me while he planned it.

I knew I had been busy lately, but I didn't like having things kept from me. I thought back to how Chris used to plan things without my knowledge and then get mad when he thought I hadn't pulled my weight. Sal didn't seem like the kind of guy to hide things from me like Chris did, but I'd been wrong before.

I reminded myself that Sal was not Chris and looked back up at him. "What can I do to help?"

His eyes lingered on my face for a heartbeat. "Are you upset with me?"

I tried to relax my forehead, to push some joy into my eyes to hide my apprehension. "No, not at all. I'm just worried you took on a lot when I could have been helping." I really hoped he believed me. It was mostly the truth, anyway.

After a second he asked, "Will you find out how long the rehearsal will be? The party bus can pick us up at The Pacifica, but I need to know what time to tell them to be there. Oh, and do you know how many of Maggie's friends are going to be there? I'll need a final headcount for everything, too."

"No problem. I'll find out at work tomorrow what time we can book the rehearsal, and *Maggie* sent me an email with the list of girls she wanted to invite. It'll be easy." I ate another piece of ravioli and reminded myself that this man was nothing like my ex-boyfriend. He wasn't being sweet because he was hiding something or doing nefarious things behind my back. He was a great friend and cared so much about the people I loved.

He leaned forward and asked quietly, "You're really not mad?"

I sat my fork down on my plate. "About what?"

"That I planned the whole thing without you?"

I raised my eyebrows at him. "You stepped in when I lost my house, you feed me a ton of meals, you advocate for me at work, you planned a party I was dreading, and you think I'm going to be mad at you?"

Okay, so I was a little upset that he hadn't involved me, but when I listed everything he had done for me lately, a little more doubt crept in. I sounded like a total mooch, like that Dustin guy I had gone on a date with.

Sal laughed at my answer. I could listen to that sound every day for the rest of my life and not get sick of it. He clapped his hands and said, "Well, when you put it that way, I can see what you mean."

"Speaking of losing my house," I started, happy to tell him about my conversation with my mom. To move the topic away from the party. "I put in a bid for a house today, and Theresa is showing me another one next week as a backup. Want to come?"

One side of his mouth lifted in a smile. "Oh, I'm busy that day."

"I didn't tell you what day!" I laughed. I adored how even when I wasn't sure of something, he could make me smile. He wasn't Chris. He wasn't going to hurt me.

His smile was brilliant. "I'll go if you want me to, but you've got to tell Theresa that we're dating now. I don't want her to think I'm using you to get to her."

I scrunched my eyes at him playfully. "Maybe that's been your long game this whole time."

He stared across the table at me, and deadpanned, "You figured it out, Blake. It's Theresa I've wanted all along."

I rolled my eyes at him and took a bite.

"So, tell me about these houses."

"You will not believe this, but I might get to buy the house Lina and Reece rented when they came to visit."

"Wow, that's crazy." He waved his hand toward a waitress, and when she came over, he asked, "Can we get some wine? A glass of Chianti for us both?"

I turned to her and smiled. "I'm fine with just my water, but thank you." I didn't like to drink before driving, and I knew Sal didn't have a lot of time for dinner.

"Just one for me, then," he said, and then he smiled at me. "Sorry, I didn't mean to cut you off."

I told him about the bungalow and how my mom helped me bid on it before it made it to the market. Then I told him about the other house I was going to check out. The waitress brought him his glass, and he drank it much faster than I'd expected him to. There wasn't an open seat in the whole restaurant, and I wondered if that made him a little nervous. "It's not as nice as the house on the beach, but it's got good bones."

"Well, I hope whichever one you end up with is perfect." I had worried he would be upset that it meant I'd be moving out in a month or two, but he didn't seem to show anything but happiness. He shifted in his seat, taking a rather large bite of food. After he swallowed, he asked, "How's Valerie's new store going?"

"She's a little more stressed than usual, but I think that's normal for what she's dealing with. Her grand opening is a week from Saturday. Are you going to come to that with me?" I gave him a wink. "Or do you have secret plans with Theresa?"

"As long as you don't tell her I'm free, I'll be there." I

loved the way we could joke around with each other so easily.

A waiter came up to the table, whispering something in Sal's ear. Sal murmured something back that I couldn't quite hear, but the waiter nodded and went back to the kitchen. I asked, "Do you have to get going?"

He shook his head, scanning the room. "No, I have some more time."

I picked up my fork and scooped up another ravioli. "So, tell me more about your weekly Dungeons and Dragons games."

He smiled again, and it was probably just my paranoia with a new relationship, but I wasn't sure if it met his eyes. I wondered if his head was in the kitchen, like how my mind sometimes stayed at work well after I'd left for the day. "Have you ever played before?"

I admitted I hadn't—that I didn't really know anything about the game, and the smile I'd worried about a heartbeat before warmed his entire face. "Oh, you're going to love it . . . ."

Chapter Thirteen

Kicking off my shoes at the front door had been the most refreshing part of my day. Maybe the whole week. The last room renovations were finally done at the resort, and the contractor had promised me the kitchen would be done in a month. I had begged him to get it done sooner, for the sake of Lina's wedding, but I also knew Sal had the reception dinner under control. I was just going to have to deal with the mess for a little bit longer.

The rooms looked great, and I was so proud that the board of directors had let Lizette and me choose the interior designer. The biggest worry I'd had during the corporate takeover last year was that The Howell Group would take our boutique-style hotel and turn it into some strip-mall cookie-cutter facility.

But now that the renovations were done, the property was still warm, inviting, and homey. Only now the rooms had hideaway tv screens and shiplap paneling on the accent walls behind plush headboards.

After dropping my purse on the entryway table, I

pulled my phone out and sent Sal a text: *I just got home. Can't wait to see you when you get off later.*

I flipped on the hallway light while I walked to my room. I knew he wouldn't be home for several hours, but I didn't like being in the house while it was completely dark. His reply came quickly: *I'm going to be pretty late tonight. We're short-staffed and slammed.*

I started to make a joke that I'd show him a thing or two about being slammed if he came home and climbed into my bed, but I stopped myself. I'd never made those kinds of jokes with anyone before, let alone a boyfriend. He really was bringing out something fun, more relaxed in me already.

We had slipped into a comfortable routine this past week, which was surprising for how quickly everything between us had happened. I was still staying in the ugly orange room, since sleeping in his room would feel like we were actually living together, and I didn't want him to think I was rushing things. Especially since I was still planning on moving out soon.

But I certainly didn't complain when he slipped under my covers each morning around two to sleep near me before making love to me every morning before I left for work. I finally replied to him: *Well, I'll be here in this creamsicle bed when you get home,* before lying on my bed, thinking about how well he had taken care of me this morning.

I stretched my arms over my head, remembering how he had crept under the covers, pulling my pajama shorts down to my ankles.

My phone rang, jolting me out of my memory. "Hello?" I answered.

"You said you would call me hours ago." My mother didn't sound disappointed, although I would have understood if she did.

"Sorry, Mom. I got really busy." It was a lame excuse, but she didn't call me out for it.

"Well, how was the house?" I had gone to see the one with the crappy backyard during my lunch break today. Sal hadn't been able to get away from work, so I went on my own. In the end, it would have been a waste of his time, so I was glad it had just been me.

I closed my eyes. "You're going to say I'm being too picky, but it really didn't feel like me."

"In what ways?"

"Well, the kitchen countertop was great from far away, but up close, it looked like it was peeling apart. Which, I know, can be fixed, but oh my gosh countertops are so expensive." I rolled onto my side. "Not to mention the gold light fixtures and faucets in the bathrooms. What is this, 1993?"

She laughed. "You weren't even around in 1993."

"True. But you get the point."

"I have some good news, then." I could hear the smile in her voice. "The owner of the bungalow house, as you called it, approved your offer. You're going to be a homeowner!"

"What! Why didn't you start with that?" I sat up, folding my legs under me.

I could imagine her smile. Bright, maybe a little

proud. "You've got to agree to a thirty-day escrow, which is typical."

She filled me in on the rest of the details, telling me about the paperwork I would have to sign and fax to her office in the morning. It was the first time since Chelsea had called with the news of my living situation that I felt like things were lining up the way they should. Even if this meant that I had to start saving for my own bed-and-breakfast from the ground up.

Which was also something that felt pretty doable.

I wasn't sure where this positivity was coming from, but I liked it. "Hold on real quick," I told her as I sent a text to Lina and Val, letting them know the house was going to be mine. They both replied almost instantly, sending me congratulations.

Mom and I talked for another hour. She told me about her latest sales, and I shared the ridiculous things that had been going on at the resort lately.

I hesitated before telling her about Sal, but near the end of the conversation, I admitted I was seeing someone. Was serious about him.

She said she was happy for me and couldn't wait to meet him.

When we hung up, I laid in bed, thinking about how different my life was from how it had been just two months ago.

I must have fallen asleep, because Sal's arms wrapped around me tightly, his body tucking against mine. "Are you planning on sleeping in your work clothes all night?" His whisper sounded like a dream.

Reaching for the zipper, I tried to pull my skirt off. "What time is it?"

"Here, let me do that." He undressed me slowly, his fingers gentle. When he finally asked me to move so he could pull the covers over us, I found he had also undressed himself in the process.

He pulled me against him again, spooning his legs behind mine before kissing my neck. "How was your night?" I asked groggily.

"It was busy. Rewarding, but busy." He sounded exhausted. It was nice that even after working late, he felt compelled to come to my room instead of his own.

I turned around in his arms, pulling him closer to me. "I think I bought a house tonight. The one Lina stayed in."

He smiled, kissing me slowly. "Congratulations, babe."

I pressed my head against his chest, savoring his warmth. His strength. "I can't wait for you to see it."

His fingers ran through my hair, and I started to doze off again. "I'm sure I'll love it" was the last thing I heard him say before falling back to sleep.

We held hands as Sal pushed the door open, the bell tinkling somewhere over our heads. We were greeted by excited staff members, the one closest to us sporting a blue pixie cut and a hot pink nose ring. I remembered her. She was the woman who had rented Lina's room after she moved out of Val's house.

"Welcome! Everything in the store is 10 percent off for our grand opening sale. Let any one of us know if you need any help finding something."

I had been in this record store a dozen times already helping set up, so I didn't think we'd need assistance, but I gave Berkley—that was her name—a little wave. Before we could take another step, Val yelled from the opposite side of the large room, "You made it!!"

She launched herself toward us, wrapping both Sal and I in a tight hug. "We wouldn't have missed it for the world!" I told her, excited to be here on the day it officially opened.

I hugged her back before she pulled away, gesturing to the rest of the store. "I can't believe it's really happening."

I looked around the building. This store was twice as large as her other location, with rows and rows of records all organized by genre. There were also tables set up sporadically with knick-knacks from every fandom imaginable. "It looks amazing, Val. I'm so proud of you."

Sal said something similar, and Valerie's smile turned a little bashful. He added, "My cousin is meeting us here, too. She's excited to have a new record store so close to her house."

The front door jingled again, but it wasn't anyone we recognized. Val moved to welcome them to the store. "Have a look around, and let me know if you have any questions."

I took my boyfriend by the hand, pulling him down the aisle. "I'm going to have to get a turntable for the new house so I can build my record collection."

He put his hand on my hip, pulling me a little closer to him. "Maybe I'll get you one as a housewarming gift."

We browsed section after section until Sal found his favorite punk band. He pulled a couple of albums out and was tucking them under his arm when the front door opened again.

Marianna found us immediately, walking straight to us while waving at the employees who welcomed her. I reached out to shake her hand. "It's nice to meet you for real. I'm Blake."

She ignored my hand, instead pulling me into a bone-crushing hug. "I'm so happy the two of you finally got your shit together." She pulled back, grinning, and I didn't know how I'd missed it when I'd seen her before at his restaurant. She and Sal definitely had genetics in common. "This dude's been pining for you for God knows how long. I've been rooting for him the whole time."

She stepped back, giving him a punch on the shoulder. His icy look didn't phase her. "I'm so glad we invited you, Marianna." His voice was flat, maybe a little nervous.

Marianna shrugged, dismissing his tone, and pointed at what he held in his hands. "Find anything good yet?"

He showed her the albums he had picked out, and the two of them discussed what other bands they might be able to find before they dove into the stacks, searching for the next great find.

I wandered down the next aisle, not really interested in flipping through albums, since I had spent plenty of time over the last several days placing them here. It was fun watching them interact, though. The way they joked and teased each other made me happy. Like their joy was something I got to have more in my life now that he was mine.

His phone rang, and he handed her the stack of albums in his hands. "Hold on, I've got to take this." He looked up at me. "It's my dad." He turned toward the door, walking out to the parking lot for some privacy. I watched him through the window as he took the call, as he paced back and forth and ran his fingers through his hair.

Marianna snuck up next to me, bumping her hip into mine. "Thank you," she said.

I looked over at her, finally peeling my eyes away from Sal. "For what?"

She reached to the stacks in front of us, flipping through records. "He's been obsessed with you since last summer. We even had a friend who tried to set him up on a blind date, and he turned it down. So seeing you two actually together is great."

This was new information, but I liked it. It was sweet to think that I had such an impact on him. Too bad we had lost so much time being stupid about what we really wanted. "Well, he is a pretty great guy."

She pulled an album out of the stack, flipping it over and reading the back. It was some pop band that I vaguely remembered from the radio a few years ago. "When I came up with the idea for him to ask you to fake date him, I was shocked he agreed. We'd all worried he'd resigned himself to never date again, but then when you said you'd go along with it, we were all so excited."

I paused, trying to process this. Not only did she know everything about us, but so did other people. "Um," I started, trying to find the right words. I flipped through some albums, not even seeing what they were. "So who are the other people that know about my and Sal's . . . situation?"

She went on, not noticing that my demeanor had shifted. Or maybe I was doing a good job hiding my internal stiffness. "Oh, just our Dungeons and Dragons group. We talk about everything, don't worry."

Except that I was worried. I knew I had told my best friends, but he hadn't even mentioned these other people. Who else was in on it?

And it was her idea? Not Sal trying to get his dad to talk to him again? Had they made this all up to trick me into dating him?

I patted my phone in the back pocket of my jeans, hoping someone from work would choose right now to call, so I could have an excuse to ditch our lunch plans and get out of here. I spotted Val across the room, helping an employee with something, but knew if I told her about my issue, it would dampen her grand opening day.

The bell jingled and Sal strode back in. He reached for my arm, pulling my hand into his. "Is everything okay?" I asked.

"My dad actually called me." He looked like he had gone into shock, his breathing shallow and his eyes wide. "He invited me to Easter mass next weekend."

I covered my mouth with my free hand, trying to

forget the gossip Marianna had just dropped on me. "That's great news. Did you tell him you'd be there?"

He shook his head, still not looking either of us in the eyes. "I told him I had to work. I don't know why I did it. It just came out."

That's when I realized he was terrified. He dropped my hand, and his fingertips wiggled back and forth at his sides, like he had to get the nervous energy out somehow. "It's not like you lied to him," I tried to assure him.

His eyes finally met mine, the brown taking over almost all the green. "That's what I've been telling myself since I hung up. We're always fully booked on Easter. It's not like I would have time to go to mass."

I ran my hand down his arm, hoping to calm him a little, and Marianna added, "Your mom invited me to mass, too. How about I go and put in a good word for you?"

His smile was definitely fake. He was too trapped in his own head for any real emotions. "He said that he understood, that my business was important. And then he told me to call Camilla and ask her for details about the anniversary party." A genuine smile met my own. "We did it, Blake." Then he grabbed me, pulling me into a tight hug. "Thank you so much."

I squeezed him back, happy that he was taking these first steps to being back with his family. "It was all you, Sal. I'm just here to help."

The two of them started chatting about what Marianna could say or do at mass to give him a boost with his parents, so I slipped away from them, collecting the albums Sal had picked out in my arms and pretending

I was browsing further down the aisle. I replayed what Marianna had said to me while he was outside, picking apart every second of our conversation.

I barely knew this woman and had met none of their friends, but it felt like they knew my entire life story. I wasn't sure why this rubbed me the wrong way. Why I felt a little sour watching the two of them converse, even though it seemed like the goal of our scheme had been met.

It was difficult for me to share personal stuff with my best friends, and now I knew there was a whole group of strangers who knew all about my sex life.

What else had Sal told them?

What if all of this was some trick to get me back into his bed? Or worse, to humiliate me for giving him the wrong number? Had he lied to me about needing a girlfriend so I would feel bad for him and go along with his plan? Because it worked. And now I was falling for him.

I tried to relax my shoulders, but they were cranked all the way up, practically touching my ears. This was a lot to mull over. A lot to figure out.

"Should we head to lunch?" Sal asked as he approached me, taking my hand in his.

I nodded as he led our group to the checkout counter even though I wasn't sure if I wanted to go to lunch with them anymore.

Val came and stood next to Berkley at the streamlined-looking tablet, helping her navigate the point-of-sale system. "Sorry, we upgraded to a new system, and neither of us know it all the way through just yet." Val smiled, her pride rolling off her in waves.

Sal paid for his albums, after taking Marianna's from her to pay for them too, and turned to me. "Ready to go?"

Val answered for me. "Actually? Can I steal her for a bit?" She smiled brightly at them. "Bridesmaids duties, and such." I knew she was full of shit, but I was sure neither Sal nor Marianna had a clue. I also had no idea what she needed me for, but I knew it had nothing to do with Lina's wedding.

I waved my hand toward them. "You two go on ahead. I'll meet up with you at the restaurant." I had to admit, I was a little relieved to have a moment to think about all of this without either of them around, but I knew whatever Val wanted to talk to me about might be worse.

Sal's brows furrowed, but he nodded. "I'll ride with Marianna. But don't take too long, okay?" I knew immediately that he saw right through Val, too. Luckily, he had ridden here with me, so I had an easy way out if I needed one.

"Yeah, I'll let you know when I'm there," I promised. He gave me a quick peck, and the two of them walked out the door.

Val came around the counter, looping her arm through mine. "Come check out the break room with me."

She pulled me toward the back of the building. "Val, I've seen the room already." She was up to something.

When we were almost to the table in the cozy back

room, she responded, "Yes, but you just got real weird out there, and I wanted to check on you." Her hands gripped my shoulders for a moment, showing me that I had tensed all the way up again.

She made me sit next to her, tugging on our chairs so her knees touched mine. "Everything's fine," I lied.

She just stared at me.

"Okay, everything is going to be fine. I don't want to dump my baggage on you today, of all days." Or ever, really.

She put her hand on my knee, and I knew I had to be completely honest. "Okay, so while Sal was on the phone, his cousin told me it had been her idea for us to fake date and that all of his friends knew our history." I folded my hands in my lap. "Our entire history."

"Good. I'm glad she encouraged him to go after you."

"But Val, he told a bunch of strangers about us. Doesn't that seem intrusive to you?"

"They're not strangers, hun. They're his friends. It's like you telling me and Lina." Her words were soft, and I knew she made sense.

"But he already told Reece and Joey. Don't you think that's a lot of people knowing our business?" Business I wasn't even fully aware of until recently.

"So you have a man who is not only hot, but has the ability to talk to his friends about his emotions? And that bothers you because?"

"I know I'm being so dumb right now. I just—I don't know. I wish he would have talked to me about it. Instead of a group of people."

Her eyebrow went up skeptically. "You weren't exactly

in the headspace to talk to him about a possible relationship, remember? Didn't you say something about gouging both of his eyes out with your thumbs?"

I cringed. I had said that to her once. "Okay, but now there's a bunch of people who know about us."

She rolled her eyes. "Who actually gives a fuck if you love him?"

I felt my cheeks blanch. "I never said I loved him."

She rubbed her forehead. "You don't have to say it. It's written all over your face when you look at him." She pushed my shoulder gently. It had relaxed a little all on its own. "It's all over his face, too, you know."

I sighed, knowing that this wasn't a roadblock worth arguing over. "Thank you for this. I'm sorry I took you away from the store." I stood up, pulling her into a hug.

"Honestly, my feet were killing me, and I was just looking for an excuse to come back here and relax." She pulled back, winking at me. "Now go have lunch with your man. You can talk to him about your boundaries later."

Chapter Fourteen

The night of the anniversary party had finally come, and I could feel the tension coming from Sal, even though we were on opposite sides of the house. Neither of us had taken a day off since Val's store opened, which didn't help the nerves I was sure both of us felt. Once the party was over, though, we would have the rest of the weekend together. To spend with our friends and each other.

The party had a 1920s theme, and with Val's help, I had found a dark green vintage dress covered in sequins that fit like a glove. I put the last bobby pin into my hair, securing it into a bun at the nape of my neck, just like the YouTube tutorial instructed me to. Spinning in a circle in front of the full-length mirror in my room, I felt like I could have perfectly blended into the background of an episode of Downton Abbey. My patent-leather shoes and stockings had really tied the entire outfit together, and I was ready to meet the people who had raised the man I was falling for.

I made my way to the foyer, where my beaded clutch

was sitting on the round table. I was placing my cell phone, ID, debit card and a bit of cash inside when I felt him come up behind me, putting his hands on my waist.

"Holy shit, you look amazing," he murmured into my neck before biting me lightly.

I turned around in his arms and found him wearing a black suit with a green bowtie. The color matched my dress perfectly, but what stood out to me the most were those tortoise-shell glasses.

I reached up, pretending to adjust his tie. "You look gorgeous, too."

He leaned forward, kissing me. "It's too bad we're going to be late." His voice was wobbly, like he was a little on edge.

I shook my head, looking toward the clock in the other room. "No, I think we're actually a little early."

Without another word, he grabbed me by the hips, propping my ass onto the table. "Oh, if we left right now, we'd be early, but I have to fuck you in that dress before we can go anywhere." One hand pushed my dress up my thighs, and the other wrapped around the back of my neck, pulling me in for a kiss.

I reached forward, unbuttoning his pants, and pulled back a fraction of an inch. "Please be gentle with my hair. It took a really long time to put together."

The hand that was gripping my thigh slipped under me, yanking my panties down to my knees. "No promises. I need to get inside of you. Now." His pants dropped to the floor, and he pulled me to the edge of the table. His free hand found my core, and he slipped a finger inside of me, just the way I'd liked it most. "Fuck, Blake. I love you so much."

His mouth found mine before I could reply. I knew he didn't mean it. This was still too new, but I loved the thrill of him saying those words right before making me come. We'd have time to have the awkward conversation later. Right then, I wanted nothing other than him inside of me, too.

Forty minutes later, we stood back where we had started, at the entryway table. He put the last bobby pin back in place, having done his best to help me fix my hair after destroying it with those thick fingers of his.

"Ready?" He asked, fiddling with the key to his Audi.

I tried to offer him a smile, but I was almost as nervous as he was. "No time like the present, right?"

We stood for a few more seconds before he nodded and led the way out the door. Once we got into his car, his hand found mine. Other than when he reached down to shift, he clutched to me like I was his life raft.

At a stoplight about halfway there, I was desperate to cut the tension. I had been obsessing about the words he had said while we were on the table. If he had meant them or if he'd forgotten he'd even said them. And I'm sure he was worrying about every breath he would take, every word he would say, once we got to the party.

"What should be our reward when the party is over? To celebrate that we made it through the night?" I asked, breaking the silence.

"Hmm." He rolled his shoulders, relaxing a little. "We could go out for milkshakes?"

I turned in my seat, knowing just what to say to get his

thoughts off the party. "I was thinking more like a blowjob on the couch. But milkshakes could work, too."

I didn't think I'd ever said the word blowjob out loud before, at least not while sober, so I knew it had hit its mark when he looked at me with a mix of a gasp and a grin on his face. "We could skip the party and go do that instead."

I laughed, "Nope. You're going to have to earn this one."

He shot me a playful glare. "Thanks for being here with me, Blake."

I shrugged. "I know you'd do the same for me."

The car went silent again as we slipped back into our own personal fears. I wondered what else Marianna might tell me tonight, what other things I would have to find the courage to talk to Sal about.

He spoke first this time. "I finally convinced Cami to let me help take care of Nonna." He had been practically begging her for weeks to let him take some responsibility for their grandmother's declining health. "She told me this morning that she's ready for support."

"That's amazing. I'm happy she's letting you help." He had been worried about the toll it was taking on Camilla. The rest of the family, too.

"I know it's going to get harder as the disease progresses, but I want her to know I want to be here for all of it. No matter how bad it gets." He shifted gears as he pulled into the parking lot. "I want all of them to know that I'm here. I want to be part of this again."

I was glad we had talked about his future with his family on the drive here. It helped put a bit of my nerves at ease. Sure, it might lead to some not-easy conversations with his family over the next several weeks, but I supported him, and I wanted him to be happy.

Maybe I felt those little words he accidentally slipped out earlier, too.

We entered the ballroom an hour after we were supposed to, but the venue was spectacular. It looked exactly like a speakeasy during prohibition, with dozens of people standing around high-top tables, drinking cocktails out of art deco glasses. Camilla had gone above and beyond with this party.

I reached up and patted my bun, making sure all the pins were in place. "Stop worrying. You look great," he whispered into my ear, calming my nerves. I wondered if focusing on my anxiety helped him lift a little bit of his.

Lucky for us, the cocktail hour was still going strong. The room was arranged much like the way we sat tables out for receptions in the ballroom at The Pacifica. The cocktail area was on one side of the dance floor, and several round tables for dinner service were on the other side. Near the back wall stood a large rectangular head table with eight chairs facing the rest of the venue.

Sal grabbed me by the hand and pulled me onto the dance floor, stepping in time with the music. "You look so beautiful tonight."

"Thank you." I looked around the room. "I'm glad you wore your glasses."

He kissed me on the cheek. "I had a feeling you'd like them."

He spun me in a circle before pulling me back to him.

I fought the urge to lay my head against his chest, knowing we were on a mission. "Shouldn't we go find your parents and say hello?"

"I was kind of hoping we could just stay on the dance floor all night. We don't even have to tell anyone we came." I'd never seen him so wound up, so out of his element. Gone was the man with an easy smile who moved through the world with a graceful swagger.

I laughed, trying to help with his nerves. After another twirl, I caught sight of his grandma from the corner of my eye. "Let's at least go say hi to Nonna." I had been texting back and forth with Camilla this week, and she had told me that Nonna had been better lately. A pleasant break between the episodes that slowly took their grandmother away from them.

He pressed his forehead against mine, slowing to a stop. "Fine. But I'm going to avoid my father as long as I can."

"Then why did we come?"

He leaned down, kissing my earlobe. "I don't even remember. Let's go home instead. Wasn't there something we were supposed to do on the couch?"

Instead of answering him, I grabbed his hand, dragging him over to where his grandmother stood with two other women that looked to be about her age. They all wore varying shades of blue, and their dresses screamed 1920s elegance.

I called out to Nonna and held my arms open for a

hug, one that she welcomed with a smile. "I'm glad you made it, *cara*." she said before introducing me to the women she was standing with—her cousins she had moved to America with when they were all little girls.

Sal wrapped his arms around me from behind and kissed me on the neck, distracting me from the conversation. Nonna took the fan she had been holding and smacked him in the arm. "You haven't visited me in ages, young man. Were you planning on coming to see me anytime soon?"

He reached past me, gently placing his hand on her shoulder. "I was just thinking, what if I take you to a movie this week?"

Their smiles made the entire night worth it already, their happiness making up for any bad blood within this room.

We talked with the older ladies for a few minutes until the DJ announced it was time to be seated for dinner. The group dispersed quickly, claiming they wanted to sit before the good seats were gone.

His hand wrapped around mine tightly, and I felt him change. He stood up straighter, his breath shallow. I looked at him, realizing he wore an invisible mask, covering the panic flowing through him. I placed my hand gently on his chest. "Just breathe, Salami." It took a few seconds for his eyes to move from somewhere across the room to meet mine. The nickname earned me the smile I had hoped for. "We're here together."

"Can you do me a favor and remember that when dinner is over?" Concern filled his gaze.

I looked over at the tables filling with people. There

had to be at least two hundred people here. "They can't all be that bad."

"It's not all of them I'm worried about." I wished I had asked him more about his parents, more about why he was so afraid of their opinions.

I tugged on his hand and walked toward the tables. Spotting Camilla at the head table, I gave her a wave. She stood and pointed to the empty seat next to her. "Come sit next to me!"

My eyes scanned the rest of the head table, which included who I assumed were Sal's parents. I saw that there were only single seats left, one next to his father, and the one next to Camilla. We were not going to be able to sit next to each other there. "Want to sit somewhere else?" I asked quietly.

His father, who looked like he was used to getting his way, stood from the second seat at the table. "Have a seat next to me, son." He pointed to the chair at the end.

Sal's body tensed even more than it had been before. I could feel him freezing in place. "I can take the spot next to your sister if you want to sit there," I offered.

He gave me a curt nod and kissed me softly on the cheek. "You sure you don't want to go home?" His voice wavered. This was a moment he had been anticipating for a long time.

"It's too late for that, babe."

He walked me to the seat next to Camilla, and once I assured him I was fine; he left to go to his own. The head table was now complete: Sal at the end, then his father and mother, Camilla, me, and the three grandmothers.

A weird image of the last supper flashed through my

mind, but I told myself it wouldn't be as bad as Sal had worried.

The salad course came out first, and luckily there wasn't much conversation to be had. Camilla and I chatted about work and the guy she was dating, and everyone else kept to themselves. I glanced down at Sal, but it seemed like his parents were having a discussion he wasn't involved in.

Camilla seemed concerned about their conversation as well, her eyes darting to Sal and their father every few moments. By the time the main course had been placed in front of us, Sal's mother finally looked over at Camilla and asked her how work had been lately.

After Camilla answered her, their mother looked over at me. "Sorry, what was your name again?"

"Blake." I placed my hands in my lap and smiled, hoping I was making a good first impression.

"Isn't that a man's name?" she asked with a sweet smile. I noticed Camilla tense, but she didn't say a word.

"I'm sure there are men named Blake out there, just like there are men named Ashley and Kelly."

Camilla smiled at me, but I could see the cringe in it. "Blake, this is my mother, Lucia, and my father, Antonio. They're a delight to be around."

Lucia just nodded and went back to her dinner, missing her daughter's sarcasm. I looked from table to table, hoping to find a face I recognized, and finally spotted Marianna. She sat at the table with Bianca and Giovanna. It was nice to see familiar faces in the sea of strangers.

As if she knew I was looking her way, Marianna

glanced up at the head table, looking at me and then over to Sal. She flashed him a thumbs up I wasn't sure I was supposed to see and then smiled like he had given her one in return. I was glad that he had her, even if he may have told her too much about me.

After I picked up my fork again and took a small bite of my overcooked steak, Lucia asked, "So, Blake, what do you do for a living?"

I covered my mouth with my hand, swallowing my food. "I'm the general manager of The Pacifica Resort."

Her lip went up in a sneer. "So, what exactly do you do? Check people in and out of the hotel?"

It wasn't the first time someone had asked me this question, and usually I was pretty good at brushing it off, but I had a feeling this woman had something out for me. "Sometimes. But I also handle all the other issues that arise while running a billion dollar property."

She must have been satisfied with my answer, because she turned in her seat, focusing her attention on her son. "Salvatore, what do you think about that nice Cohen girl? Wouldn't she make a beautiful bride?"

His reply of, "Mother," was a warning to tread lightly. He had warned me that his father could get vicious, but I hadn't expected such hostility from Lucia.

She obviously wasn't satisfied, since she turned to me again. "Oh, that's right, my only son has decided that marriage is beneath him."

Sal's father put his hand on her thigh. "Lucia, we've talked about this before." Maybe Camilla was right. He was warming up to Sal again. "Our son has no intention of real commitment. That's something we're going to have to learn to deal with."

I would have been lying if I said that didn't burn. "His level of commitment is just fine for me," I admitted, hopefully loudly enough for Sal to hear me.

His parents both laughed, and I hated that their voices together sounded like one of my favorite of Sal's laughs. Deep, heady, soulful. They really were a delight.

Antonio leaned toward me. "If there is one thing I know about my son, it's that we unfortunately spoiled him and he will never settle down. I'm sure it will be a different woman in that seat next year." Sal's fist landed on the table, like he was going to lose his temper, but Cami shot him a warning glare.

She spoke to her parents, trying to break the tension. "Did you know Blake is planning on opening her own hotel? A bed-and-breakfast, actually. I'm thinking of investing."

"Oh, that's interesting." Lucia replied. "Are you planning on using my son's money to finance it, too? Nonna tells me you're living in his house." This was exactly what I had worried about. She only saw me as a woman with dollar signs in her eyes.

I opened my mouth to tell her I had been saving and investing in stocks for a decade, that my plan had always been to do it on my own, but now that I had signed the paperwork to buy a house, all of that money was gone.

I stopped myself from saying anything. For this dream to happen, I would have to rely on others—people like Sal and Lizette—to help me open my bed-and-breakfast.

But wasn't that what I had been avoiding this whole time?

The last person I wanted to be was the girl who depended on other people. The best thing for me was to take care of myself.

Sal had said something to his parents, but I hadn't heard a word of it.

My stomach churned. "Please excuse me. I need to use the restroom." These people were horrible, but they also held up a mirror in front of me. I was living in their son's house. I was depending on friends to invest in my dream. Everything I never wanted to do.

Tossing the napkin from my lap onto my plate before I stood on unstable legs, I was halfway to the restroom when I felt a hand on my elbow. "Blake, slow down." I stopped, turning to face Sal. "The way they treated you is not okay."

I fought back the tears forming in my eyes. I had to be strong for him, even though all of my faults were cracking open. "No, Sal, the way they were treating you is not okay. I'm just a stranger. They don't even think they'll see me again. You're their son."

He pushed his glasses up his forehead, pinching the bridge of his nose. "This isn't anything my therapist hasn't heard before. I'm worried about you right now."

I pointed to the table where the rest of the family ate, ignoring the two of us. "The reason we came here tonight was for you to talk to your parents about your relationship. To get them to see your point of view. All the work you've put in will be worthless if you don't get back over there and smooth things over."

My words must have clicked inside of him as his face went stony again. He pushed his glasses back into place. "You're right. Fuck. Are you sure you're okay?"

"Yes, I'm just going to freshen up in the bathroom, and I'll be back in time for dessert."

He spun on his heel and went back to the party as I ducked into the bathroom. I couldn't admit to him that I felt like a giant piece of shit. Just like his mother had mentioned, I would be nothing if it wasn't for the charity of other people. Without her son's money.

After using the restroom and touching up my eye makeup in the mirror, the door swung open and Camilla stepped in. "Everything okay in here?"

I smiled at her. "Yep, just fine."

She didn't seem to believe me, but moved out of the way when I stepped back into the reception hall just as Sal's parents stood before a large cake, cutting it like newlyweds. How on earth two people could look so happy after being so cruel, I would never understand.

I hadn't realized that I had been standing at the back of the room watching them until Camilla wrapped her arm around mine. "They're really not that bad. They're just looking out for him."

I tried to see it from her perspective, but failed. "I'm sure every family has a different dynamic." Was this one I wanted to be a part of? I wasn't so sure.

She leaned into me, tugging tighter on my arm. No doubt trying to comfort me. "Let's forget those jerks right now. How's the house hunt going?"

I appreciated her trying to take my mind off her

parents. "Actually, I'm in escrow with the perfect beach bungalow."

"Do you have any pictures?"

"Just the ones from my realtor." I pulled my phone out of my clutch, ignoring the missed calls on the lock screen, and opened the report my mother had sent me a few weeks ago.

I handed the phone to her, and she looked more confused than excited. "This is my brother's house."

"What? No, it's the house that Reece rented while he was here. That's probably where you've seen it before."

She handed the phone back to me, concern bunching her eyebrows together. "No, I was there the day we did the final walk-through, and I was there when we moved the furniture in. Sal owns that house. Hell, he did most of the renovations himself. It's his rental property."

The meal I had barely eaten threatened to come up. "He would have told me if he owned a rental house. Especially since I told him I was buying this one." Had I heard Lina earlier this year telling me that the house was owned by one of Reece's friends? Jesus, was the house really Sal's?

My fingers went numb. This had to be a mistake. Maybe he owned the house next door? Maybe Camilla had drunk too much tonight. She had to be wrong.

Fuck, I felt just like I had when I found Chris sleeping with Maxine. Or any of the other lies he told me and then made me feel guilty about later.

I thought about the first time I had asked him if he had cheated on me. How he told me I was overreacting about his work schedule, but then he bought me a nice designer purse. Had I not been so dumb, I would have seen that he was just trying to smooth over his bad decisions with nice gifts.

Both men I had felt deeply for had hidden things from me and expected me to just roll over and be happy about it.

I was going to have to cancel the escrow. I couldn't go through with this sale. Especially now that I knew why a house like this was in my budget. I would email my mom as soon as I got home.

Home. Where even was that?

I didn't want to stay at Sal's house tonight, knowing that he had been lying to me about being the owner of my dream house.

I needed to find out what he was trying to get out of me. Why had he been using me, lying to me?

I started to think of an excuse to get away from Camilla, but my phone rang in my hand. I didn't recognize the number, so I sent it to voice mail.

"You need to find my brother and talk to him. Soon. Whatever trick he's playing is not cool." She pulled her arm from mine but touched my shoulder as if I had just experienced a devastating loss.

Which I guess I had.

Either I was losing my boyfriend or my future home. Or both.

My phone rang again from the same number, and I answered it. The voice on the other end was deep, maybe a little tired. "Hello, is this Blake Thomas?"

"This is she. How can I help you?"

"This is Fire Marshal Jameson. I hate to make this

call, but there's been a fire at The Pacifica, and I was told you're the general manager."

My body turned to ice. This was the worst news imaginable. "Oh my God, is everyone okay?"

"Yes, we were able to evacuate all the hotel guests and employees, and we've successfully put the fire out, but we're going to need you to come to the property to discuss the situation." He sounded calm and professional. Like it either wasn't that bad, or he was well-versed in bad-news phone calls.

"Absolutely. I'm on the way." I hung up the phone and looked for Sal, but as I scanned the crowd, I knew I should have asked the fire marshal more questions. I should have asked him to stay on the line until I got there. How bad was the damage?

I was going to be sick.

Several people had moved from the tables to the dance floor, and I couldn't find Sal anywhere. Camilla must have heard my conversation, since she walked away from me and went across the dance floor like a woman on a mission. My eyes followed her as she found Sal, who was standing with Marianna and a few other younger people. She leaned in and whispered something to him, causing his eyes to shoot up, meeting mine.

The last thing I wanted to do right now was look into those eyes. Staring into them felt like a punch to my gut. How could someone I had trusted so quickly betray me this easily? And with a smile on his face while he did it.

He rushed over to me, his eyes never leaving mine. The worry and compassion painted on his face made me think back to earlier, when he had told me he loved me. I hated that I had let him get close enough to me to say such a thing, even if I knew in my heart he had said it accidentally. Someone who loved me wouldn't have anything to hide. "Blake, we need to talk. Camilla told me you—"

"I have to go. There's been an emergency at the resort, and I need to talk with the fire marshal." Fuck. The resort. How was I going to handle this without breaking down? My entire life revolved around that building and the people inside of it.

Was I losing my home and my work?

Was I going to have to move back to Bakersfield for real?

I wondered briefly if the house I had looked at, the one with the concrete backyard, was still available. Probably not.

Panic crossed his brow, pulling me from my worries. "Okay, I'll drive."

I put up my hand, stopping him. "No, I'm going on my own." I didn't want to be around him right now. I couldn't think clearly with him near.

"But Blake . . . ." He reached into his pocket, pulling out his key fob.

I shook my head. "I've already called for an Uber. He's two minutes away. You came to handle this situation with your parents. Please don't waste the time we spent together."

He paused, knowing I was set in my decision. "I'll see you at home?"

I raised an eyebrow at him. "I'm not going to either

of your houses again." Taking a step toward the door, I was ready to get the hell out of here.

"Blake, that's not fair. Let me explain."

I gave him the most serious look I could muster as I noticed several heads turning our way. "Let's not make a scene. I have to go. Alone."

He nodded, frustration clear on his face as I spun around and jogged to the lobby.

I stood at the Valet booth, feeling a little guilty that I had told him I'd already called an Uber. I looked over my shoulder several times, worrying that Sal had seen through my bullshit and would follow me out here while I waited for the actual car I'd just hired to pick me up. But he had listened to me and stayed at the party.

A tiny crack of disappointment spread through me, like I had secretly wished he'd follow me anyway. But he hadn't.

The slight breeze in the air wasn't too cold, but I couldn't fight the shiver running through me.

As I stood there, hoping that Dwayne in his black Chevy Equinox would hurry the fuck up, I saw a couple sitting on the only available bench, making out like their lives depended on it.

The guy looked a little familiar from behind, and my eyes lingered over him. The Valet startled me as he jumped out of a red Ford Focus. "Chris?" he called out, and then my brain connected the dots.

The PDA king and queen stood, and as if I had

conjured the devil himself, I came face to face with my ex-boyfriend. The one who had fucked one of my closest friends almost the entire time we had been together. The one who had hidden everything from me for years.

As if this night could get even worse. Was I about to be struck by lightning? Hit by a bus?

I turned away from them, hoping to melt into a shadow, but I had apparently used all my luck for this year. "Blake, is that you?"

I turned around and gave him a fake smile, ignoring the lipstick spread across his face, looking like he just huffed a can of red spray paint. "Chris. Hi." I glanced at the girl, who was very clearly not his pregnant wife. She didn't even look old enough to be out this late. Fuck this guy. "You're not Maxine."

She turned to him, twirling her hair between her fingers. "Who's Maxine?"

Thank goodness for Dwayne. The black SUV pulled up to the curb. "Chris's wife. Who's about to give birth to their child any day now. Do yourself a favor and run away as fast as you can."

"Thanks a lot, Blake." Chris called out as I opened the back door, like I had been the asshole.

"Go fuck yourself, Chris." I yelled before closing the door. At least I could burn off some anger yelling at him, but the stress of running into him might have made the heart-crushing sadness inside of me worse.

Dwayne and I barely made it out of the parking lot when it all came tumbling out. Once the first tear fell, I couldn't stop the flow. As I started ugly crying in the back of this stranger's car, without a single tissue in my little purse, I wondered how I even got here.

How was I breaking up with my boyfriend, homeless, maybe even jobless, all at the same time?

And why the fuck was Chris even there? Remembering his hands on whoever that girl was made me fucking sick. It was just like finding him with Maxine.

I wondered how many other girls he had done that to. How many girls were riding in the back of a car right now, heartsick that their partner couldn't be honest with them.

I'd played it safe. I'd taken care of myself, not relied on a single other person. And here I was, alone.

The universe was being such a bitch right now.

"Rough night?" My driver's voice startled me. Falling apart back here had somehow made me forget there was someone sitting in the front seat. I looked up at the rearview mirror and met his gaze. Without another word, he passed me a box of tissues.

"You have no idea." I pulled one out and blew my nose. "Love is dead, and my career just literally went up in flames."

"Here's the thing. I've got three grown daughters, and every time one of them went though a heartbreak, they found their footing again. No matter what."

"I don't know, Dwayne. I thought I was on the right track. Like I was finally figuring it all out." I blew my nose again. "But boy was I wrong."

"You know what? No one has it figured out." He stopped at a red light and looked at me over his shoulder. "Not a single one of us."

I had no idea why I felt like opening up to this stranger, but for once I didn't stop myself. Maybe because I knew I'd never see him again. "Have your daughters ever dealt with men who lie? Like really lie? About finances and investments?"

He laughed, but focused on the left-hand turn he was pulling off flawlessly. "Everyone lies. You just have to find out if the truth is worth it."

I laid my head back on the seat. "I don't know if I'm ready for the truth. I just want to crawl into a hole and never come back out."

He shrugged. "You could do that. But I don't think you will." We pulled onto Cabrillo Boulevard, and I could see the resort up ahead. I debated closing my eyes, avoiding the damage, but I knew I couldn't avoid the truth forever.

"I hate to admit that you're right. I'm just going to have to sleep on a couch for a while." Maybe Val and Joey would let me stay on their couch . . . or I could dip into the money I didn't want to spend and get a hotel for a few days while I figured something out.

"You'll end up on top. I'm sure of it." There was absolute certainty in his voice, and part of me really wanted to believe him.

He pulled into the main drive, and I scanned the front of the building. There wasn't anything wrong that I could see, other than the fire truck and ambulance still parked outside, and relief flooded through me.

Unfortunately, I had learned the hard way that just because something looks beautiful and stable doesn't mean you can trust what's going on underneath.

Chapter Fifteen

Dwayne dropped me off in front of the fire truck and ambulance. I thanked him for taking care of me and got out. It was kind of him to give me a chance to be vulnerable and let out my feelings before putting my work hat back on, so I tipped him more than my usual amount on the app as I walked to the entryway.

It was time for me to be all business. To assess the damage and plan for the future. To stand up tall, pull my shoulders back, and pretend I knew what the fuck I was doing.

Except I knew on the inside that I didn't know shit. There wasn't a single aspect of my life that gave me the *"You've got this"* attitude I needed to portray.

I wished there was anyone else who could take care of this for me so I could go home and sleep.

But home wasn't a thing I even had right now, so I guessed it might as well be me.

Looking around the covered driveway, I still didn't see

any fire damage, and it only smelled like a campfire had been lit in the distance, somewhere far away from here. No signs of a raging inferno, which eased a few of my worries.

I pushed through the oversized door that led to the lobby, figuring that if it was off-limits, they would have blocked it off. After tossing all of my gross tissues into the nearest trash can, I found the room full of firefighters.

I didn't know which one could be the fire marshal, so I asked the closest guy in uniform I could find. He pointed to a gray-haired man on the other side of the room, and I was in front of him in just a few steps. "Fire Marshal Jameson?"

He looked up from his clipboard at me. "You must be Blake Thomas." I nodded at him and reached my hand out for a handshake. "I'm sorry to have taken you away from the event you were at this evening."

I didn't know what he meant until he gestured to my outfit. I had spaced that I was standing here in a bejeweled 1920s flapper dress. "Sorry, I must look like a time traveler who's a bit lost." I waved my hand around the room. "It doesn't look like there was much damage?"

"No, your property was extremely lucky. The alarm went off and one of your employees acted quickly. He was able to keep the fire contained in the kitchen."

The kitchen. Of course.

I felt the world tilt under me, but he reached out for my arm. "Would you like to sit down?"

I nodded and let him lead me to the leather chairs across the lobby. Someone handed me a cold bottle of water, but everything else was a blur.

He asked me a series of questions, and I answered them as best as I could, trying to remain as professional as possible in this ridiculous outfit, but there was such a ringing in my ears that I couldn't focus on much.

I felt like I had left my body. I was above the small crowd, watching the conversations happening around me. I didn't snap back into my own head until he mentioned securing the property and moving people back to their rooms.

I knew I would have a ton of complaints when I made it to the office on Monday, but there was nothing I could do about that right now. I thanked him for being so kind to our patrons and I hoped he didn't see that my businesswoman shell was cracking into a million pieces.

Mr. Jameson told me they would send someone to double-check the damage, but they were pretty certain the fire had started because of an electrical issue during the renovation. There was nothing any of us could have done to prevent it.

When he was sure I could walk without fainting, I followed him through the kitchen and made notes in my phone about everything he showed me. He was right. The fire had been relatively tame, and there wasn't much damage. It was the first time I'd been thankful that the kitchen had been sitting here gutted for so long.

I thanked all the firefighters for coming out and helping us and waved them goodbye from the front drive. The party I had left in a hurry felt like it was days ago, like I had been trapped in a loop at the resort for hours.

I tucked my purse under my arm and made the walk to the parking lot, wishing I had worn a shawl. The ocean breeze was strong tonight, freezing me to the bone. Halfway to the staff parking lot, I remembered I hadn't driven here.

Dammit, I was going to need a ride.

I needed a place to stay.

If I tried to check into a room upstairs, the staff would find out and ask me a million questions I didn't want to answer. Especially if I had to do the walk of shame tomorrow morning in this dress.

Besides, they couldn't even keep their gossip about a smoothie delivery to themselves, and Paige would be concerned if she found me here in the morning.

I wondered if they would whisper about my breakup once they heard about it. Another relationship failure.

At least all my past ones had been easier to hide from everyone.

My skin broke out in goosebumps from the breeze as I came up with a plan. Val was always out this late on Friday nights. I could call her.

I just kind of wanted a hug from my mom. I wondered how much an Uber to Bakersfield would cost.

I stared at my phone for a few minutes, mentally listing pros and cons of my possible next steps. Movement up the sidewalk stole my focus—or lack thereof—and I looked up, spotting Sal walking up the path, holding something dark in his hands. His tie was undone, and so were the first few buttons of his shirt. He had his head down, like he was concentrating on the cracks in the concrete.

I was hurt, for so many reasons. And had so much to

figure out. The last thing I wanted to do was talk to him. I wanted to take off my shoes and crawl into bed—to sleep for a month.

He finally looked up when he was ten feet away and stopped in his tracks. Instead of speaking, I just stood silently in front of him. I could feel my heart beat several times, unable to say a single word.

Holding up the bundle in his hand, he said, "I brought you a sweater. I wasn't sure how long you'd be here, and I didn't want you to get cold."

"Thanks. I'm fine though." I hoped it was too dark for him to see that I was clearly freezing, but I crossed my arms just in case my goosebumps were visible.

He lowered the sweater and pointed toward the front door of the resort with his other hand. "Was everything okay in there? It looks like it's still standing."

"Yeah, it was just the electrical in the kitchen, and everyone was safe." An awkward silence filled the space between us. I didn't want to say anything, to risk letting everything out.

"I'm sorry I didn't tell you the truth about the beach house."

He sounded genuine, but I was too mad to think clearly. And not nearly ready to hear his excuse. I spent years listening to Chris's lies, and I was always so quick to forgive him and forget why I had been mad. But I had learned the hard way through that relationship that when someone hurts you, they'll just keep doing it forever. "I don't want to talk to you right now."

"Can I at least drive you home?"

Since I didn't know where home was anymore, I lied. "Actually, Val was out late, so I'm going to catch a ride with her." It was an easy fib, since Valerie was often at the store until midnight and usually went out on the weekends afterward.

Now wasn't the time to be concerned about telling him the truth about anything, since he wouldn't trust me with it, either.

"Just text her and tell her I'm here instead," he said. I took a step backward. There were too many thoughts running through my head. "Babe? Talk to me."

I closed my eyes briefly. "Please don't call me that. I'm not your babe." I felt tears pool as my chest felt like it was tearing open. I already knew my ruined makeup was a dead giveaway that I'd been crying, but I didn't know how bad it was, since I hadn't seen myself in a mirror since the party.

"Look, I'm sorry I didn't tell you everything. I was going to, I swear. I just didn't want you to find out like this." I hated hearing the pain in his voice. He had made this choice. He didn't get to feel heartbroken over this.

I took another step backward. "I need you to leave."

"Babe." He started to follow me, but stopped himself, closing his eyes for a second. "Blake. Don't do this. Let's talk about it."

"If you wanted to talk about it, you would have told me well before you tricked me."

"I just wanted to help." He looked absolutely ruined as he ran his hand through his disheveled hair.

But I didn't care.

"No, Sal. You've helped enough. I need to handle

things on my own. Being with you right now is too much and I just can't do it." My voice echoed across the walkway, and he stood there, looking dejected. "I don't want to talk about it tonight, and I don't want to go home with you. I've had enough of your handouts, and frankly, I'm not sure when I'll want to see you again."

His bottom lip quivered a little before he bit down on it. How was this the same man who had told me he loved me earlier tonight? It's a good thing I hadn't taken him seriously then, because I definitely didn't believe it now. "Okay. Just please call me. When you've had a chance to process."

I nodded, hoping he would believe me enough to leave.

He held the sweater out one more time, and because I didn't actually know where I would be sleeping tonight; I took it.

Without another word, Sal turned around and walked away toward the parking lot. Possibly out of my life forever.

I went back into the hotel, trying to figure out what I was going to do next. After checking on each member of the nighttime staff—especially Frank, who had jumped in to put out the fire but refused to take the rest of the night off —I crept into my office.

I sat down at my desk and took off my shoes, hoping Valerie would still be awake. I sent her a text: *You up?*

And then I turned my computer on. I opened the

email thread from my mother that had all the information about the beach house and sent her a message saying something had come up and I wouldn't be able to go through with the sale. I explained I understood I would lose my escrow money, but this was an unavoidable situation and I didn't want to discuss it any further.

As soon as I sent it, my office phone rang. I wondered if it was the fire department with more information. Hopefully it wasn't my mother. "This is Blake. How may I help you?"

"Hey," It was the nighttime concierge, Davis. "There's a couple here saying they're here to come get you."

Who had shown up to talk to me now? "Thanks. Can you send them back here?"

A minute later, Val and Joey came into my office. Val sat down in a chair across from my desk, and Joey stood in the doorway. He looked sweaty and exhausted, probably from a show.

"Were you going to call us and tell us we had agreed to drive you home tonight or were you just going to stay in your office by yourself?" She had that angry mother-hen look to her.

I stood up, coming around the desk. "How did you find out?"

She barked out a laugh, like she thought I was insane. "Your boyfriend called us in a panic. He said there had been a fire, and you ran out of his parents' anniversary party to talk to the fire crew, but when he tried to bring you home, you said I was already on the way to get you."

Had Sal really not believed me and called her to check up on me?

Or had he been worried that she was going to be out later than expected and wanted her to know I was here waiting?

No, it was definitely the trust thing. He wouldn't still be trying to take care of me like that.

Right?

"He's not my boyfriend anymore."

Joey cleared his throat. "Does anyone else want a glass of water or coffee or something? I'm going to go see what I can find."

"Waters would be great. Thanks, hun," Valerie said to him before he left. When the doorway was clear, she turned her attention back on me. She patted the chair next to her. "I had to pretend that I already knew all about it to cover for you, so now you owe me. Sit down and spill your guts."

"There's nothing to spill. The fire was small and won't affect the hotel. We won't have to cancel any events or lose any reservations."

"As great as that is, I'm not actually concerned about the fire. What's going on between you and Sal?"

"It would have ended between us anyway, so what's the point of delaying the inevitable?"

"I don't believe a damn word you just said. Sit down." I listened, plopping down in the empty chair facing her. "Just the other day you were dancing around my store acting like you were going to run away with this dude forever."

"And you know what? I felt the same way about Chris, and look how that turned out."

She leaned back in her chair. "What the fuck does this have to do with that asshole?"

"I saw him tonight, when I was waiting for my ride here. And you know who wasn't with him? Maxine."

"Okay. So?"

"So men don't change, and love isn't real."

She rubbed her face with her hands. "I'm not tracking this conversation at all." She scooted her chair closer to me and put her hand on my leg. "Blake, honey, what's really going on?"

At her touch, the tears I had been holding in rolled down my cheek. "I thought I had sacrificed my happiness for Maxine. Like I went through a ton of shit with Chris, but at the end of the day, she was getting her happy ending. She had found her person, even though he had hidden their relationship from me for so long. Their happiness made my pain worth it."

"Oh, Blakey, that's simply not true."

I shook my head; the tears flowing on their own now. "And Sal's mom basically called me a charity case, and she's right. She saw right through me. I'm just a fucking loser relying on my friends all the time." Shame flooded through me. I hated letting people take care of me, but here I was, doing it yet again. My parents paid for my college, and now Sal was paying all of my bills.

I continued my miserable thoughts. "Camilla knows all about how I've been relying on her brother's good fortune, which means our friendship is probably over, too." Then it got worse. "And Camilla and Lizette are best friends. That woman offered to back an entire hotel for me. What is she going to think when she finds out I'm a fraud?" That I was pretending to buy a house from my boyfriend so I could use his grandmother's house as my own hotel?

I covered my face with my hands, unable to see a way out of this.

Suddenly, Val pulled me into her lap, which would have been hilarious if I wasn't in the middle of losing my mind. She pulled me against her, and I started crying harder. "You are not a charity case. You're a badass bitch with a fucking MBA."

"Yeah, just barely." I had worked so hard to get my MBA, but I was the first to admit how much help I had needed during the entire program.

"Who's been helping me with my finances since the day we met? You're the reason I was able to afford a second store, Blakey. You've got to see that."

"Lizette is going to think I'm out for Camilla's family's money, too. They're not going to want to help me with my bed-and-breakfast. Not that I'm going to have one now."

When I sniffled into her shirt, she said, "Lizette would not have promoted you to general manager and then begged you to work for her corporation if you were a charity case."

"She just did that because I'm her brother's wife's best friend. I'm practically a nepo-baby."

"Okay, so let's be logical here. Your concerns are that all men keep secrets and no one thinks you're a capable adult."

Being under a microscope was making me uncomfortable. I stood up and paced the floor for a few moments. "Well, when you put it like that, it sounds flippant."

Val scoffed, and when I looked up at her, she was dead serious. "What aren't you telling me?"

I gave up and slumped into the chair across from her again. Not ready to share my terrible news, but knowing I needed to. "Sal owns the bungalow."

"The one Lina and Reece are staying in?"

"Yep. The one I thought I was buying."

"Did you know it was his this whole time?" Val's brow furrowed.

"Nope. And I don't think he was planning on telling me." I clenched my fists, just as angry at him for hiding this from me as I had been two hours ago. "You know how I found out? His sister told me!"

"But did he say anything when you asked him about it?"

I practically growled in frustration. "I didn't have time to ask him about it! I found out right before they called me to come check on the fire damage."

"And you don't think there's a chance this was a weird miscommunication?"

"Oh yes, I definitely misheard him when I told him I was buying a house and he told me he was the damn owner."

She put up her hands. "It makes sense that you're angry when you say it like that."

Joey picked the right time to pop back into the room with two bottles of water in his hands. "Sorry, it took me a while to find these, and then I got to chatting with the guy at the front desk, Davis. He knows Lyle from The

Great Escape!" When we just stared at him blankly, he said, "Remember the band we met in Europe?" It was the most I'd ever heard him speak in one breath.

Val nodded. "Oh yeah, the one with the red hair?"

I used their conversation as an excuse to stop talking about my problems. "Is it okay if I crash on your couch tonight?"

I had a feeling Val was going to tell me I had to go home, but before she could protest, Joey said, "Sure, I don't see why not."

"Thanks so much, you guys. Let me turn off my computer, and I'll be ready to go."

I shifted in my sleep, wondering why my back felt like I had slept weird all night. The bed I was in felt wrong, like it wasn't mine. I stretched my legs out, and suddenly all the emotions and thoughts from last night flooded through me.

I wasn't in my bed. I was on Val's couch.

As soon as I opened my eyes, I let out a scream. Val was perched on the coffee table, watching me sleep. "What the hell, Valerie?"

"Well, it's after ten, and you never sleep in. I was worried you weren't breathing."

"I'm going back to sleep," I grumbled as I rolled away from her.

Instead of giving in, Val slid onto the couch next to me, shoving me into the cushions. "Fine. I'll go back to sleep with you."

I shoved at her with my elbow. "Get off me!"

"I'm not on you. I'm next to you. Because I love you."

I pulled the pillow out from under my head and smacked her with it. "Why won't you leave me alone?"

"Because our best friend gets to practice getting married in a few hours, and you're wearing my leggings and some random sweater." She tugged at the fabric. "Where did you find this thing, anyway?"

I sat up, almost knocking her off the couch. "Oh shit. I don't have any clothes."

"You have a ton of clothes. At the house in which you live. Which is not here." I hated that she was always the person who had her shit together, especially when I was the messy friend. Even lately, when she was frazzled, she was the glue that held us all together.

Last night when we had gotten here, she had tried to get me to talk, but I feigned exhaustion. Now I realized I couldn't go through this weekend without first going to Sal's house and, second, spending the entire evening with him. And right now, I didn't want to do either of those things.

She slapped her hand down on my thigh, bringing my attention back to her. "Put your shoes on. Let's go."

"I'm not going anywhere."

She stood up, walked to the table by the door, and picked up her purse. "Yes, you are. We're going to get your car and grab what you're wearing this weekend. Come on."

"Do you have any gum?" If I was going to risk bumping into Sal at the house, I didn't want to do it with morning breath.

She reached into her purse, pulled out a pack of gum, and threw it at me. It thumped into my chest, and I watched it fall to the ground. "You're really making me do this?" I asked her.

"Absolutely."

We pulled up to the house, and Val parked between my car and Sal's motorcycle.

I begged the universe that he wasn't here. That he had taken the car somewhere, but I knew I would be let down.

I pulled my keys out of my clutch as Val asked, "Do you want me to wait in the car?"

"No, come inside with me." I didn't want to be alone with him.

We made it to the living room before I found him, lying on the couch with his arm covering his face, wearing all but the blazer, tie, and shoes of the suit he'd had on last night. His glasses were on the coffee table like he had tossed them there before lying down.

I started to creep down the hallway toward my room, but Val opened her big mouth. "Hey, how's your head this morning?"

He moved his arm and squinted at her. I tried not to look, but my eyes scanned over him anyway. The bags under his eyes made me doubt he had slept. Which was just fine with me.

Ignoring their conversation, I went to my bedroom and started collecting what I would need for the weekend.

I thought about packing for longer, but I only had an overnight bag and didn't want to wrinkle anything.

I grabbed a cute dress for tonight, with a cardigan that actually belonged to me, and my bridesmaid dress for tomorrow. Lina had picked beautiful dresses for Val and me to wear. They were strapless and form-fitting, making us look like sirens rising from the ocean. The only difference was that Val's was purple and mine was teal. I couldn't wait to wear it tomorrow.

After putting all the other clothes and accessories into my duffel bag, I steeled myself and walked out to the living room.

Val was sitting on the arm of the couch, drinking a cup of coffee while Sal sat on the couch, talking normally —like a giant bomb hadn't gone off a handful of hours ago.

"Are you ready?" I asked her.

She looked up at me, down at him, and back at me. "Actually, I think I'm going to go introduce myself to the horses. I'll be back in a little while." Then she stood, coffee in hand, and walked right out the back door. Which left the two of us together.

Valerie was a traitor.

Sal looked up at me, and I just stood there, debating if I should just walk out the front door. After a few seconds, he patted the couch next to him and asked, "Can we talk?"

I gestured to the dress in my hand, trying to ignore the freckles dusted across his nose. How I never wanted to think about them again. "No, not really. I need to grab Val so we can get ready for the rehearsal."

He propped his elbows on his thighs, cupping his face in his hands. "Don't do this, Blake. We can't let this happen again."

I put my free hand on my hip. "Let what happen? Let you hide something important and life-altering from me?"

He looked up at me again, and my heart skipped a beat at how tortured he looked. There was genuine sorrow in his eyes, but I wasn't ready to hear him out. He had wronged me, and I was allowed to be angry.

"Yes, I hid that I owned the house from you, and I'll have to live the rest of my life knowing that I hurt you. But I need to tell you why."

It was hard to look at him any longer, so I pretended to be checking the time on the clock on the wall across the room. "I really can't stay. I've got a lot to do before the rehearsal."

He stood up, moving in front of me. "Can I ask you a question, then?"

"Fine. One question."

"Would you have bought the house if you knew it was mine?"

I opened my mouth to speak, but stopped myself. I honestly didn't know the answer. "I'm leaving."

His fingers grazed my elbow as he reached toward me. "Please, we need to fix this."

Shaking his hand off me, I squared my shoulders. "I went to your parents' party. I put up with their rude behavior and snide comments, which was more than what I expected from this bargain to begin with. And then I had to hear the bombshell of a secret about my house from your sister. So please excuse me as I spend the rest of the weekend focusing on my very best friends as they make what might be the dumbest decision anyone could ever make."

I walked away from him, grabbing my car keys from the table in the entryway. Val would have to forgive me for ditching her, but there was no way in hell that I would stay for another minute.

Chapter Sixteen

After giving Valerie a pinkie-promise that I wouldn't run away to Bakersfield if she left me alone, I drove to the resort to get things ready while she and Joey picked up the bride and groom.

I loved my best friends. I was so glad that Lina had found the person who made her heart light up.

But I also didn't want to see the house that had almost been mine, and I really didn't want to be alone with Reece, knowing he was Sal's best friend. Which meant he was probably in on the big secret, too.

Luckily, the contractor had replied to the voice mail I'd left him at midnight and agreed to meet me before the rehearsal. I couldn't wait to read him the riot act. His negligence almost cost us the entire resort.

While I waited for his appointment, I sat in my office, checking my emails. Sure, it was my day off, but if I could get some work done today, I wouldn't have to handle it on Monday.

There was a knock at my door, and I told them to enter, hoping the contractor was early.

Lizette entered with a light air around her for the first time in a long time. "Blake, why didn't you call me last night? I would have come in and taken care of things."

She sat in the chair across from me as I told her, "There wasn't really much to talk about. But the contractor should be here in about ten minutes, if you want to tag along with that meeting."

"That would be great." She kicked off her shoes like she always did.

I hadn't expected to see her on a Saturday. "Any reason you're here today?"

Her eyebrow arched like she thought I should know and then smiled a little. "I'm going to marry my brother." Her lightning bolt of a laugh that came afterward threw me off completely.

"You're going to what?"

"Reece needed an officiant, and since I am one, I told them I'd do it." The more time I spent with her, the more interesting she became.

"That might be the weirdest fact I've heard about you."

She shrugged, laying back in the seat. "I thought it was sweet when he asked me. I have a feeling it was only because they ran out of people that could do it, but I think it will be pretty cool, regardless."

"Are your parents still not coming?"

She shook her head. "No, they're not even in the country right now. And to be honest, even if they were, I don't think they'd come."

The thought of not having my parents around for such a special day broke my heart. And then I thought of Sal and his parents. If he actually wanted to get married one day, would they support him? Or would he have two missing people on his side of the altar, like Reece?

I wanted to pull out my phone and text him that I hated how much his family sucked, but then I remembered I was still so angry at him.

The phone on my desk rang, and when I answered, the front desk attendant told me that the contractor had arrived. "He's here. Ready to check out the kitchen?" I asked.

"Hold on real quick." She put her hand on my desk. "I want you to know that it's okay with me if you don't take the promotion. I was just worried that you'd realize how great you are one day and leave us. The promotion was my way of trying to keep you in the corporate umbrella."

I sat back in my chair, surprised at her honesty. "Wow. I'm flattered." When I took a second to think about what I really wanted, an idea occurred to me, almost out of thin air. Now felt like the right time to ask for support. "I actually have a plan that could keep me in the corporation."

She grinned. "I'm listening."

"I'm not ready yet," I started. My words came out slowly as I wondered if this was a smart decision. She was best friends with Camilla. Would she still want to be my friend when she found out about me and Sal not being a thing anymore?

No. I had to give myself a chance, friends or not.

Lizette was a businesswoman above all else and would understand. I was finally aware that this dream was the most important thing in my life. "Hell, I don't know when I'll be ready, but how would you like to invest in my future bed-and-breakfast?"

She clasped her hands together, her eyes lighting up. "I thought you'd never ask!"

"Don't get too excited. We've got a contractor to go harass." I stood as she slipped her shoes back on.

"This guy better stop costing us so much damn money so we can start planning our next property together." She winked at me as I opened the door. Maybe my own hotel was closer to reality than I had thought.

Thankfully, the repairs wouldn't be as substantial as we had anticipated, and Lizette threatened legal action from the entire corporation if the job was not made the top priority of the construction company.

She said something about no longer settling for table scraps as she lit into the guy. It made me want to ask her more about what was going on at home. I knew she was still friends with her new ex-husband, but she still carried some anger just below the surface.

Thinking about staying friends with an ex made me think of Sal.

What was his deal? Why couldn't he have just been honest with me from the start?

Lizette and I spent more time than we had originally planned in the kitchen, so I sent her to the rehearsal before discussing the new agreement with the contractor. I figured it would be rude for them to get started without the officiant. After walking the contractor out, I walked through the crosswalk to the spot on the beach we would hold the ceremony tomorrow evening. It was still early enough in the afternoon that the sun was bright in the sky. The small group that had gathered either had on sunglasses or were shading their faces with their hands.

I waved at Kathy, who was showing Lina and Reece where they would stand for their vows as I approached. I specifically avoided the man who stood to the right of them. The best man, who was also the worst man. "Sorry I'm late. The fire threw a wrench in a lot of things."

Lina came toward me, wrapping me in a hug. "I've missed you so much," she said before whispering, "We shouldn't be worried about the fire, right?"

I squeezed her tightly before letting go. "Nope. The kitchen issue won't affect your big day whatsoever."

Reece came in for a hug, too, and it took everything in me not to demand he tell me what he knew right then and there. He looked a little guilty, but I wasn't sure if it was nerves from the wedding or knowing that his best friend was a jerk.

But there was a time and a place for everything, and now belonged to the wedding party. I would play nice.

Kathy told me where to stand, right next to Val in front of the wooden arch that was decorated for the wedding that would take place in two hours for a group of complete strangers. She went over where we would come in from and where we would stand, and I felt fairly confident in the process as a whole.

My phone vibrated in my pocket—thank goodness for designers who were finally making dresses useful—and I wondered if it was my mom. She hadn't replied to my email and hadn't called me at all today. I pulled it out while Kathy discussed the pros and cons of using a microphone with Lizette and found a notification from the geocaching app.

There was a brand new geocache nearby. It said it was medium-shaped, and when I zoomed in; it looked like it was in the bushes by the sidewalk, not over thirty feet away from me.

I tucked my phone back into my pocket, knowing it would be burning a hole through my dress for the rest of the night, begging me to come back and look. Since no one I cared to talk to at this party was interested in treasure hunting, I would come back and see what I could find tonight, after everyone else had gone home. It would be a nice little boost after a crappy twenty-four hours.

"Is everyone ready to go?" Val clapped her hands, getting our attention before wrapping her arm across Lina's shoulder.

Sal said something along the lines of, "The bus is parked on the East side of the building," but I was trying to ignore him, so I just followed my friends.

The group was fairly small—the bride and groom, four members of the bridal party, and both Lina and Reece's sisters. Lina tried to talk Kathy into joining us, too, but she turned us down, saying she was way too clumsy to try her hand at axe throwing.

I was the last one to get onto the bus, which, other than looking like a bus from the outside, had nothing in common with an actual bus. It was just a limo that was tall enough to stand up in.

"Before we get started, I'd like to give a toast," Sal announced to the group as he moved through the bus with a tray in his hand. He handed out glasses of champagne and water bottles to everyone, and when he came up to me, I snatched a water bottle without making eye contact.

I had decided I wasn't drinking tonight, and probably not at the wedding either. The last thing I wanted was to make another drunken mistake.

Sal held up his water bottle. "My best friend has been through a lot. He's had to fight inner demons and outer demons, all the while thinking he had to hold the whole world on his shoulders. Last year when he met his Maggie, all I had to do was look at her to know how deeply she loved him and how perfect they would be together. To my friends. May you find happiness forever."

Everyone clapped and took a drink, but I slumped in my seat, preferring to pick at the label on the bottle than to seem like I was paying attention to him. Sal and his perfect word choice, his perfect composure all the time. It made me sick. I knew I should be pretending to have fun so my friends wouldn't ask any questions, but I just didn't have it in me.

Soon we were off, and in just a few minutes, the bus let us out on the sidewalk by the axe-throwing club. It looked like heaven for lumberjacks. Wooden walls, tables, and floors filled the room. Red and black checkered plaid fabric covered anything soft, and for a moment, it felt like we were deep in the woods somewhere in Oregon. The long wall had eight bays, each with a chewed-up target hanging on the wall.

The guy who greeted us at the counter went through the safety regulations and made us sign waivers before walking us to the first bay to show us proper axe-throwing techniques.

The group started splitting into twos like they had instructed us to, and I panicked I would get stuck with Sal. I looked around and found Lina talking with her sister, so I took the opportunity to steal her groom.

I bumped my shoulder into Reece. "Care to join me?"

He smiled, said, "I'd love to," and we found our little table in the target bay. After getting situated, he threw his first axe, and when it hit the target, he asked, "So, how have things been?" like he hadn't taken part in keeping an enormous secret from me. Luckily, Sal and Lina were on the other side of the room, out of earshot, so I could speak candidly.

"You knew he owned the rental house, didn't you?" I asked and then flung my first axe. It bounced off the edge of the target and hit the ground.

"You're just going to dive right into it, huh?" He stepped up to the line, preparing to throw his next axe.

"There's no use in wasting my time. I'm thirty years old and sleeping on a couch. What's the point of not being direct?" I was tired of everyone's bullshit.

His axe flew through the air, landing a little off center but still finding its way into the target, before he turned to fully face me. He looked so out of place in his blue button-up and slacks, but I didn't think I'd ever seen him in anything other than business attire. It made me think of Sal and how good he looked in his tight black T-shirt and dark jeans tonight. How he looked like he could throw an axe without even concentrating.

"I'm going to be honest, so please don't stab me in the chest the day before my wedding." He held his hands up like he honestly felt I would chuck a blade at him at any second.

I picked up an axe and lifted it up and down, like I was analyzing its weight. "It depends on what you say, I guess."

"I did know about the house." He paused like he was weighing his next words. "He told me he was going to sell it to you because he knew how much you loved it. And he knew you wouldn't buy it directly from him, so he didn't tell you at first."

"Does Lina know it's his house?" They'd had issues with his honesty in the past, and I wanted to know what kind of man she was tying herself to for all of eternity.

He sucked in a breath. "She does. But only because I told her the whole truth when we got to the house last night." He must have seen the anger in my eyes, because he took a step back. "Sal told me he was going to tell you. When he told me you signed the paperwork, I told him you would not appreciate being deceived, and he said he was going to find a way to tell you." A resigned smile crossed his face. "I thought he had told you until we settled into our flight and Mag mentioned she wanted to get you something unique for a housewarming gift. I asked her if she had heard any news, knowing that if he had told you, she would say something, but she didn't.

That's when I knew he'd chickened out. So I told her everything."

"Why couldn't he have just told me from the start? I don't understand why he hid it from me."

Reece's eyes trailed over my shoulder, and I followed his glance. Across the room, Sal and Lina were chucking axes and laughing hysterically. "He knows who you are. How you are." As I turned back to face him, ready to argue, he went on. "Blake, I've only known you for a year, and I know we haven't always been on the best footing, but you are so independent and headstrong that I believe you would have turned it down if he offered it to you, too. Just like you turned down moving in with him until it was your last option."

"I can accept help when I need it." This guy didn't know me at all.

He faced the target, picking up another axe and throwing it. "Sure, when you know you need it. But when do you ever think you need help?"

His words sank in a little. When was the last time I asked for help? I thought back to my house hunt, to anything at work lately, and came up short. Shit, he did know me. "I think the last time I asked for help was in third grade when I couldn't get the knot out of my shoelace at recess." I threw my next axe, this time sinking it into the target.

"I think that was his point. It was easier to beg for forgiveness than to ask for permission."

"But a whole damn house, Reece? This isn't like a nice leather jacket or a kitchen table. He tried to sell me a house for way less than he should have. How will I not look like a gold digger to his family?"

He tucked his hands into his pockets. "Does it really matter what they think? If you care about each other and you know he was doing it for you and your happiness?"

I looked over at Sal as Reece took his next throw and caught him looking right at me. His eyes were so sad, remorse painted across his face.

I turned away and picked up another axe before my legs wandered over to him on their own. I hated how much I wanted him. How much I knew that deep down, he thought he was taking care of me. And maybe I needed him to when I didn't have the courage to ask for it myself.

Tonight needed to be about Reece and Lina, though. Now that I had gotten the information I needed from the groom, the rest of my problems could wait until later.

The next stop on the party bus tour was dinner. The food was delicious, even though it was a far cry from the food I'd been eating lately. I thought about sitting near Sal but was worried I'd turn it into a whole thing if I started talking to him.

Instead, I sat at the other end of the table with Lina's sister Ester and Lizette. Ester worked at a marketing firm, and so the three of us slid into easy conversations about running businesses and keeping them afloat.

I even hung back while a couple of the more

intoxicated members of our group—mainly Lina and Val —tried to play bocce ball on the dirt field in the back patio of the restaurant.

It was almost midnight when the bus dropped us back at the hotel. I made sure everyone had a safe ride home, as usual, and we said our goodbyes. This time tomorrow, Reece and Lina would be married.

Instead of following Joey and Val home, I told them I needed to check something in my office. I even went all the way through the lobby and down the hall, just in case they didn't believe my terrible excuse.

After waiting a few minutes, I pulled out my phone to double-check the new geocache on the beach. There had been no check-ins logged online, and I got a small thrill thinking I would be the first person to sign my name inside.

At the last second, I rushed into my office, pulled open my top drawer, and grabbed a little compass I had taken from Sal a few days ago. I was sure he wouldn't mind if he found the same cache later on and his trinket was already there.

A part of me wished he was here with me, but he had been in a hurry to leave when the bus dropped us off. It made me wonder if there was something going on at one of his restaurants.

I waved at Davis, who was at the main desk, and crossed the grassy field between the hotel and the road across from the beach. Without waiting for the crosswalk to light up, I looked both ways and ran across the street.

One more check of the app helped me see which direction I needed to hunt, and I started looking.

There were a few different plants I tried to dig through, but it was dark and the moon wasn't bright enough to help. I turned on the flashlight on my phone and scanned the base of the thick pink sand verbena my hand was halfway through.

There it was!

A little wooden box.

I lay down on my side, probably filling my dress with sand, and reached for it. My hand wrapped around the wood, and I could see that it was heart-shaped. The lid was carved to look like a puzzle, with a little piece that slid out to unlock it.

This one felt different from the usual ones hidden throughout the city. It was fancier by far. More special.

I flashed the light on it, looking at the little details carved into the wood.

You must allow me to tell you how ardently I admire and love you had been etched across the top.

What a sweet little box. I immediately recognized the quote and wondered how many other people who would find this cache would recognize it, too.

I slid the locking piece out and opened the lid. The box was full of tiny compasses—there wasn't even space for the one I was planning on adding myself.

I gasped, my free hand landing on my chest. He had done this. He was probably the only person who could guess my favorite line from my favorite book, so I knew he had put this here.

I knew now, looking at this little box filled with compasses, that my heart belonged to him and always would. We could figure out all the messy stuff later.

In the darkness, I looked up and down the beach, wondering if anyone was nearby.

I dug my fingers through the compasses, looking for a log. I didn't find one, but it wasn't necessary. I knew without a doubt that Sal had placed this geocache.

Knowing that I couldn't wait another minute before talking to him, I put the box back together and pulled my phone out of my pocket.

It only rang once before he answered. "Hello?"

"Hey. It's me." I was so nervous but had a feeling I didn't need to be.

"Where are you?" He sounded quiet, not his usual boisterous self.

"I bet you could guess." I looked up and down the beach again.

He paused. "I'll be right there."

"Okay."

He was breathless when he asked, "Stay on the line, okay?"

"Yeah, I'll be here." I thought about asking him where he was, but I didn't want to break the silence.

In less than a minute, I saw a figure in the crosswalk. "Is that you?"

"Yeah, it's me." He jogged down the sidewalk toward me.

"How did you get back so quickly?" I whispered into the phone. He was twenty feet away from me, and I probably could have just called out to him, but this felt more intimate somehow.

"I never left. I've been waiting in my car, hoping you couldn't resist looking for it."

And then he was in front of me. It had only been one day, but somehow I had missed him so badly. I hung up my phone and he followed suit. I put mine in my pocket before holding the box up to him. "When did you do this?"

He scratched his neck, probably subconsciously. "My tattoo guy also makes wood carvings. When you told me who your favorite author was, I commissioned him to make it."

I glanced down at the box again. "It's from Pride and Prejudice." I rubbed my thumb across the letters. "How did you know it was my favorite line?"

His hand wrapped gently around my elbow, and I looked up to see his face barely lit from the moon. "Because it's how I feel about you."

I looked into his eyes, wishing it was brighter so I could see more of the color in them. "But it's right before she tells him to go to hell."

He laughed. "I know, but you probably want me to fuck off anyway, so it fits."

My eyes welled up, thinking about why I was upset with him. "The house. You hid it from me."

"I know, and I regret it. I wish I could go back in time and tell you from the start. I hate that I put you through this." He bit his bottom lip, and I felt his words through my whole body.

I tucked the box under my arm and wiped my eyes with my fingertips. "But you were right."

He pulled me closer to him and wrapped his arms around my waist. "No, I completely messed things up."

"Only because you know I wouldn't have taken it. It

really is my dream house, but it's just too much. I can't buy it from you."

He kissed my forehead before pulling back to look me in the eye. "Then come live in it with me. Let it be our house. Together."

I shook my head. "I can't take any more handouts. I have to do this on my own."

"That's a bunch of crap, and you know it." His eyebrow went up, challenging me.

I was about to protest, but I knew he was right. Even Reece, who'd been on the opposite side of the world for months, could see right through me. But the more I thought about what Reece had said, the more I knew that Sal really did know me better than I knew myself. "So?"

He ignored my question. "We're partners in this, right? Just you and me?" His hand slid from my elbow to my hand, and I moved slightly so I could twine my fingers through his.

He had a point. Partners asked for help and stepped in when the other needed them the most. I had to focus more on accepting his help rather than trying to do things by myself. "You're right. We are," I said, thinking of how my hand felt so perfect in his.

"I love you, Blake." This time his words rang true, and I knew with certainty that I felt the same way.

I had never felt this content before, despite our issues. "I love you, too." I admitted.

He kissed me then, tenderly, sweetly. I felt myself melt into him, but I needed to clarify some things before we went too far. I pushed against his chest, and he pulled back a few inches.

"I'm not a charity case, though." I wanted to be just as independent as he was.

"I know you're not. Please let me take care of you." He tightened his grip on my waist. "Let's do a quick deed. I'll put your name on the house with mine. Fuck, I'll let you pay the annual taxes if it means you'll move in with me. Let it be ours."

"Ours?" I should be worried about the prospect of sharing property with him, but my steady heart knew where I was meant to be.

"Not just mine. Not just yours. Both of us." His fingers tightened around mine.

"Can I think about it?" I knew my answer already, but I was still afraid of jumping in just yet.

He pulled me against him again. "Of course, I would worry you were sick if you didn't ask for more time." He pressed his cheek against my temple, and I felt so secure, so protected. "Can we go home now?"

"One more thing." I needed to get everything off my chest before we started fresh. I pulled out of his embrace, but grabbed his hand with mine. "Marianna said it was her idea for us to pretend to be together. That you had been talking about me, about us, for months. Is that true?"

One side of his lip perked up. "It's mostly true, I guess."

"You guess?" It was cute that he seemed a little shy on the subject, but I was dying to know everything.

"I told my gaming group about you the first time I met you. I couldn't help myself. You were so beautiful and funny. Something about you just made me want to be with you. And then we . . . . Well, after we spent that night together, I thought we were going to be something more. So I told them about us."

I felt my eyes go wide. "You told them we slept together?"

He shook his head. "No, I just told them we connected. That we stayed up late talking. Which was the truth."

"Okay. Go on," I instructed him, wanting to know more. I was relieved knowing he hadn't shared our intimate moments with his friends, but I needed more.

"And then when things didn't happen between you and me, they—well, mostly Marianna—kept asking about you. Asking how my dating life was going. I guess I had been pretty obvious that I didn't want anyone else. Just you."

"So, how did this turn into the grand scheme?" I was more flattered than upset now that I knew how badly he had wanted me from the beginning.

"I told Marianna that I had offered for you to move in with me, and she jokingly mentioned fake dating. She didn't even mean anything by it, but since I might have mentioned that I was seeing someone to my sister to get her to stop asking me personal questions, too, it just kind of worked out on its own." I must have looked a little skeptical still, so he added, "It's not like we were sitting around a table plotting our relationship like some grand adventure."

I looked up at him, knowing in my heart, in my soul, that even if he had planned it all out, I would have still loved him despite it. "Well, are you going to take me home?"

He looked at the bush where I had found my treasure. "Are you going to put the geocache back?"

I laughed, gripping it tighter. "Hell no, this one is mine. You'll have to get another one."

"Maybe I can talk to the general manager of the resort and see if she'll let me install a Little Free Library somewhere on-site. The one I put up by Nonna's house is always busy."

It was too early to ask him to put one outside our new house, too, but I knew in that moment that I wanted one. And I wanted it to be just like my favorite one up in the hills, the one that he had always taken such great care of. It felt like the universe kept bringing him to me and I couldn't see it until now.

"I need you to agree to something, though," I said as we made it to the grassy field in front of the resort.

"Anything," he said, and I knew he meant it.

"You can't hide shit from me anymore. My ex used to do that, and it really messed me up."

He stopped me and pressed his lips to mine. Our arms wrapped around each other, and it felt like the first real kiss of our new relationship. When he pulled away several moments later, he said, "I'm going to share so much with you that you'll get sick of me. I promise not to keep anything from you ever again."

Sal and I stood across from each other at the altar, and even though I never wanted to get married myself, it felt like one of the most romantic moments of my life.

We turned and watched Lizette and Reece walk down the aisle, he in a deep navy suit and she in a black pencil skirt and matching blazer. Since the ceremony was on the beach, we had all left our shoes on a table by the sidewalk, and it was the most relaxed and happy I'd ever seen Lizette. When she stood under the floral arch, she hugged her brother tightly and turned to the small crowd—no more than fifty people—and said, "Please stand."

The wedding guests stood from their seats and faced the aisle as quiet cello music began to play from a hidden speaker. Lina and her mother began their walk toward her groom.

Lina was so beautiful, her smile bright and her dress shimmering. She really had picked out the most beautiful gown. She looked like a mermaid about to dive back into the sea, with her dress tight around her hips and thighs, fanning out at the bottom. The pearls braided into her hair, hanging over one shoulder, were a nice touch, too.

Halfway down the aisle, her hand reached up and grasped her heart-shaped locket. It was amazing to me how that little trinket had brought all of us together. We were one big family now and forever.

Lina's eyes never left Reece's, and when she was halfway here, I turned to see his expression. His eyes were filled with tears, and he had a smile so big his dimple was visible to everyone.

I looked over his shoulder and saw Sal standing there,

his eyes already on me. He mouthed "I love you," and I whispered it back.

The ceremony was beautiful; Lizette did a great job officiating. She spoke about the importance of partnership and trust. Telling the truth and admitting when you're wrong.

All the things Sal and I had struggled with. Things that maybe everyone struggled with from time to time.

When Reece and Lina came together and kissed for the first time as husband and wife, I couldn't hold back the tears. Valerie reached over and held my hand, and I squeezed it back.

Then it was time to pair off, following the bride and groom toward the reception hall. Val and Joey went first. He gave her a sweet kiss on her temple before they embarked. I loved how happy they were, how supportive they were of each other through every challenge. No matter what.

Sal held his hands out to me, and I reached for him. He took the bouquet out of my hand, tucking it under his arm, and pulled me in for a kiss. His body pressed against mine, and the small crowd cheered.

We stopped to take a few pictures with the rest of the bridal party while the guests walked to the reception hall, and he never let me go. I knew this was fresh and new, but I didn't think I would ever tire of his hands on my hips, the small of my back, and anywhere else for that matter.

The reception was just as beautiful as the ceremony. The newly married couple looked blissful at their sweetheart table, and as soon as dinner—which was not overcooked—was over, Sal pulled me onto the dance floor, where we stayed until most guests had called it a night.

My sweet boyfriend gripped my waist, pulling me close during a slow song, and I laid my head on his chest. "So, have you thought about moving in with me?"

I breathed in his sandalwood and eucalyptus scent, wanting to be enveloped by it for the rest of my life. "Actually, I think I will."

He leaned back, looking down at me. "Really?"

I nodded. "Yeah, in the bungalow. I like the idea of it being ours. Together."

He kissed me quickly and then asked, "Does that mean what I think it means about Nonna's house?"

I gripped his back, squeezing him close to me again. "I think we should do it. Let's turn it into a bed-and-breakfast."

He stopped dancing and cupped my face in his hands, looking into my eyes. "You're absolutely sure?"

I smiled nervously. "Maybe not right away, since I still have to handle the kitchen renovations and talk to Lizette about what my role here at The Pacifica would look like. I don't know if I can stay at both locations or if I have to leave here completely." I paused, thinking about what I really wanted. "And I want to talk about how involved you want to be. You've got so much going on, but I want you to be a part of it, too. If you want to."

"There's nothing I'm more certain of. Other than how much I love you." He looked a little bewildered, which I understood. Just yesterday I had fantasized about throwing an axe at him, and today I was willing to sign a deed with him.

"If it means letting you help me make my dream come true, I'm in."

He kissed me sweetly before pulling back and spinning me, dancing to the music again. "I can't wait to go on this adventure with you."

"Me either, Salamander."

Epilogue

Three Years Later

I came up the walkway to the front door of Nonna's Bed and Breakfast to double-check that everything was in place for the family that was checking in at the main office. I was technically off the clock and should be on my way home, but they had rented the entire property for a week, and I wanted it to be absolutely perfect for them.

We had built a little casita next to the garage that looked like a mini version of the main house. It held our administrative offices so we could be on-site while giving our guests the privacy they came up to the hills of Santa Barbara for, and it worked out perfectly.

I had originally planned on converting the garage for our offices, but Sal said the only thing he wanted out of this whole conversion was to keep his garage. Since he was giving me an entire estate to work with, I thought it was fair.

We had been up and running for six months now and

were fully booked for another six. We had scalped a bunch of employees from The Pacifica, but since The Howell Group was a major investor, they didn't mind.

Paige came over as my assistant, Davis was our concierge, and Kathy was doing her magic right now in the casita. She took care of our scheduling, booked our events, and still worked for Lina and Reece part time.

They had finally moved back to town, just in time for their first baby to be born in a few weeks, and Lina said when her maternity leave was over, she wanted to use our property as one of her photography locations. Of course, I said yes without hesitation.

In return for Lizette's investment, I took a project manager job at The Howell Group, which meant I got to be in charge of the bed-and-breakfast and also had a small role in The Pacifica, as well as my say in any new projects she and I decided to take over in the future.

Her role at the company had also changed since her brother's wedding, and I took comfort knowing that we were both content doing what we loved in places that brought us the most joy.

I opened the front door and smelled dinner cooking. A table full of food would be the perfect way for our guests to be welcomed into their home away from home.

I came into the kitchen and was surprised at who I saw. "What are you doing here?" I asked Sal, who was chopping vegetables in his dark jeans and chef's coat.

He turned, smiling. "Hi babe. I heard we were fully booked this weekend, so I canceled my shift downtown so I could come and give Marco some help tonight."

I said hi to Marco, the full-time chef Sal had hired for

the property, as Sal came around the island and gave me a kiss.

It had taken some time, but Sal had decided it was best if his parents weren't in our lives, and I supported his choice.

We had his sister and his cousins who took turns taking care of Nonna with us, and we had my family—all of whom agreed that he brought out the best in me. They practically begged us to come visit every holiday, so of course we did.

Uncle Sal, who wrestled on the floor with Jake's kids and promised to take them on rides on his motorcycle when they were older, was always a big hit. What we had was all we needed, so it didn't matter to us if his parents were around or not. We had enough love in our lives to make up for their loss.

I wrapped my arms around him. "How did I get so lucky?"

"Well, I figured it would be a nice way to spend our anniversary."

"Is it, though?" We always argued about what day our anniversary really was—the day we met, the day we first kissed, or the day we finally took our relationship seriously —so I had a hard time keeping track of it.

He pulled away from me to unbutton his chef's coat, folding it over his arm before grabbing a large canvas bag from one of the bar stools. "We'll be back in a little while, Marco," he said before grabbing my hand, eager to get me out of the house. "Come with me."

I followed him out the back door, around the pool, and down the grassy hill. I rubbed my hand across my arm, warming the skin that was now covered in a floral tattoo—we had gotten matching ones in Oregon last summer while on vacation. "Where are you taking me?"

We made it halfway down the hill before he opened the canvas bag, pulling out a thick blanket. He shook it open and laid it on the grass. "Have a seat."

I followed his direction, sitting on the blanket, and he sat next to me, his long legs stretching in front of him. He pulled out a bottle of wine and two glasses, and I noticed his hands were shaking as he handed one to me. "What's going on?" I had to ask.

He winked and gave me that grin I adored, the one that meant he was up to something I wasn't going to be able to turn down.

Pulling the cork out from the bottle, he said, "I've loved you from the moment I met you. I'm so happy to be your partner in all of this."

He poured wine into each glass before putting down the bottle. "And I love you too." I looked out as the sunset painted the sky pink and purple, my favorite colors.

Sal reached into the bag again, pulling out something else.

It was the heart-shaped box I kept on our dresser, the one he had used as a geocache down by the beach.

He handed it to me as he asked, "Blake, will you not marry me?"

I laughed, sitting my glass down. "What?" I slid the top off the box and found two plain black rings lying inside.

"Well, we have everything we need. We're happy, and we're going to be happy forever. I want you to know that you're it for me, and you always have been." Pulling the rings out, I looked between him and them. The smaller one had a thin stripe of black diamonds in the center, which caused it to sparkle like glitter in this low lighting. It was perfection.

When I looked back up at him, he leaned closer and continued, "I know that neither of us wants to get married, but I thought it might be a nice way to celebrate these years together, and to look forward to our many years to come."

I held the larger ring up, smiled through my tears, and grabbed his hand. "Of course I'll not marry you." I slipped the ring on his finger. He sat his glass down and took the smaller ring from the box, sliding it onto my finger.

Then he wrapped his hand around the nape of my neck, pulling me in for a kiss. "I love you so fucking much."

I shifted to his lap, straddling him as I kissed him deeper. "I'm going to love you forever."

His kisses trailed down my neck. "We should probably get going so the guests don't leave a bad review because the owners were fucking on the lawn."

I tugged at his T-shirt, challenging him. "What's one bad review?"

From start to finish, this book took just under 500 days to complete. From that little spark of an idea I had while writing A Liar and a Thief—if you've read it, you'll know the moment I had the idea to pair Sal and Blake together —to today, when I made my final edits on a story that I couldn't put down.

The last 500 days have not all been pleasant. Don't get me wrong, there have been some completely awesome moments in the last year and a half, but the losses were heavy. That being said, it wasn't until I was almost done with the first draft of this book that I realized I was writing Blake for myself.

Extremely independent woman who refuses to ask anyone for help, even when it might tear her apart is my entire personality. Taking the time to write a story where Blake learns that it's not weak to ask for help has taught me to give myself grace. To be kind to myself. To love myself. And I hope that maybe someone out there reading this feels the same way.

So, I want to start this acknowledgments thanking everyone who has been there for me for the past 500 days (and all the days before that, obviously). This story would not be what it is without you. I would not be this woman who strives to keep learning and bettering myself every day without you.

Thank you to every single person who made this book happen.

I have to thank Beth Stedman first and foremost. She is a literary queen, and I still can't believe that I found her randomly on the Internet one day. Thank you for holding my hand through initial outlining and being there for me as I drafted Sal and Blake's story, as well as Lina and Reece's before this. You're such a gem, and I'm the luckiest writer in the world for having you in my life.

Next, I have to give huge props to my beta reader goddesses. You all deserve a million thanks for taking the time to read Blake's story so I could make it the best it could possibly be. Brennan, Tamara, Catie, and Mandy, this story has so much more depth because of your thoughts and ideas. Thank you for asking the best questions so I could get to know Blake (and myself) better.

My writing community, including the QC Hedgies, has been invaluable in my life. Having women to throw ideas at, to share jokes with, and to huddle around me on bad days has filled a void I didn't even know I had. Thank you for writing with me nonstop, no matter where you are in the world (even if by "writing" I mean staying up after midnight and eating weird candy while we gossip on Zoom about the funniest slang words).

And to Clara. Thank you for making sure this story was ready for readers. Your editing is like no other, and I'm honored to work with you on another project.

I can't go any further without telling you how thankful

I am for my family. Like wildly, enormously, beyond thankful.

My hot husband, who doesn't mind me objectifying his body "for research," who wrangles our wild kid so that I have time to write, and who prioritizes my mental health better than I do. You are THE BEST man who ever existed.

Thank you to my parents who continue to do all the babysitting when I have a looming deadline. Who continue to feed me and let me sleep at their house when I'm sick. I won the lottery. Being your kid, even as a grown adult with my own kid, has been wonderful.

To my brother and his amazing partner. Thank you for introducing me to geocaching so that one day I could write a book about a cute couple who plays Dungeons and Dragons and has a Little Free Library at the end of their driveway, just like you.

Thank you ZJ. For loving Jane Austen just as much as I do, for finally being old enough to watch Hallmark Christmas movies with me, and for being the smartest person I've ever met. One day you will read this book, and I'll probably be completely mortified because you're my kid, but right now you always tell me how proud you are that I wrote a book, and I think that's pretty cool.

My heart is broken that you can't read this, but thank you, Lynda. For giving me the courage to stand up for what I believe in, to fiercely support what I love, and to try new things. I am who I am because of you, my other-mother. I would not have started writing if you hadn't introduced me to Goodreads all those years ago. I hope I can continue making you proud.

To my village, which has doubled in size over the last 500 days. The people I eat lunch with mean more to me than they will ever know . . . especially the ones who invite me to do Secret Santa exchanges and send me ridiculous memes that fill my cup every day. I would not survive without the memes, Alexandra. Please continue sending them until we are old and gray.

And last but not least, I want to thank my readers. There is never enough time in our lives, so knowing that you used some of yours to read this book is such an amazing gift. I'm grateful to all of you for diving into my stories and loving my characters as much as I do.

Thank you all, I love you. Here's to the next story!

FOLLOW THE AUTHOR

Instagram | Facebook
DeeRollingsBooks.com

Join my Newsletter to access exclusive content, news, and get access to bonus scenes coming soon!

BOOKS BY DEE ROLLINGS

Discordant Memories

The Pacifica Resort series:

A Liar and a Thief

Love and Reservations

First Loves and Last Resorts

**When you've given up on love . . .
but he finds you anyway.**

Lizette Howell-Xu is married to her work. She didn't even cry when her husband of fifteen years left her for his very muscular, very male personal trainer. But now it's time for her ex to break the news to his family—and he's asking Lizette to help him do it. All they have to do is find a way to talk to his parents alone . . . At a family reunion, that's easier said than done.

Convincing herself that she needed a vacation was the easy part; juggling lost luggage and a major business opportunity from a tiny cabin in Michigan is trickier, especially while pretending to still be married. Luckily Ben, the rugged handyman with a British accent, doesn't mind offering Lizette his desk, especially since he's in on her secret.

But the more Lizette gets to know him, the more willing she becomes to step away from her computer and spend some quality time with a man who finally stirs something deep inside of her. Something she hasn't felt in years.

As their romance threatens to turn into a family scandal, Lizette must decide what parts of her life are the most important, which may mean breaking a few hearts . . . including her own.

First Loves and Last Resorts, the third book in **The Pacifica Resort** series, is a first person POV romantic comedy that will leave you swooning.

**The best way to meet a man is . . .
breaking into his house?**

Lina Herrera hates risks. So prying up the floorboards in a stranger's house isn't her usual MO — but real estate agents are jerks about lost property. And technically, this *was* her childhood home.

Interrupted by the dreamy, tousle-haired owner, Lina is mortified — but Reece Howell is un-bothered by her break-in. Not that it matters. They're just two strangers…right?

But when Lina's lukewarm situationship stands her up a week later, it's Reece who saves the night.

New in town and with more in common with Lina than a shared crime scene, Reece's charm ignites an unlikely spark. But then a management change makes him Lina's new boss, and her aversion to risk puts Reece in the friendzone.

As she struggles to find the courage to break her own rules, can Lina learn to trust her desires — both at work and in the bedroom?

A sweet and steamy, first person POV, contemporary romance novel, **A Liar and a Thief***, the first book in* **The Pacifica Resort** *series, will sweep you off your feet.*

A car accident, amnesia, two supposed lovers, and many dark secrets. In a race against time, who will come out on top?

Catrina Banks wakes up with bruises on her body and no memories from the last six months. An illustrious painter, she feels as though someone has stolen the colors from her canvas.

Under the teeming hospital lights and white coats crowding around her, Catrina faces questions she has no answers to. How did she end up in a city far from home? What was she doing there? Where is her phone, her ID, and most of all: *Who assaulted her?*

Struggling with intermittent flashbacks, Catrina tries to piece her life together. Cradling a gray hoodie and wedding bands she has no memory of, Cat returns home with her boyfriend Danny.

Even after she's safe at home, she can't shake the weird feeling that something is *off,* nor can she ignore the haunting glimpses she gets of a different life with another man.

Discordant Memories *is a* **gripping romantic thriller** *that will have you on the edge of your seat, desperate to flip the pages to find out what happens next.*

About the Author

Dee Rollings was born and raised in the big city, but her heart lives in the forest. She does her best writing on the porch of her tiny house in the woods when she's not wrangling her kid or her dogs and having one-sided conversations with chipmunks.

She's a multi-genre author, penning both romantic thrillers and romantic comedies, but there is one thing for sure about all of her books—they'll make you think a little differently about society and the world, exploring topics such as addiction, grief, womanhood, and self-worth.